CLAIMED AT THE STROKE OF MIDNIGHT

ZOE RAY

CHAPTER 1

Audrey

Stafford family tradition unofficially dictates that all family members must be present for all holiday festivities because my mother insists. Everything in me wanted to skip this year's annual tree trimming party, but here I am as always waiting for the moment I can say I knew I shouldn't have come in the first place. We get along well enough, but my issue is that Christmas is my favorite time of year, and my family has a way of ruining it for me.

I'm constantly criticized and scrutinized by the people who are supposed to support me. Last year for Christmas, my mother gave me a gift certificate to get my eggs frozen. The year before, my sister gave me a membership to an elite matchmaking service. Apparently, it's a crime to be single in my family. Everyone is accomplished, polished, and most important married. Everyone except me, that is, and no one lets me forget it.

Despite the critique of my family, I'm happy with my life, and though my family doesn't understand me, my accomplishments are real and I'm fulfilled by my work.

The fireplace is lit. The smell of apple cinnamon fills the air. Christmas music plays in the background. I have a glass of champagne and smile to myself as I watch the children make their ornaments for the Christmas tree. There's no way that my mother Maxine will have them placed where they can be seen in the window or the front of the foyer. The house is perfectly decorated in red, green, and gold and the giant Christmas tree in the foyer is a thing of beauty.

I hum along to my favorite Christmas song, Silent Night by the Temptations while I sip. My thoughts are interrupted by my sister, Brenda.

"Audrey, guess what. I showed your picture to a guy from work, and he wants to meet you."

"I told you not to do that. I don't need you to find dates for me."

"You also told me you haven't been on a date in at least six months, and you haven't had sex in over a year. One of us had to do something. I decided to be proactive in case you changed your mind. Christmas is around the corner. Wouldn't it be nice to have someone jingle your bell?"

"No, I'm too busy to date."

"Don't lie to your big sister. No one is that busy."

"I'm not looking for just anyone. I need the right man to jingle my bell. I'm not interested."

"He's a successful, black, lawyer. You'd better get interested."

Brenda is older, married with two kids, and she acts more like an overbearing mother than a sister. Maybe I see it that way because Brenda is the spitting image of our mom. They're both tall, thin, athletic, gorgeous, and perfectly poised at all times. They both have dark silky hair. Brenda's hair hangs down her back, and our mom's hair is neatly cut in an elegant bob that accentuates her diamond-shaped face. I, on the other hand, am short, curvy, and a bit clumsy, and while I'd like to think that I'm easy on the eyes, I could never compete with my big sister. Brenda has always been the center of attention, so I faded into the background while Brenda would shine. She was the star student who always brought home awards and good grades. She was a cheerleader and a basketball star in high school. I was smart and introverted. My goal was to get through school and get out unscathed.

"Brenda, why do you keep doing this? What do you even know about this guy? Does he treat women with respect? Does he like music and art? Is he kind? Is he fun? Is he generous?"

"Why don't you go out with him and find out?" Brenda asks.

"Because I don't need to be defined by a man, and I don't need you to pimp me out."

"What's your plan then? You have to put yourself out there before it's too late."

"Is there a man shortage I'm not aware of?"

"Yes, there is, and the women out here aren't playing around. Finding a mate is a competitive sport. You can't sit on the sidelines."

"I'm not going to have this conversation with you again, Brenda." I reach for our little brother as he walks past us. "Marcus, save me."

Marcus is tall, lean, and handsome. He's also no stranger to the spotlight either. He was a high school and college basketball star, and he has a degree in engineering. He stops and puts his arm around my shoulder.

"What has she done now?" Marcus asks.

"She's trying to set me up with a lawyer. Make her stop."

"Before you try, remember that I set you up, Marcus. Look at you now, married with a baby."

"She does have a point," Marcus says.

I punch Marcus in the shoulder. "You're not helping."

"Brenda, leave Audrey alone. If she wants to be sad and lonely, that's her prerogative."

I push Marcus. "Go away."

He kisses me on the cheek. "I'm just playing, sis. You know you're my favorite."

"I need a drink." I excuse myself to refill my empty glass of champagne.

"Honey, make sure you watch the top." My mom,

directs my dad, Jim, on how to hang the lights on the Christmas tree. After thirty-five years of marriage, my dad knows exactly how my mom wants the lights hung, but that never stops her from micromanaging.

I can hear the frustration in his voice. "I got it, Maxine. Why don't you go check on something?"

"I am. I'm checking on you."

He closes his eyes and calms himself. "I love you, baby."

"I bet you do."

I shake my head.

"Hi, baby girl."

"Hey, daddy. Are you hanging in there?" I joke.

"As well as can be expected."

"What's that supposed to mean?" My mom asks.

"Nothing."

"The lights look great, daddy."

"Thank you, baby girl."

My mom eyeballs my glass of champagne. "Audrey, make sure you don't drink too much, baby."

"When do I ever drink too much?"

"Don't get sensitive, sweetie. I'm not saying you have a problem or anything. I just don't want you to have another outburst like you did the other day at Thanksgiving."

"I didn't have an outburst."

"You raised your voice at your mother like you don't have any home training." She pinches my arm. "If I talked like that to my mama, y'all would've had to pick me up off the floor."

"Ouch. I didn't raise my voice. I was just pointing out that my cake was not dry, and that's not why I don't have a man."

"Don't contradict your mother."

The front door opens before I can respond. "Hi, everybody. Sorry, we're late. We're still a little jet-

4

lagged."

Ugh. It's my cousin Michelle. She poses in the doorway like a supermodel at the end of the runway. Michelle has long legs and long, blonde hair that compliment her flawless golden-brown skin. She only wears designer clothes and never leaves home without a full face of makeup. Michelle's husband Andre, stands behind her. Andre is the definition of tall, dark, and handsome, and also the definition of my ex-boyfriend.

They claim they got together after we broke up. They claim neither of them was looking for the other. It just happened, they say, but Michelle has always tried to outdo me. First, she starts her beauty channel after I started mine. Then she winds up with my boyfriend.

Michelle runs to hug my mom. "Aunt Maxine. Sorry, we're late."

"Hey, honey, we're just getting started. You look more beautiful every time I see you. I love this color on you." My mom tugs on Michelle's red sweater.

"Thank you, auntie. You look fabulous as usual." My mom's honey-colored skin has never known a wrinkle. She wears a casual powder blue pantsuit with a navy shirt.

My mom gives Andre a polite hug. "Andre, how are you?"

"Doing well. You look beautiful Mrs. Stafford."

"Thank you, dear."

Andre smiles at me and gives me an awkward hug. "So do you, Audrey. Good to see you."

My hands remain stiff at my side, but in the spirit of not wanting Andre to think he has any effect on me, I muster all my energy to force a smile. Everything about Andre is smug, and he comes around acting like everything is normal, like nothing ever happened between us. I would love to smack that perfect smile off his face.

"Thanks."

"How are you, Audrey? One of your videos popped up on my feed the other day. How's business?" he asks.

Michelle interrupts before I can reply. "Oh, Audrey, I didn't see you."

"Hi, Michelle."

Michelle gives me a fake ass one-handed hug and an air kiss. "Don't you look cute. What did you do to your hair?"

"I was feeling adventurous, and I wanted something different." Unlike the rest of the women in my family, I choose to wear minimal makeup and my hair in its natural coils, and I recently added a vibrant red color.

"It looks good, doesn't it Andre," Michelle asks.

Andre's phone rings. "Yeah, excuse me," he says.

There's a brief flash of disappointment on Michelle's face. "Can't it wait?"

"It's business."

Michelle keeps her eyes glued to Andre as he walks out the front door and closes it behind him.

"It's temporary, isn't it dear?" My mom smooths my hair with her palm.

I try to dodge her hand as I respond. "It's a temporary color, but I might do it again. I love how it turned out."

"It is something." My mom forces a smile.

"Here we go. I'll be back." My hair has been a topic of discussion at family functions ever since I cut it off. It's grown tremendously in the last two years. It's healthy and thick, and it's never looked better, but I still have to constantly defend my decision to wear it natural.

My mom and Michelle continue to gush over one another so no one pays attention when I slip away.

Another glass of champagne is definitely in order if

I'm going to get through this event. My family drives me crazy, but I love them. My cousins play spades and the children are busy with their crafts. Marcus is in the corner with his wife, whispering sweet nothings in her ear. They look so in love, and I can't remember if a man has ever looked at me that way. Suddenly I'm hit with a feeling of longing. I hate it when this happens. It's usually unexpected, but the good thing is it won't last long. With everyone being coupled up, maybe I should let my sister set me up. I'm proud to be single, but there are moments when I get lonely. I try to tell myself to think about something else.

My grandfather taps me on the shoulder. "Sweet pea, what's happening?"

"Nothing, just enjoying family time."

"It's alright, sweet pea. What does Papa always tell you?"

"I don't know what you're talking about."

"You are special, and whoever you're meant to be with is also special. They have to prepare for you, and when they're ready, it'll be worth the wait."

My grandfather, with his cinnamon skin and salt and pepper hair, is the only person in my family who never judges me. He's always full of kind words and encourages me to trust myself and my decisions. "How can you be so sure?" I ask.

"I'm old and wise, and you're young and beautiful."

"I don't know Papa. I don't know if I'll ever be that happy." I point at my brother and his wife.

"Everybody married ain't happy, and everybody happy ain't married. You remember that. Now smile for Papa."

I flash my teeth.

"That's the smile that's going to make your future husband crazy for you." He pinches my cheek.

"Thank you, Papa."

"Hi everybody," Michelle shouts as she steps into the living room. "We didn't come back empty handed. We've got gifts for you all from the Cayman Islands." Michelle reaches into a big bag and walks around the room handing out souvenirs. She approaches me last holding out a red bag with a big smile. She's a little too excited for my liking. I thank her and sit the bag on the table next to me.

"No, open it now. I found the perfect gift for you."

"Perfect?" I question.

"I promise."

My gift is the only one in a bag. Michelle is definitely up to something. I smile sweetly. "I'll just open it when I get home."

"No, do it now."

"I'd rather not."

"Come on baby, just open it," my mother says.

Why is saying no never enough?

"Fine," Michelle grabs the bag. I instinctively reach for it, but Michelle is quicker, and she begins tugging at the tissue paper. "I'll open it for you," she says.

I roll my eyes.

"See, look." Michelle is loud enough for everyone to hear. She pulls a black and gold box out of the bag and waves it proudly for everyone in the room.

I squint through my glasses as the box comes into focus.

"It's a hot comb," my mother says with excitement.

"It's supposed to be the best," Michelle adds.

I look at my mother, then at Michelle in disbelief. "When was the last time you saw me with straight hair?"

"Exactly," Michelle says with a smug smirk that only I can detect. "I figured that since you went old school, this was a perfect way to straighten your hair. This one will definitely work all those kinks out. Now your hair can look pretty."

"Excuse me," I say.

"It's about time you did something to that hair of yours," Michelle says.

"I like my hair the way it is, and I already have a hot comb. I just don't straighten my hair because I don't want to. Don't act like you don't know that."

My mother tries to calm me with a rub on the shoulder. "This is for when you're ready to try something different. You're getting older and you need to get married and have babies. Don't you think you need to focus on attracting a man? Men are visual creatures, and your hair is your crowning glory."

"I like my crowning glory the way it is, mother. It took years to grow my hair this long, and any man who can't appreciate my natural hair the way it was created can kick rocks."

"That's why it'll look so good when it's straight. Imagine how long and silky it can be. You'll have men lining up to be with you."

"Aunt Maxine is right. When was the last time you had a boyfriend or a date? Aren't you tired of being alone?"

My cheeks heat. The entire family is watching the spectacle.

"Audrey is beautiful just the way she is," her grandfather states.

"Michelle, my personal life is none of your business. Don't start with me."

Michelle is quick to judge everyone else and pretend that her life is perfect. Everyone knows she's lonely and miserable because her fiancé is always on the road or working late, and there are many rumors as to where he really is when he's away from home.

"I've got a man. You should take notes."

"You've got a man today. Where is he every other

day? Where is he right now?" I ask.

"He's taking a work call. You'd know what it was like if you could get a man, let alone keep one."

"Does it count as keeping one if he's keeping busy with everyone else in town?"

My mom interrupts me before I can really let Michelle have it. "Honey, don't get so angry. I think it'll be nice if you try to wear it straight and see what happens. You used to be so pretty when your hair was done."

"Really, mom?"

"That's all I'm saying," Michelle says.

"My hair is done. This is a style. This takes time and effort, and I love it. I shouldn't have to defend my hair to my family of all people."

They can talk about her being single all they want, but I will not let them insult my hair. I finally got it trained and my curls to act right. Thanks to my new conditioner and styling cream I can run my fingers through it without using too much product, and my curls have definition. It's a major accomplishment, but since I'm the only woman in the family who wears my natural curls, no one else understands.

"You're the only one who loves it," Michelle says.

"That's fine with me."

"When you look around and you're old, dried up, and all alone, don't say we didn't try to help you."

"I'll just call you, Michelle. You know what it's like to be all alone, don't you?" I ask.

"Audrey, don't be rude."

"You're reprimanding me, mom? She's the one being rude."

"Honey, I think you're just being sensitive. Your cousin tried to do something nice for you. She just wants to help."

"I don't need help. I'm happy and healthy. I have a

career that I love, I do what I want, and I don't have to answer to anyone."

"Yet none of those things will keep you warm at night," Michelle points out.

"Don't worry about me. I do just fine."

"Doesn't everyone think Audrey would look beautiful with straight hair?" Michelle asks the room.

"This is ridiculous." I look around in disbelief as my family members nod in agreement with Michelle.

Papa puts his arm around my waist. "Don't listen to them, sweet pea, your hair is beautiful and so are you."

I manage to muster a half smile.

"It's true. They're just jealous because you're happy with yourself," he whispers.

"I love you, Papa. I need to get some air." I walk out of the room.

On my way out, Andre walks in the door. "Hey, Audrey."

"Did you have something to do with that?" I ask him.

"What are you talking about?"

"You and your fiancé want to taunt me. Is that it? Let me tell you something. I love my hair, and there's nothing either of you can say to make me feel otherwise." I storm off.

Andre follows me outside. "I don't know what you're talking about."

"Do the two of you just sit around and laugh at me?"

"No, of course not."

"I have no desire to straighten my hair so you can take your hot comb back to the Caymans and throw it in the ocean. I don't want it."

"What hot comb?"

"You didn't know your wife brought me a hot comb from your vacation and pulled it out in front of the "whole family."

"No, I had no idea. I'm sorry. I'll talk to her."

"Yeah, right."

Andre gently grabs Audrey's hand. "I mean it."

I snatch my hand from his. What the hell? "Don't do me any favors."

"I don't know what's going on with Michelle, but I like your hair. You're beautiful." He places his hand on my shoulder. "I can't help but wonder." He stares into my eyes.

"Wonder what?"

Michelle opens the door. "Andre, are you finished with your call?"

"Yeah, I was about to head in."

Michelle gives me a cold look and holds out her hand. "Well, come on. It's cold out here."

"I'll catch you later," Andre says to me. He takes Michelle's hand and she kisses him on the lips as he crosses the threshold.

I rest my head in my hands on the porch rail. Even their dysfunctional relationship is better than my nonexistent one. The air is cold and crisp. A gust of wind caresses my cheek, and I close my eyes. It's not like I don't want someone, but I want someone who can't live without me, who has to have me. What would he look like? That's not important. What's important is how he feels about me. I imagine a hand, brown skin, long, with strong, hard-working fingers gently touching my face before a pair of perfect lips touch mine. I long for the warmth of a strong pair of hands peeling my clothes off piece by piece, exploring my body as his kisses my neck. It would be nice to have someone to go home to. A slight moan escapes my lips.

"Audrey, it's cold out here." My mother's voice jolts me back into the real world. I can feel my cheeks grow hot.

I stand up straight and clear my throat. "It feels good to me."

"You're not even wearing a coat. Come inside."

"I'll be right there."

My mother puts her arm around me. "Honey, you know I love you, don't you?"

"Yes ma'am."

"I just don't want you to be alone. I don't want you to miss out on a family of your own. Who's going to take care of you?"

"I take care of myself very well."

"I know you do, honey, but that's not what I'm talking about. Don't you want a man to be a man, to take care of all your needs to be there with you through the good times and the bad times?"

"Do you think straightening my hair will make that happen?"

"I think it'll show off your pretty face."

"I'm more than a pretty face, and I can't believe we're having a conversation about hair in this day and age. I'm looking for someone who wants more than that. I want someone kind, strong, passionate, masculine, sensitive, thoughtful, dominant, smart—"

"Girl," my mother interrupts me, "no wonder you're still single. That's unrealistic. No one man is all those things. It would take at least three men to give you what you want."

"Excuse me for having standards."

"Those are not standards. That's a fantasy."

"Mom, I'll be fine."

"I know you will. You're smart and you're beautiful."

"You think I'm beautiful?"

"Of course I do, sweetie."

"Even with my hair like this."

My mom puts her hands in my thick mane and

13

sighs. "Even with your hair like this."

"Thank you." My smile is genuine as I hug my mother. I know she means well.

"But mama would like to see you straighten your hair at least once. Just for me. We don't know how much longer I'm going be around."

I laugh. "That's so unfair, and you know you're going to be around, criticizing my hair, for a long, long time."

"When my mama asks me to do something, I'd do it out of respect."

"Why don't I go inside and ask grandma how respectful you are of her wishes?"

"Don't you dare," she says. "I'll never hear the end of it."

"Interesting," I say.

We share another laugh and a hug.

"I love you, Audrey."

"I love you too mom."

"Don't be so hard on Michelle. You know she's going through a lot that she doesn't talk about."

"Why do you always take her side? I'm your daughter."

"When my sister passed, she needed someone. She never came to terms with losing her mother, and I try to do my best to honor my sister. I try to fill that void for her, but no one can. You could be a little nicer to your cousin."

"She already got my ex. What more can I do for her?"

"You handled that whole situation with such grace. You were too good for him. Trust me, there's someone much better than Andre for you."

"You think so?"

"Mama knows."

"I know you're right. It's just one of those things you

just don't do, but whatever. If they belong together, who am I to stand in the way?"

"Just try to cut her some slack. She doesn't have your strength."

"Well, she needs to quit pretending that her life is perfect and leave me alone."

"She's harmless."

"She's evil, and I don't know why you all don't see it."

"She's family. She wouldn't do anything to hurt you."

"Mom, she did not bring me a hot comb out of love and concern. She tried to embarrass me."

"What did mama tell you? Nobody can embarrass you without your permission."

"That doesn't stop them from trying."

"Come on, let's get inside where it's warm."

I follow my mother back into the house.

"Everything okay?" my father asks.

"Yes, daddy. I've got some work to do tonight so I'm going to say goodbye to everybody. I hug him and a kiss on the cheek."

"Why are you leaving so soon, Sweet Pea?" Papa asks.

"I want to get some things done before it gets dark outside."

"So you're just gonna leave me here with these people?"

I laugh. "They're your family too."

"I guess neither of us had a choice," he says.

"At least we have each other," I say.

"Don't you forget it. Now, what kind of work do you have to do. You know I don't like you going out into those woods alone."

"I know, but I have to. I'm just going for a few minutes. I promise."

15

"Can't you pay somebody to do that for you?"

"It helps me clear my head. Don't worry about me. I'll be careful." I kiss him on the cheek before heading out the front door. I need a breather from my family. My hair is important to me. It's my life. It's my business. It's everything.

Three years ago, I needed a change. I felt like relaxers and heat styling were damaging my hair. I wanted to see my hair and embrace my natural texture because I didn't even know why I was straightening my hair in the first place. That's when I did the big chop. I was happy with the result. It was short, but I felt so free like a weight had been lifted off my shoulders. I thought I'd finally found myself, but soon after, I got dumped. Coincidence, I think not. Andre gave me a speech about growing apart. It was bullshit. Before I cut my hair, we were inseparable. I thought we were headed for marriage. We dated for four years, and I thought we were happy. Six months after we broke up, he and Michelle started dating, and six months after that, they were engaged. I stood on the sidelines pretending that I didn't care and that I was over Andre. What else could I do? They've been engaged for two years now. It took some time, but I made peace with it. I moved on with my life. Since then, it's just been me and my hair.

Once my hair started growing, it quickly went from cute to I don't know what the hell to do with this, and I'm a cosmetologist. The texture was nothing like I imagined it would be. It was hard to manage, and styling it was impossible. I had to figure something out. I looked for products to keep it moisturized and stylish. I was determined not to wear wigs. It was like a personal challenge. I wanted to accept my hair. I tried every natural haircare line under the sun, and nothing gave me the look or feel that I wanted. I searched online for natural hairstyles and came across a YouTube video. That's when my obsession with natural haircare began. I watched countless videos and picked up some helpful tips. That's when I started my channel, documenting my journey. I began using natural oils, plants, and ingredients to make my own conditioner, moisturizer, and hair gel. Through a lot of trial and error, I created products that worked for my hair.

My obsession became my passion. I saw aloe vera plants outside the forest near my house, and I started to get my supply from there. Venturing into the woods, I found many more plants that I used to experiment with. The further I went, the more I found. I came across the most beautiful flowers I had ever seen, and I found the sweetest berries I had ever tasted. I felt like I won the lottery, and picking plants from the forest for my conditioner became my favorite hobby. I had a crazy idea to add berries to my conditioner, and I discovered that juices from ripe regal berries helped moisturize my hair and eliminate frizz. It started with a few people noticing and requesting the products I used. My subscribers were raving about my progress. I started gaining more natural clients. I opened my natural hair salon. Pretty soon I was selling at trade shows and public events. I even opened an online store and sold to other salons in the area. Women are going crazy for Regal Haircare.

The more products I made, the deeper I went looking in the forest. That's when I saw the most beautiful flowers I've ever seen. They must be exotic. The petals are white with colorful tips, pink, blue, and purple. They have a bulb in the center, the same color as the tips, and the bulb is so bright it glows. The first time I saw them I was drawn to them like a moth to a flame. I couldn't resist taking some home with me. I put them in a vase and set them in my kitchen. They filled my house with the most intoxicating scent, and sometimes I'd wear them in my hair.

That's when I got my next great idea. Most women like to wear perfume on their bodies. I extracted oil from the flower and added it to my conditioner. Not only did my hair smell heavenly, but it was softer, more manageable, and had a shine I hadn't seen since going natural. This flower became my new obsession, but I couldn't find it anywhere. I scoured the internet. There's not so much as a picture of it or anything that confirms its existence. I gave up and continued to pick them from the forest.

I gave the flower a name, Alaria, and that's what I named the new addition to my haircare line. Something exotic, just like the flower. I visit the forest more frequently, making sure to leave some behind, hoping more will grow so I can continue to use it in my haircare line. Alaria is my new secret ingredient and once my customers try it, it's sure to be a game changer for my company and the industry.

The sun will be setting soon, and I need to get some plants, so I park my car and grab my basket. These woods are always peaceful. They help me relax. It's beautiful, like an oasis. I inhale as I walk a familiar path ready to clear my head, and put today behind me.

CHAPTER 2
Darius

She's back. I can feel her.

It's been three months. I have to put a stop to this. I stalk through the forest, following her scent. There she is, this foolish woman. She has no idea I'm here. She never pays attention to her surroundings. She comes here all alone. Her head is always down, looking at the ground. She doesn't carry a weapon. Anyone could attack her, and she wouldn't have a clue until it was too late.

My wolf is infatuated with our mate and angry with me. I've been able to keep him at bay by allowing him to be near her. She's never seen us but we watch her as she picks plants from the woods. My wolf longs for her, and why wouldn't he. She's beautiful, perfect, and her scent drives both of us wild.

She's never come this far before. She must be looking for more flowers. I have to put a stop to this now. I hope she doesn't hate me. Then again, I hope she does. I stand over her while her back is turned to me. She has no idea I'm here. Her curly hair is parted on the side and the red color is intensified by the sunlight. I like this new color. It looks good on her. She's wearing a black sweater dress that clings to her body. I can't deny I want to touch her, caress her, feel her body against mine, taste her brown skin. I lick my lips as I watch her body move. I have to snap out of it.

I stand with my arms folded. "What are you doing here?" I startle her with my most threatening voice.

She jumps and turns around with her hand over her heart. Before she can respond, she stops in her tracks and stares at me. Her beautiful brown eyes trail my body, my feet, my abs, my biceps, and her heart races. She's five feet, four inches. I'm six feet, seven inches, all muscle. When our eyes meet, I swear time stops.

She's frozen and so am I. I've never been this close to her. I can feel her desire. It surrounds me, pulling me in. Her shiny lips look supple and beg to be kissed. I desperately want to fuck her right now.

She backs up and tries to run.

I reach for her arm and grab her hand instead. "I asked you a question," I say as I pull her close to me. Electricity crackles, it starts at my fingers and works its way through my body. My dick jumps.

She must feel something too because she pauses, and for a moment, she succumbs to the pull between us. I can see it in her eyes before she struggles to break free of my grasp. "Let me go," she shouts.

"Why should I?" I ask. I grab her arm. She bites her bottom lip. My wolf stirs and my grip tightens.

She stomps on my foot, slams her elbow into my side, and pushes me.

She's so tiny. I chuckle. The more I think about it, the harder I laugh. I can't remember the last time I laughed so hard. I think I needed this.

With my grip loosened, she snatches her arm away from me and turns to run. She suddenly stops and watches me. "What are you laughing at? Are you laughing at me?"

"That was cute," I say. I clear my throat. I need to focus. I make sure my face is serious, threatening. "This is no laughing matter. You've been stealing."

"What?" she shouts. "I've never stolen anything in my life. How dare you?"

"You're a thief, and if I ever see you here again, I'll have you arrested."

"Arrested? What are you talking about? Arrested for what?"

"Trespassing, for starters."

"I'm not trespassing. This is public property."

"What makes you think it's public?"

"It's the woods. You can't own the woods."

"Who told you that?"

"Common sense."

"You have a lot to learn, lady. You can't just make assumptions, and you can't steal from me without there being consequences."

"Steal? I don't steal."

"I've watched you. I hoped you'd stop, but you keep coming back, taking what's mine. I won't tolerate it any longer. You're not welcome here."

"You've been watching me?" she asks.

"The point is, you need to leave here and never return."

"How do I know what you're saying is true?"

"This is my land, and that is my house." I point beyond the flower bed to my cabin.

"Why have you been watching me? Why didn't you say anything before now?"

"It's time for you to go," I reply.

"What is your name?" she asks.

"That's none of your concern, Audrey."

She pauses. "How do you know my name?"

"You ask too many questions. Get off my property. Stop stealing from me, or you'll be sorry. Do I make myself clear?"

Audrey stands with her mouth open. I can see that for her, nothing is clear.

"GET OUT!" I shout.

Audrey jumps. Her glasses fall, and she drops her basket as she takes off running. She doesn't look back until she reaches her car, out of breath.

I don't move until Audrey drives off. "Damnit," I shout. Sending her away is one of the hardest things I've ever done. My wolf whimpers. I try to tell him it's for the best, but now I'm finding it hard to believe

21

myself. I can only hope it's enough to keep Audrey away for good. I'm immediately filled with sorrow.

I pick up her glasses and basket from the ground. I don't know what I'll do with them. I'd like to mail them to her, but I don't think that would be a good idea. I touched her. I don't think that was smart. I won't be able to get her out of my mind. As I take her things inside the cabin, I'm angry at myself, and my wolf is angry with me. I remind him that I want her as much as he does, and I'm doing what's best for Audrey. That's the end of it.

I need to clear my head. I change into a pair of basketball shorts and go for a run. I bought this land because the soil is rich and healthy. The proof is in the plants and trees that grow here. I found a hidden gem. My forest is thriving and the fresh air is good for my spirit. I stop when I reach the lake. I look out into the water and center my thoughts. Audrey is safe and happy, and I want her to stay that way. Keeping her away is what's best.

I hear my father, Jonas, approach from behind. "Woman problems?" he asks.

I continue to look at the water and hold out a bottle of wine that I got for him.

"Thank you. This is nice."

"You're welcome. How are you, dad?"

"I'm fine, son."

"Do you need anything?"

"Don't worry about me boy. I know how to get anything I need."

"I know you do."

"I'm more concerned about you. What's your problem?"

"I talked to her today," I inform him. My father is the only one I've told about Audrey.

"That's new. What happened?"

"I yelled at her. I told her to stay away."

"Why did you do that, boy?"

"Why do you think?"

"Not only are you keeping yourself from happiness, you're keeping it from her too. Is it fair to do that to someone you love?"

"I'm more concerned with protecting her than her happiness. I can't drag her into this life. It's not right."

"It's not right not to give her a choice. Do you really expect her to stay away?"

"I made it clear."

"That's why you look like a lost pup right now. I don't feel sorry for you. You're doing it to yourself."

"I don't know why I expected you to understand."

"My life is my life, and you have to live yours. Not only are you betraying your mate, you're betraying your pack. It's not right. If you want to go at it alone, do that, step aside, but I raised you to have integrity."

"Can't you see I'm not doing this for me?"

"Son, you're the one who's getting his way in this situation."

"I'm the one who's being selfless."

"You're not being selfless. You're selfish. You're hiding behind your pain and fear. You're stronger than that. You're better than that."

I hug my father. "I have to go, dad."

As I run back to my cabin, I can't shake what he said to me. He's been saying it for months, and I've been convinced that I was right. Part of me is trying to protect myself, but the bigger part of me wants to protect Audrey. If I'm being honest, I'm working off of assumptions. My father's right. I made the decision for her, but I know this world better than she does, and if she has the opportunity to live a full life without this, shouldn't I let her.

I've been telling myself that what my pack doesn't

know, won't hurt them. Am I selfish? My pack is small but powerful. And I like it that way. There are twenty of us, all alpha wolf shifters, and I'm alpha in charge. I rule alongside my beta, Felix, and omega, Damien. It was fate that brought us together, the three white wolves, the most powerful of our kind, and we're connected. I love my pack, and my pack will love Audrey, but I don't know if Audrey would love this life. She's human, and she wouldn't choose this for herself, so I've resisted every urge, to touch her, take her, and mate her, for her.

CHAPTER 3

Audrey

I pull my car into my garage as the sun sets. The sky is turning dark, but I can't move. My mind is consumed with the man I saw today. His green eyes pierced my body, and his deep voice penetrated my soul. He smelled like fresh rain. I can't shake the thought of him, his light brown skin, his big, and strong hands. He's the tallest man I've ever seen, not to mention he's sexy as hell. He did something to me. He awakened something in me, and all I want is for him to touch me, hold me, fuck me. I've never felt like this before. Like I have no control over my desire. I want him like I've never wanted anyone, and I don't even know his name.

He may think he scared me away with his angry old man act, but I see through him. He didn't mean the things he said. If he wanted to have me arrested he would've done it already. I ran out of the forest for dramatic effect, making sure to leave my glasses and basket behind. There's no way I'm not going back. I'm no thief, and I hope he and I can at least come to an agreement about his plants. I bang my head on the steering wheel. My body is going crazy, craving his touch like an addict.

If I don't relieve some pressure soon, I'm going to burst. When I think about the spark I felt when his calloused hand touched mine, I can't stop myself from imagining those hands all over my body. I close my eyes and squeeze my breasts. Intensity builds in the hardened buds of my nipples as my palms slide across them. I need more. I lift my dress. If only I knew his name, I'd be calling out to him right now. I slip my hand inside my tights, underneath my panties, and touch myself. I'm so wet I can hear my juices as I press my fingers in and out. I recall every inch of his beautifully sculpted body, beginning with his sparkling green eyes. My hips grind against my leather seats. Pleasure courses through my body, and I can't control my moans.

A knock on the window startles me. I scream. My heart leaps out of my chest.

"What the fuck?" I shout as I quickly adjust my clothes and look around. I focus on the figure to my left. "Andre? What are you doing here?" My cheeks heat, but as he licks his lips, I see a desire in his eyes I haven't seen in a long time.

"I'm so sorry," he says.

"Go away," I shout with my eyes closed.

"I didn't know you were in here. I just saw the garage door was open, and I wanted to make sure you were safe."

"As you can see I'm fine."

"I need to talk to you."

I adjust my clothes and jump out of the car. "Why are you driving past my house? Where's Michelle?"

"She's still at your mother's."

"Does she know you're here?"

"No, I told her I had to go to the office."

"I'm not sure what's going on, but you shouldn't be here." I look around paranoid. This could be some kind of set-up or trick.

"Everything happened so fast before you left. I just wanted to make sure I didn't do anything to cause you to leave. Are you okay?"

"What? I'm fine."

"You snapped at me today, and you've never done that before, not even when we broke up. You've changed."

"For better," I say.

"Definitely better," Andre says.

"Well, if that's all, you should leave." This feels

strange. I haven't been alone with him since we broke up. He came to my house to get his things, and I don't know why or how, but as he stood at the door and gave me one last look, something happened. We were drawn to one another, and we ended up making love. It was better than it had ever been, so good that it still pops in my head from time to time, but that was our goodbye. We didn't speak afterward. He just left, and that was that. The next time I saw him, he had my cousin on his arm, and I had the wind knocked out of me. I never said anything about it because I never wanted Michelle to think she had anything over me.

I know Andre well. He looks like he wants to say something. I watch his nervous movement. I can see the wheels turning in his mind.

"You made me think. I always assumed you were okay with me and Michelle."

"I am."

"I'm not so sure anymore."

"It's water under the bridge."

"Still I want to make sure there's nothing unresolved between us."

"There's absolutely nothing between us."

"I'd like to believe you, but I was hurt that you think I'd do or say anything to hurt you."

"You were hurt. Am I supposed to care?"

"I know you care because you're a good person. I know you, Audrey."

"I'm no longer your concern, Andre. What is all of this? You've barely said anything to me since we broke up, and now you want to have a heart to heart."

"I've changed also," he says.

"I noticed."

"I hope you know that I never stopped caring about you."

"Yeah, sure Andre. You care about me. Got it. You

can leave now."

"Can I talk to you for a minute? I mean really talk like we used to."

"That's not weird at all."

"Please. Can we go inside?"

"Hell no." I lean against the wall. "What's up?"

"Have you ever felt lost?"

"Yep."

"What did you do about it?"

"I took a look at myself, who I was, and who I wanted to be. I figured out what made me happy, what I wanted to contribute to the world, and I accepted myself and my flaws."

"I don't think I've ever done that."

"It's not too late."

"I've been thinking about us lately, about everything we lost."

"Did we really lose anything?"

"We lost a friendship. I regret that all the time."

"You do?"

"We don't even talk anymore."

"That's what happens when people break up. They don't talk."

"It doesn't have to be that way."

"I'm pretty sure it does. We don't have anything to talk about."

"It's weird being on the sidelines. You opened a business. You're making moves and I can't even celebrate with you. It's like I'm watching you grow, and I don't get to be a part of it."

"You're pretty busy these days, Andre. You're never around. Do you even have time for a friendship? You're always working."

He shrugs. "Michelle is high maintenance. I have to do what I have to do to keep her happy."

"I suppose you do."

"I don't know if that woman can ever be pleased. What am I supposed to do?"

"I know you didn't come here to ask me for advice about my cousin."

He looks sad. "I'm sorry, not at all. I wouldn't do that. I was just thinking out loud."

I sigh. "Look, Michelle likes to show off. It's who she is. I don't know if there's a way you can balance work with putting her on a pedestal, but try, or at least let her know you're trying. She doesn't only want the perfect picture, she wants it all. She wants you on her arm when she goes out, so try making a little more effort to spend time with her. Take her on dates. You can at least dedicate one day a week to spend with her."

"Maybe you're right." He looks into my eyes. "You're too kind."

"I'm not."

"I know she gives you a hard time. There's no excuse for her behavior, but you're still nice to her, even though she doesn't deserve it." He moves closer to me.

I inhale his cologne. I don't like the way he's looking at me. I turn my head to avoid his gaze.

He touches my cheek and gently turns my head to face him. His fingers tangle in my hair. "You never could accept a compliment. Don't turn away from me."

I forgot how well he knows me. "You shouldn't touch my face," I say.

"I know," he says. His voice turns deep and raspy. "I can't help it. I can't help but wonder."

"You said that earlier. What are you wondering?"

He pauses before he speaks. "I wonder if I made a huge mistake."

"Regarding what?"

"I thought our relationship had run its course," he says.

"It did." I push his hand from my face.

"Maybe, or maybe we didn't fight hard enough."

"Or maybe you were a superficial asshole who didn't want me when I cut my hair off. Don't come here trying to play me. You're were full of shit then, and you're full of shit now."

"You don't know what you're talking about."

"If you don't want to be honest we have nothing to talk about." The shock on his face is priceless, and it feels so good to finally call him out.

"Maybe you're right," he says.

"Right about what? I want to hear you say it."

"Say what?"

"Tell me why you broke up with me."

"We grew apart."

"Bullshit. You can leave now." I shout as I push him.

"What do you want me to say?"

"The truth. Just say it. Don't be a coward. I want, I need, to hear it.

"What's gotten into you?"

"I'm sick of your phony bullshit. Just be honest for once in your life. Maybe that's why you're so unhappy. You lie all the time." I push him again.

He grabs my wrist. "Don't put your hands on me."

I push him with my other hand.

He grabs my other wrist.

I'm angry at this point. I hate him and his lying ass. "Just get out of here," I shout like a mad woman.

He clenches my wrists. I think he's going to yell at me. "You're right," he shouts.

"Say it," I demand.

"I broke up with you when you cut your hair because I'm a superficial asshole. Is that what you want to hear?"

"YES!"

"You didn't warn me. You didn't say anything. You just walked in the room, and your hair was gone. You didn't even ask for my opinion."

"Excuse the hell out of me. I didn't think my hair mattered."

"Maybe it did. Maybe it didn't. I don't know. I was caught off guard. It was an adjustment, and you didn't care about my feelings. You just did it."

"I thought it was my hair and my decision."

"You only thought about yourself. It was a major decision, and you didn't even consider my feelings."

"I didn't know I had to."

"What was I supposed to do? I fell in love with the woman I met and you took her away."

"You were supposed to love me for me, not my hair."

"You're right, okay. I'm sorry. I was wrong. I didn't understand that at the time, and I paid the price for it. I lost so much."

"Naw, you didn't lose anything. You gained so much more, someone more superficial than you could ever imagine. You two deserve one another, and I hope you're happy together."

"I'm not happy."

"You must be. I mean, we were together for years, and you practically proposed to my cousin instantly. She's what you've been waiting for your whole life, isn't she?"

"Like I said, I've changed."

I jerk my wrists from his grasp. "Oh well."

He steps closer to me. I can feel his body against mine. "I'm sorry, Audrey. I'm sorry for the pain I caused you. I'm sorry for not looking back and making sure you were okay. I'm sorry for all of it."

Before I know it, a tear falls from my eye. I told myself I would never cry in front of him. He doesn't deserve my tears. Damn him. The tears start flowing and I can't control them, but I'm not sad. I'm relieved.

He wipes my tears away. "Please don't cry. I already feel like shit. I'm sorry."

"Thank you," I say. I didn't know I needed to hear his apology until he said it. I feel like a heaviness lifted from my chest and I can breathe.

His hand is rested on my cheek and he leans his forehead against mine. He embraces me, and I stiffen, but he holds me tighter, and my body begins to relax.

"I'm sorry, Audrey."

"It's okay."

"I can't get a hug," he says.

I reluctantly hug him back.

"I made a mistake," he says.

"No, you didn't. You did what you felt you needed to do."

"I miss you."

I try to speak, to tell him not to say that to me, but before I know it, his lips are on mine, so soft and gentle. I resist, but then I'm sucked in by an old familiar feeling, and I slowly kiss him back. I allow his tongue to tease mine and his hand to caress my back. It takes me a moment to come to my senses and I pull away. I try to stay calm. "Stop, Andre."

"It felt good."

"No, it didn't," I lie.

"You're not a good liar."

I can feel his dick, hard against my leg. "You should get going."

"How long has it been since someone fucked you?" he asks.

"What?"

"When I walked up to your car, I saw what you were doing."

"That was private."

"I can't stop thinking about it. I used to make you moan like that. Remember?"

32

"No."

"Was I the last one?" he asks. His finger trails my arm.

I turn my head away from his gaze.

"I was," he says. "That pussy is still mine."

"No, it's not."

"Your body begs to differ. Let me take care of that ache, Audrey."

"No," I say. I push him off of me. "You're engaged to my cousin."

"I know, but I belong with you."

"No, you don't. I should've known you were up to no good."

"Are you telling me you don't feel anything for me?"

"I'm telling you that what you're doing is foul. You can't go back and forth between us. I don't know what you think this is, but I'm not the one. You made your choice, and you have to live with it."

"I need to find what makes me happy, and that's you."

"That's not me. You can't find happiness in someone else, only yourself. I don't know why you're here or what you want, but I'm not interested in you or us. If you and Michelle have problems I don't want anything to do with it. You keep my name out of it, and stay away from me. Don't come back here."

"Audrey, don't be like that."

"Go now, or I'll call the police. You're trespassing."

"What the hell are you talking about?"

"Now," I shout.

"Audrey, just listen."

"Leave."

He turns to walk away.

"Andre," I shout.

He turns around.

33

"You'd better do right by my cousin. Do you understand me?"

He walks away. He looks a little sad, but I don't care. I can't believe he just did that. I also can't believe myself. I finally confronted him. I don't feel haunted by him anymore. Stupid jerk. My mother was right, I can do better.

CHAPTER 4

Darius

I try to get Audrey out of my head as I sit by the fireplace and read the Sunday paper. What's done is done, and I may never see her again. That was my plan after all, and now I feel sick about it.

The words leap off the page, and I can't focus. My wolf stirs. He's excited, and I know there's only one reason he'd feel that way. I sniff the air around me. I can scent her. Audrey's back, and she's pacing outside my front door. I can feel her nerves. She wants to see me as much as I want to see her.

Finally, she stops pacing and knocks on the door. I pause. Now that we've met, I can feel her desire. Our bond is too strong to ignore. I should've known she couldn't fight the pull.

She knocks again. "Hello," she shouts. "Sir, are you here? I need to talk to you."

I stand next to the door in contemplation.

"Please. I see your truck outside. I left my glasses here, and I can't see anything," she shouts.

I open the door. I didn't expect company so I'm only wearing a pair of sweatpants.

She stops in her tracks when she looks me over. I can barely contain myself, looking at the want in her eyes. "Hello," she says. Her mouth hangs open as her gaze is fixed on my dick. I'm trying desperately to fight this erection, but this is a fight I won't win.

"If you can't see anything, how did you drive here?" I ask.

"I got lucky," she says.

"I told you not to come back here."

"I'm sorry, I didn't get your name when you yelled at me yesterday."

"I didn't give it to you," I say.

35

"Why don't you tell me so we both know who we're dealing with?"

"That won't be necessary."

"Did I do something to offend you? I didn't know this was your land. I never intentionally set out to steal from you."

"Alright then." I step back to close the door.

"Wait," she pleads. "I dropped my glasses. Did you find them?"

"I did."

"Do you have them?" she asks.

"I do."

"Can you give them to me?"

"There's something different about you," I say.

"Like what?"

"I don't know. You just seem different."

"I had to wear contacts since you have my glasses."

"Something else."

"I feel pretty good today."

"You look good too." I probably shouldn't have said that, but she does look good.

For a moment, she's speechless, but she can't fight the smile forming on her lips. "Thank you. You look good too."

"Flattery will get you everywhere."

"I'm counting on it," she says.

"Don't tempt me, Audrey."

"I didn't know I could."

I lick my lips. "You definitely can."

"You threatened to call the police on me yesterday."

"I meant what I said. You can't steal from me, and you need to stay off my property."

"Let's talk about something else." She rubs her hands over her arms and blows into her palms while she rocks back and forth on her feet.

I can't focus. I keep looking at her breasts and her

hardened nipples in that tight black shirt that perfectly displays her cleavage. "Why aren't you wearing a coat?" I ask.

"The air feels good to me. The weather is never too cold so I rarely wear one."

"You're freezing. Come inside."

Audrey looks around. "I don't think so. I don't go into serial killer homes."

I smirk and lick my lips. "But you would knock on a serial killer's door?"

"Are you admitting to being a serial killer?"

"The case is still pending," I say.

Audrey smiles at me. "You warned me to stay away multiple times. Now you want to invite me inside."

"I'm not going to leave you freezing outside. What kind of man would do that?"

She looks around.

"Come in while I get your glasses. It's warm in here. I won't bite."

She reluctantly steps inside, and I close the door behind her. "I wanted to talk to you about something."

"Give me a minute. I'll be right back." I walk to my office to get her things.

As I return I see the curiosity on her face as she looks around the cabin. It must seem strange that a man like me has so many plants in his home.

"Here." I hold out her basket with her glasses inside.

"Do you live here alone?" she asks.

"I don't see how that's any of your business."

"No need to be rude. Look, if I offended you by picking some plants, you could've said something a long time ago. I didn't know anyone lived here."

"Now you do."

Audrey grabs her basket, and the moment her hand touches mine, she sucks in a breath through her teeth. Her scent overpowers me, and her body begs for me.

"Are you still cold?" I ask.

"No," she says softly.

"You should get going."

"No," she says.

"I think it's best." I lick my lips.

"I'm sorry. I lost my train of thought. While I'm here, I didn't only come for the glasses. I was hoping to talk to you about your plants."

I stare at her lips as they move. My dick jumps in my pants. I can't hear a word she's saying. "Audrey, stop."

"If you would just hear me out, please."

"You're killing me."

"I'm sorry. I'm not a thief."

I grab and kiss her hand, and her body shivers. "You don't have to apologize to me, Audrey."

"I don't?"

"But you should leave while you can." I kiss her forearm.

"You're making it hard to leave," she says.

"Believe me. You have no idea how hard it is."

Audrey instinctively looks at the bulge in my pants. Her eyes widen. "I, I think I have some idea."

I place my palm on her cheek and she closes her eyes at my touch. Fiery passion scorches my veins. "You came to get your glasses, and you have them."

"I came to talk to you." She touches my abs, gently grazing my skin with her soft fingers.

I step closer to her. "Damn, Audrey."

Once our bodies touch, neither of us can speak. Her chest heaves as she takes deep breaths.

I gently push her against the door and press my body against hers. My dick pokes her hip.

She looks at me with anticipation.

I whisper in her ear. "What did you want to talk to me about?"

Her basket falls to the ground.

I lick her ear. "You smell so sweet. I want to taste you. Can I taste you, Audrey?"

She freezes.

I kiss down her neck. I'm delighted when she pulls me closer. She runs her hands over my back and chest and tugs at the elastic on my pants. I grunt, trying to fight the urge. She stands on the tips of her toes and wraps her arms around my neck. My hands roam her body, squeezing and holding her close. I can't resist her lips. I gently take them between my teeth.

She mumbles something but I can't understand what until I release her lip.

"You said you wouldn't bite."

"I lied."

"What's your name?" Audrey asks.

I kiss her lips and tug her hair. Her body melts into mine. Her mouth tastes like peppermint, and her lips feel like satin. She slips her tongue into my mouth, and I take over with an urgency I've never felt. I lift her shirt and feel her skin. "Damn, Audrey," I say as I suck her neck.

"Tell me your name," she moans.

This has to stop. I removed my hands from her body and place them on the wall on both sides of her. She holds me tighter. *Stop. Stop. Stop.* I tell myself. This is what I was trying to avoid. I panic and remove her hands from my body and force myself to step away.

"Please," she pleads.

"Forgive me," I say tearing myself away. "I shouldn't have done that. I meant what I said. I don't want to see you here again. You have to go."

"I don't understand," Audrey says breathlessly.

"I know, but I'm busy. I have to go."

"Wait."

"You have to go." I reach behind her and open the door.

"Can we make an appointment to meet later?"

"I don't have any time available."

"It'll be quick. I just want to talk to you. It's business."

"Goodbye, Audrey." I gently guide her out the door and close it. I immediately lean against the wall and smack my forehead. "Stupid," I reprimand myself.

Audrey knocks on the door. "Sir. Excuse me."

I don't answer.

"What the hell just happened?" she asks herself out loud.

"I'm sorry," I whisper, but I know she can't hear me. I hear her pacing my porch. I hang my head and notice her basket is on the ground. If I open that door, they'll be no stopping me. I won't be able to let her go again.

I watch her through the peephole. She turns to knock on the door but decides against it. My heart is heavy when she walks toward her car.

I look out the window. Before she gets in the car she turns back and heads for my flowers. I shake my head with a grin as she helps herself to my plants. I can see that she's determined, something I like about her. My attempt to scare her hadn't been effective enough, and my inability to keep my hands off her surely sent mixed signals. I sigh. I'm too busy trying to fight the bulge in my pants to get angry. Watching Audrey look around to see if she'll get caught excites me. I inhale her scent. She's ripe for mating. Without thinking, I reach into my pants and tug at my hard dick. Every movement of her body causes me to stroke my erection. Damn, I want to give her every hard inch.

It was frustrating, to say the least, watching her for so long without being able to touch her, hold her, kiss her, pull her hair until she screams my name. "Shit," I say as Audrey bends over. Her ass is in the air in her tight jeans. I want to take her just like that, bent over in the forest. I stroke faster, imagining how it would feel to be inside her pussy and her mouth. My eyes close and the thought of filling her with my seed brings me close to the edge. I cup my palm over the tip of my head, spreading the slick moisture that drips from my slit, as I pump harder and faster. My hips buck with every stroke. I need her. I don't know how much longer I can resist.

Audrey screams at the top of her lungs, piercing my ears.

I open my eyes. "Shit!" I yell. I wish I could've told her not to scream, but it's too late. I have to act fast.

A grizzly bear lunges for Audrey before I can blink. My wolf is outraged and the primal instinct to protect our mate forces me to shift without a second thought. My enormous white wolf jumps through the window, shattering the glass. The bear knocks her in the head and scratches her shoulder. Audrey covers her body and struggles to break away from the bear's claws. With tears in her eyes, she attempts to run away. The bear growls and knocks her to the ground.

Audrey covers her face and upper body. Another high pitch scream escapes from the depths of her lungs. She must've opened her eyes and seen me ripping into the bear. Touching my mate is the last thing he'll ever do, and my wolf will be the last thing he sees.

I unleash every bit of fury onto the beast. The bear will pay for any scratch on Audrey's body, any blood spilled, and any fear or pain she endures. I knock the black grizzly onto his back. He fights with all his might, but he's no match for my rage. It consumes me. I can smell his fear. I sink my claws into the bear's neck. I howl at my victory and growl at him, spewing spit in the bear's face as blood oozes from his body. I claw at his eyes. The bear whimpers from the pain and struggles to move, but my wolf is determined. Blinded by rage, I tear through the bear's fur and thickness of his flesh, ripping him apart, exposing his insides until he lies lifeless on the ground.

Audrey lies on her back and rests on her elbows attempting to rise. This is all my fault. If only I hadn't pushed her away, this would've never happened. I circle her as my wolf takes in her scent. My wolf whimpers as he nuzzles Audrey's soft skin and licks her face.

Audrey panics at first. Then she's at ease. She must feel our connection. "Thank you," she whispers as she pets my white fur. Her head falls to the ground and tears stream down the sides of her face. As I hover over her, she looks into my eyes with recognition.

I shift and sit next to her, and she gasps. I hold her hand in mine and rub her hair. "Forgive me, Audrey," I say as she closes her eyes. I know this was a lot.

I cradle her in my arms and carry her inside. There are many rooms in my cabin, but I can't help but carry her to my bed where she belongs. She's alive, and her vitals are good. She just needs to rest. I sit next to her for hours, listening to her breathe and her heart beat before I kiss her on the forehead and walk away.

While she rests, I board up the window I broke in the front of the cabin. It'll be an eyesore until I fix it, but I don't want Audrey to be cold when she wakes up, and I don't want to leave her alone. I'm almost done when I hear the sound of a vehicle approaching. I silently curse. It's Felix and Damien. This is exactly what I've tried to avoid.

Damien steps out of the car wearing a button down blue shirt and black slacks over his six foot, four inch frame. He's just a bit shorter than me with skin like cocoa and blue eyes. He's dressed nicer than usual, and he's wearing cologne.

Felix is the same height as Damien with medium

brown skin and dreadlocks that hang past his shoulders. He's wearing a tailored blue suit with a crisp white shirt and no tie.

"Where are you two going?" I ask.

"Nevermind that. What the hell happened here?" Damien asks as the two men inspect the damage.

"Minor incident," I reply.

"This doesn't look minor. Who did this? We need to act now," Felix says.

"Were you attacked?" Damien asks.

Felix sniffs the air. "Is that bear?"

"It's nothing, just an accident," I reply.

"This is some weird shit, Darius," Felix says.

"I don't want to talk about it. Don't ask me about it again."

"You're acting strange. Your energy is off. Are you nervous?" Damien asks.

"No, I'm just trying to get this done."

"Well, it looks like you're about finished, which brings us to why we're here," Damien says.

I'm pretty sure I know what they want. It's what they always want. "I'm not going anywhere," I announce.

"It's a chill party. They'll be drinks. They'll be women. You'll forget that it's almost Christmas," Damien says. "Why don't you go get dressed?"

"I don't want to go out. Not tonight."

"Don't think of it as a party. Think of it as a chance to get some pussy."

"I'm good. You two have fun."

"How long has it been? Don't you want to end the year with a bang?" Damien asks.

Felix interrupts. "Who's car is that?"

"What car?" I ask.

Felix sniffs. "There's a woman."

I can feel Damien's excitement. "A woman? Who is

43

she?"

Felix tries to figure out the scent. "No one we know, but there's something—"

"You two need to leave. Now," I say.

"What are you hiding?" Felix asks.

"I don't have to hide shit."

"That scent," Felix says.

"Come on Felix. Darius needs this. Let him have some fun,"

"You met a woman. What does that have to do with this window?" Felix asks.

Knowing the guys will be able to spot a lie a mile away, I confess. "There's no need to cross examine me, Felix. If you must know, there's a woman here in my bed."

"You dog," Damien playfully hits my shoulder.

"Who is she?" Felix asks.

"She was wandering around the house looking at the flowers and was attacked by a bear. I jumped through the window and killed the bear. Now she's resting."

"Which flowers? You need to be careful. You don't know who she is. Someone may have sent her."

"Give him a break," Damien says. "He's smart. Let him have this. He needs some pussy."

"Sure," Felix says.

"What does she look like?" Damien asks.

"I'm not going to answer that."

Felix sniffs. There's something about this scent. "She's human. Does she know who you are?"

"No, she's just resting. There's nothing going on here, but you two should go. I don't want to scare her."

"You want her all to yourself. I get it, playboy," Damien says.

"Do you want this woman to yourself?" Felix asks.

"I just want to make sure she's okay before I send

her home."

"Fine, we'll go to the party. Maybe a little fling will do you some good. You enjoy your evening." Felix gets in the car.

"Are you ready for what comes next?" Damien asks me.

"What do you mean?"

"You have, what I'm assuming is a beautiful girl in your bed. You want to fuck her. Don't deny it."

"That's not what this is."

"Sure it's not. Look, you've already saved her life. You can build on that. Don't be your usual self. Do something nice for her. Get her a gift. Make her feel special, and the panties will just fall off. I promise."

All I can do is shake my head at Damien.

"Trust me," Damien says.

"Go."

"Alright, but I want all the details." Damien gets in the car, and he and Felix drive off.

That was a close call, but I'm certain that Felix is still suspicious. He will have more questions. I need to figure out what I'm going to do.

CHAPTER 5
Audrey

I'm a little foggy as I open my eyes. My head is pounding. I begin to panic as I remember what happened. *Where am I?* This isn't my bed. Candles light the room, and the intoxicating scent of lavender fills the air.

I take deep breaths. The bedroom I'm in is large. The furniture is dark wood. It looks handmade. This mattress is larger than a California king. There's a bountiful bouquet of Alaria next to me on the nightstand. A calm feeling sweeps over me until I look down and realize I'm naked. My eyes widen as I inspect my body. What's going on here?

Next to the flowers, there's orange juice, a banana, and muffins. My stomach growls. "I'm not eating that. I don't know where it came from," I say under my breath. My stomach disagrees. The muffin smells delicious, and I'm famished. I grab a muffin, sniff it, and take a bite. "Mmm." It's still warm and moist, and the tart taste of regal berries burst onto my tongue. I eat it quickly and grab another.

The last thing I remember is being attacked by a bear and the sexy man from the cabin in the woods. I touch my shoulder. It's tender. The bear scratched me here. The terror I felt comes flooding back.

"Your scars have healed."

I attempt to cover myself. The muffin falls out of my hand. The man stands in the doorway in a t-shirt and blue jeans. His voice is just as deep and smooth as I remember. His face is just as handsome as I remember. That shirt does nothing to hide his bulging biceps and his muscular abs, and my body reacts to him as she remembers. He kissed me, and I never felt so alive.

"I covered them with an ointment I made out of

ora."

"What's ora?" I ask.

"The flowers you've been stealing from me," he says.

"I didn't know what they were called, and I don't steal."

"What would you call it?"

"Picking flowers."

"Those flowers belong to me."

"Who are you?" I ask him.

"My name is Darius Huntington."

"That's it."

"What's it?" Darius asks.

"Is that all you have to say for yourself? You yelled at me. You threatened me. You pushed me out the door. Then you fought a bear for me. You have nothing to say about any of that?"

"You must be mistaken."

"I know what I saw."

"You were hit pretty badly. You probably saw all sorts of things. Things you shouldn't repeat. You can sort it out once you feel better."

"I feel fine. A bear attacked me and a wolf killed the bear. That wolf turned into you right before my eyes. I'm sure of it."

"That sounds like a dream you may have had while you were sleeping. I found you passed out in my flower bed, and I brought you here," Darius says.

"I'm only trying to make sense of what I saw. I won't tell anyone if that's what you're worried about." I assure him.

That caught his attention, but he doesn't say anything.

"How can I thank you if you won't tell me the truth?" I ask.

"Audrey, maybe you should lie down."

"How do you know my name?"

He stares.

"You called me Audrey the first time we met. How do you know my name?"

"I tracked you down after I found you stealing so I'd know who to send the police after."

"Would you really call the police on me, Darius?"

Once again, he remains silent.

"Please just talk to me. Whatever it is, I can handle it. I know you're trying to intimidate me, but I'm not afraid of you."

"What would you like for breakfast?"

"You kissed me."

"Eggs, maybe?" he asks.

"It was the best kiss I've ever had."

"You're just hungry."

I'm intrigued by Darius. As far as I'm concerned he's harmless, and his threats were purely for show. Honestly, I think it's cute. "Where am I?"

He says nothing.

"If you don't tell me where I am, I'll assume you kidnapped me."

"You're free to go whenever you're ready."

"And my clothes?" I ask.

"They were soiled so I washed them for you."

"Did you undressed me?"

"I removed your clothes."

"Did you touch me?"

"I wouldn't do that to you."

"Am I in your bed, Darius?" The covers smell like him, like fresh rain.

His reply is a single nod.

I can't take my eyes off the bulge in his pants. My nerves are on edge. My mouth waters. His boyishly handsome face coupled with his muscular frame and his stern expression make me want to pull down his pants and take him in my mouth.

I run my hands across the sheets. The blanket falls, exposing my breasts. My nipples stand at attention when the air touches them. "Oops." I take my time covering myself.

Darius clears his throat. "How are you feeling? Any pain?"

I think for a moment. I press my hand against my ribcage. "Ahhh," I wince. "Actually, there's a sharp pain right here."

Before I can blink, Darius rushes to my side. He gently places his hand on top of mine and the other hand on my bare flesh. My skin tingles.

"Where?" He asks, gently inspecting me. When I don't reply, he looks into my eyes for answers. We stare at one another as heat rises between us.

My heart skips a beat. "There's something about the way you look at me."

"I'm not sure what you mean."

"Like before. Your mouth said leave, but your eyes said stay."

Darius gulps. His eyes sparkle. "Are you hurt, Audrey?"

"I have this ache, deep inside. I don't know if you'll be able to heal it, or maybe you're the only one who can."

Silence again.

"Maybe I'm wrong."

"About what?"

"It feels like there's something between us." I'm nervous as I wait for Darius to reply, but once again, he's silent. I lean in, my face only centimeters from his. My eyes close for a brief moment before I give up hope.

Darius sits still, seemingly unaffected.

"I'm so embarrassed." I turn my head away from Darius.

"Look at me," Darius commands.

I can't bring myself to turn around. "It's fine. If you could just get my clothes I can eat at home."

"Look at me," Darius says again.

"I'd rather not. You can just leave my clothes outside the door, and I'll get them. I can leave without bothering you, and you'll never see me again. I won't come back okay. I promise."

"I said look at me. Don't make me tell you again."

I take my time turning around. "What?" I ask. I feel like a fool. I invented this attraction in my head.

Darius says nothing once again.

"I misspoke. I didn't mean that."

"What did you mean?" he asks.

"Nothing."

"I see."

"Darius, I'm not usually so forward. I don't know what's wrong with me. I must've hit my head harder than I thought."

"There's nothing wrong with you, Audrey. You're perfect."

"You mean perfect for a thief?"

"And a liar. I suspect you're not in pain."

"No pain, but I do like the way you came to my rescue, the same way you did before."

"I feel terrible. You got hurt on my property. I had to make sure you were okay."

I'm not in pain, but I do have an ache for Darius. I can't stop myself from looking between his legs. His dick jumps. "You're resisting."

"I have no idea what you mean," he says.

"Now who's the liar?"

"You're playing with fire, Audrey."

"Maybe I want to get burned."

"I should let you rest. I charged your phone in case there's someone you want to call."

50

"What exactly should I tell them?"

"I don't know. Maybe your man is out there wondering where you are."

"I don't have a man. It's been a long time since I've been with a man."

"Why is that?"

"I don't know. Is there anyone special in your life? Is there a woman of the house?"

"It's been a long time since I've met anyone as special or as beautiful as you."

"You think I'm beautiful?"

He bites his lip. "Fuck yeah."

"Even with my hair like this?" I can't see my hair, but I know it has to be all over my head. I tend to toss and turn in my sleep, and my hair isn't wrapped.

"Especially with your hair like this," Darius says. "I love your hair. It's so thick and full."

"I have a dilemma," I say. "I feel something intense, and I can't fight it. I don't know if I want to fight it. All I want right now is for you to touch me." I've never said anything like that to anyone in my life.

"I have to go." Darius stands to walk away.

I touch his hand. My body heats.

Darius clenches my hand. "Audrey."

I stand. "Look at me."

He obeys.

"Why?" I ask. "Why haven't you said anything? Why have you been watching me?"

"It wouldn't be a good idea to bring you into my world. I'm not an easy man to love."

"Love?" I gulp. My heart skips a beat. I cup his cheek with my palm.

"Yeah."

"Darius, I know a broken heart when I see one. You're going to be okay."

"How do you know that?"

I tilt my head toward his. "I'm here now."

Whatever held him back disappears between us. Our lips met in a passionate kiss that neither of us can resist. Darius relaxes in my arms which comforts me. He holds me close as if he'd die before he'd let me go. I've always wanted this, to be wanted, needed like this. His strong hands caress my skin and squeeze my behind. I need more.

"Oh, Darius," I whisper.

He kisses my neck, making a trail to my breasts. Every touch of his lips lights my skin on fire. He bites my nipple and sucks.

"Darius," I whisper.

"Yes, love."

"Why can't I stop kissing you?"

"You never have to stop kissing me."

He lowers me onto the bed, hovering over me as I pull him closer. He works his way down my body, nibbling and tasting my skin. He spreads my legs and lifts them over his shoulders, licking his lips as he dives in with a growl. I shiver with excitement.

His tongue moves rhythmically between my lower lips, then up and down, teasing me. I relax my head on a pillow and spread my legs. Darius explores me with his tongue as his fingers tease my clit. I writhe beneath him in pleasure, whimpering and thanking the heavens. He's hungry for me, and he eats me like an animal. I squeeze my legs together and he latches to my clit and sucks. My legs shake. I try to stop them, but I can't contain my cries of ecstasy as a wave of pleasure crashes over me. I touch my body and squeeze my breasts. He pulls me closer and works his tongue as I work my hips against his face. I push his head deeper as my body lifts off the bed. My moans turned to screams, and a tear escapes the corner of my eye as another burst of pleasure courses through every inch of my body in intense waves. He devours me, and I want to get on my knees and thank him, but I'm sure my legs don't work.

He lifts his head and crawls over my body. The desire in his eyes burns through me as I try to catch my breath.

I reach for him, tugging at his pants. He quickly removes his shirt clothes. His body is perfectly sculpted and his dick is magnificent. His veins pulse. He growls.

"I need you," I whisper.

"I'm yours," he says.

He kisses his way up my body. I don't know what I want to do.

"Don't be nervous," Darius says. It's like he can read my mind. He strokes his dick and takes my hand. "Touch it."

My mouth waters as I place my palm around his shaft. It's so big my fingers don't touch. He's hard as steel, and I want him.

"Feel it," he says. "Feel how much I want you." He leans over and kisses me. I adjust my hand and slide it up and down.

"Do you want me, Audrey?"

"Yes," I whisper.

"Your body was made for me, and I'm going to take what's mine. I'm going to claim you, Audrey, take all your body has to give, and when I'm done, I'll own this pussy. Do you want me to own your pussy, Audrey?"

I grip him harder, and he growls. I nod, begging him with my eyes to take me.

Darius growls. As his face comes close to mine, I swear I see canines. I latch onto his neck with excitement as he settles between my legs. He pins my hands over my head and positions his dick at my eager entrance.

"I've wanted to fuck you since the moment I saw

you."

"Why didn't you say anything?"

"Because I'm a fucking idiot. You're a fucking goddess, and you're mine."

My essence pours like a flood while Darius rubs the tip of his dick against me. He pushes in slowly. I close my eyes and dig my fingers into his shoulders as he stretches me.

"You're so fucking wet," he says. "Are you going to let me in?"

"Please," I whisper.

"So tight." Darius pulls out and rubs the head between my lips, lapping my juices. He returns to my center, pushing slightly deeper. I grab his sides and lift my hips off the bed. He pulls out again. He repeats the action again and again. Each time I grip him tighter with my nails and with my pussy.

"Darius," I plead.

"Yes, Audrey?"

"Please," I beg.

"What's that Audrey?"

"Please," I plead.

"What is it that you need, love?"

"I need you, please. Fuck me, please."

"I'm not going to fuck you."

My eyes widen.

"I'm going to claim you. Would you like that?"

"Yes," I moan.

"Don't say it if you don't mean it."

"I mean it."

He enters her me one swift motion, penetrating my body deeper than any man ever has or ever could. I cry out as I reach for his face. I kiss his lips and pull him closer. Warmth spreads through my body.

His thrusts are slow and steady. He keeps his eyes on mine. Our bodies glide together, moving as one. I study his face. Every time his eyes close or he bites his lip or he growls, I want to applaud myself for doing my kegel exercises regularly. I also want to applaud him. No one has ever made love to me this way.

His pace quickens.

"Shit, Audrey, you're going to be mine. Do you want to be mine?" he asks.

I nod.

"I can't hear you," he says.

"Yes, whatever you want," I cry.

"Shit. Why did you tell me that, Audrey?" He kisses my lips as his strokes go deeper, harder, and faster,

"I need you." I'm pissed at myself for saying everything I'm thinking and for these crazy ass thoughts.

"I knew you were perfect for me," he says. He slows down and kisses my neck as I struggle to catch my breath. "You were right, Audrey. I'm a wolf, and you belong to me. I need you in so many ways, love. I need you more than you know. I need you. Do you hear me?"

"Yes."

"I need you to do something for me."

"Anything."

"Agree to be my mate. Can you do that?" He thrusts harder.

"Yes, Darius, yes." I've never felt so good. Darius knows exactly where to touch me, exactly where to position himself, exactly what my body needs, and when. As far as I'm concerned he can take whatever he wants from me. He can claim me. He can have my body. He can own me. I can be his mate, whatever he wants.

With a kiss, Darius lifts his body from mine. "Turn over," he commands.

It takes me a moment to comply, but I rise to my

hands and knees as Darius positions himself behind me and pushes my head down. He grabs a handful of my hair and arches my back. He enters me from the back without warning and I bend to his will.

"Shit," I shout.

Darius growls. He digs his fingers into my hips and pounds me without mercy as I scream his name, begging for more, and he's happy to oblige. I feel something sharp on my hips and gasp. He sinks his claws into my thigh and digs into my skin. I feel pain, but it's met with an extreme burst of pleasure, and I'm aware of him. I feel his desire meshed with mine. I feel a connection I can't describe. Every part of my body reacts to him.

He slowly kisses his way up my spine as I tremble beneath him. "I'm close. I know you are too," he whispers in my ear. "Cum on my dick so I can mate you, Audrey."

With that, my body obeys his command and I cum so hard I think I've been transported to heaven. I lift my body so my back is pressed into his chest. We're molded into one. He licks my neck with the tongue of his wolf. I don't know how I know it, but I know.

He squeezes my breasts, scratching my skin and pulls my hair as he cums. He groans as he erupts into me, and he sinks his canines into my neck. I see sparks and the room spins. I feel like I'm having an out of body experience. Something takes over me. I can feel him, his thoughts, his desire, his love. I'm afraid of these intense feelings, but I hear Darius in my head. *It's okay, love. This is how it works. You are one with me.* I instantly feel calm, safe, protected. He grips my hips and thrusts into me. I reach behind my head and hold his neck. Our pleasure intensifies until we're both spent, and we cave in pleasure. He wraps me in his arms as we drift off to sleep.

CHAPTER 6

Darius

When I awaken, Audrey is still sound asleep. I sniff her as I move her hair from her face. She now wears my scent. Wherever she goes, she'll carry me with her. The connection I feel to her is powerful. Even in her sleep, I can feel her happiness. I kiss her cheek and squeeze her tight. Audrey is now my mate, and the pleasure and guilt that I feel are equally immense.

There are so many things I should've said and done before this moment, but I couldn't resist her any longer. I can only hope that she'll forgive me and that my alpha brothers will forgive me as well.

She opens her eyes with a smile on her face and desire seeping from her pores.

"You should probably eat something," I say.

"Good morning," she beams. She wraps her arms around my neck.

"Good afternoon," I say.

"How long have I been here? What day is this?"

"It's Wednesday."

"Shit," Audrey shouts looking around. "Tell me you're joking."

"What's wrong?"

"I missed Sunday dinner. I missed work. I missed Christmas shopping with my mom and my aunts. I missed everything," she says.

"Oh. That's not too bad."

"It is bad. I have a business to keep afloat, and my mom plans all these traditions for Christmas. She will flip out if I'm not there."

"Your business will be fine."

"What about my family?"

"They'll be fine. It's just Christmas shopping."

"It's one of our traditions."

"You're making a big deal about nothing. Don't get bent out of shape about Christmas traditions. Christmas is the fakest time of the year. It's completely commercialized. It's all about spending money on things people don't need."

"Why do you hate Christmas?"

"I don't hate Christmas. I just don't feel the need to go overboard pretending life is perfect for one day out of the year."

"Don't you feel the magic of Christmas, spending time with the people you love, singing carols, giving gifts?"

"You can do all those things any time you want."

"I know you can Mr. Grinch, but people are so busy living their lives. Sometimes they need a reminder to stop and appreciate the people they love. Is there something wrong with that?"

"What if the person you loved died on December twenty-fifth and you were waiting for Christmas to show them how much they meant to you? Wouldn't you feel like an idiot for waiting for one day?"

"That's a hell of an exaggeration."

"It makes a hell of a point." I stand. "Why don't you get cleaned up while I get you something to eat?"

Audrey sits on the edge of the bed and grabs her phone. "Oh," she says as she looks at the display screen.

"Everything okay?"

"Yeah, I'm fine."

"No, you're not. Why are you sad? What's on your phone?"

Audrey shakes her head. "I bet you think Valentine's Day is stupid too, don't you?"

"Don't even get me started on Valentine's Day, but that's not what's wrong. What is it?"

"It's stupid. You wouldn't understand." She shakes

her head.

I sigh. "I want to understand. That's why I asked. Tell me what it is. Did you get a bad message?"

Audrey shakes her head no as she tries to hold back tears.

"Don't cry, Audrey."

With those words tears stream down her face. She covers her eyes with her hands. I rush to her side and hold her in my arms. I rest my hand in her hair and stroke her scalp. "Come on, Audrey. I didn't mean to upset you."

She lays her head on my chest before she pulls back. "It's not you."

"Tell me what's wrong."

"I got a bunch of messages from my assistant. Other than that," Audrey pauses, "Nothing." She looks at her feet.

I don't know what to say. I'm still trying to figure out why she's crying.

"I guess no one noticed that I wasn't there. Looks like you were right. Maybe I believe in the magic of the holidays a little too much."

"I'm sure they noticed."

"Then they just didn't care."

"Maybe they thought you were busy."

"We made plans. I never miss these things, and nobody bothered to call and check on me. I can't believe no one even thought about me."

"Don't be ridiculous."

"The proof is right here." She shakes her phone. "I've always felt like an outsider. This just proves it. They don't care if I'm there or not."

"That doesn't prove anything."

"I thought they didn't understand me. I thought they were hard on me. I thought I was the one who went out of my way to avoid them. Turns out, they don't even want me around in the first place."

"Where are you getting this from? You're jumping to irrational conclusions."

"You don't even know what you're talking about."

"Baby, you're just hungry."

"That's it. I must be hungry. Just don't worry about it. Forget about my feelings. I'm just a silly, emotional, hangry woman, right."

"You are right now."

She looks at me in disgust. "I told you not to worry about it. Don't insist on hearing my problems if you're just going to dismiss my feelings."

"I'm not dismissing your feelings. I think you're overreacting."

She's angry now, and I'm confused.

She scoots away from me. "I'm not overreacting. We made plans. I didn't show up. No one even thought to wonder if I'm still alive or hey, she might have been attacked by a fucking bear. Let me check on her."

"They didn't know, and that doesn't mean they don't care."

"Thanks, Darius. You're so understanding."

I think she's being sarcastic. "What I mean is I find it impossible to believe that anyone who knows you isn't as infatuated with you as I am. I just don't want you to be sad. What can I do?"

"Nothing."

"I want to see you smile."

"Sing me a Christmas song."

"No."

"You don't care about me either."

"I do care about you." I take a deep breath.

"I'm fine."

"Jingle bells, jingle bells, jingle all the way," I sing quick and dry.

She moves closer to me. Her face lights up.

"Happy now?" I ask.

"Yes." She laughs.

I shake my head at her delight.

"You're infatuated with me?"

"Can't you feel it?"

"I think so, but it's strange. I feel comfortable with you. I want to be with you, and I keep saying stupid stuff like that even though we just met. How do you fall so hard for someone you don't know?"

"It just happens."

"I forgot, you've been stalking me." She sighs. "At least someone cares."

"I'm not a stalker."

"You kind of are."

I put my arm around her shoulder. "You're kind of beautiful. I couldn't resist."

"Still a little creepy, Darius."

"Yet, you couldn't resist me."

"Clearly, I have issues," she smiles.

"It's more than that. I told you, you're made for me."

"I thought you were just saying that in the heat of the moment."

"I don't say things that I don't mean. You're mated to a wolf. You and I are connected."

"What do you mean?"

I stand and walk to the doorway. "Why don't you get dressed? I'll be back with food. You'll feel better once you eat. I promise we'll talk about it when I get back. Do you need anything while I'm out?"

"No, but hurry back. I'll be needing some comfort." She winks at me.

"Make yourself at home. Everything you need is in the bathroom, including your clothes."

"If you insist."

"Do you like it here?" I ask her.

"I do."

"Come give your mate a kiss."

She gives me a peck, and I pull her in. A peck won't do. I run my tongue across her lips and she lets me in. That's better.

I growl. "I'll be ready to comfort you when I get back."

As I walk out the door, the thought crosses my mind to track down her family and have a talk with them. They've upset her, and I don't like that. I need to fix this for Audrey.

CHAPTER 7

Audrey

I think he's kind of sweet, deep, deep down. He did his best to make me feel better, even though something tells me providing emotional support is not his thing. He doesn't treat me like a random hook up. He doesn't mind leaving me alone in his home. It feels like I know him. Like we've been together forever. He said I was his, but men don't commit that easily, do they? There's also the matter of him being a wolfman, albeit a sexy-ass wolfman.

I have questions, lots of questions, and the occasional thought that I must be out of my mind for sleeping with a strange man. I'm doing this all wrong. I feel something for him. I long for him. I made confessions that will haunt me forever if he turns out to be a lying asshole. I'm usually careful. I've never fallen this hard, this fast.

Before I treat myself to a bath I google wolf mates, and my eyes bulge when I see the phrase *wolves mate for life*. That's what I click. I read aloud. "Wolves are tremendously faithful to their mates, and would die guarding their small puppies." I smile. Is that what I've gotten myself into? A mate for life?

I bathe and get myself together. I want to look nice for Darius when he gets back.

It crosses my mind to call my mom or my siblings, but I decide against it. Instead, I contact my assistant and let her know I was in an accident, and I'll be taking the rest of the week off. I know I have some things to square away for the Alaria launch, but I can move some things around and jump in on Monday. As I stare at my phone, it occurs to me that Darius has been gone for quite some time. I hope he didn't ghost me. That's crazy. He wouldn't leave me in his house if he wasn't interested, and from what I read, he wouldn't leave his mate.

He told me to make myself at home, so I look around. He's a simple man surrounded by wood and leather and an uncanny amount of plants.

"Would it kill him to have a Christmas tree," I say to myself. I can fix this place up. Add some throw pillows, new rugs, and a few accent pieces. I wonder if he's attached to the leather couches. He also has a room that will be perfect for a nursery.

"Shit." There I go, thinking like a girl. One, or five, mind blowing orgasms and a random google search, and I've mentally moved in and started planning a family. "Get it together, Audrey," I say to myself. I open a door at the end of the hall and look inside. It's an office. I can't resist sitting behind his impressive desk in his leather chair. It smells like him.

"He owns a chain of flower shops. A pretty popular chain." There's a diploma on the wall. "He's a botanist. I would've never guessed that. I thought he was a lumberjack." The questions are piling up. Without thinking I open one of his desk drawers. "That would be inappropriate." As I close the drawer, a photograph catches my eye. It's a younger Darius with a woman. She's pretty. They're both smiling and happy. They're bundled up. His arm is protectively around her waist and she leans into his chest. They were in love.

She and I are opposites physically. Now I wonder what his type is. This must be the woman that broke his heart. I want to know what happened. The sound of the front door closing makes me jump up from his desk. I scurry out of the room and quietly close the door. After checking the hallway, I tiptoe to the bedroom and sit on the bed.

Darius goes in and out of the front door a few times.

"Audrey," he finally shouts.

That's my cue. I head for the living room. "You took your time, didn't you? I'm starving."

Darius stands in the middle of the room with a grin on his face.

"What's going on?" I ask.

I look behind him. There's a Christmas tree peeking over his head.

"You got a tree?" I squeal. I don't know why I'm so excited. "Did you get this for me?"

"I certainly didn't do it for myself."

I run into his arms. "I can't believe you did this."

"I also went to the store and got decorations."

"You didn't have to do that."

"I know. I wanted to see that beautiful smile on your face, the one you have now."

"This is the nicest thing anyone's ever done for me. Thank you." I go through the bag looking for decorations as Darius stands back and watches.

"Wait. Not this one," Darius grabs a black bag from my hands.

"What's in that one?" I ask.

"None of your business."

"You've got a lot of secrets, don't you?"

"A few but none that I'll keep from you."

"I'm going to hold you to that."

He looks nervous. He wants to say something, but I can feel his hesitance.

"Is something wrong, Darius?"

"No."

"Why are you looking like that?" I ask.

"I was just… never mind."

"No, you were just what?"

"I was hoping that you'd spend Christmas with me."

My mouth hangs open. "You mean like celebrate the holiday together with music and mistletoe and the magic of Christmas."

"Yes, but not quite so Disney."

"I'd love to spend Christmas with you."

"Really?" he asks. The excitement on his face is adorable.

"Yeah."

"I hope we can start our own holiday traditions."

"I'd like that. Is it okay if we visit my family too?"

"Anything you want."

"You're saying you want to meet my parents and my brother and sister and my aunts and uncles. Are you sure about that?"

"If that's what it takes to be with you."

"You're perfect."

"Why don't we eat, and then you can decorate the tree?" Darius suggests.

"Are you going to help me decorate?"

"Wouldn't you prefer to do that alone?"

"I'd really like to do it with you."

"I'll think about it."

I grab his hand as he leads me to the table where he laid out the food. He brought my favorite chicken alfredo, and I don't waste time trying to be cute. I dive right in. "This is delicious."

Darius smiles while he watches me scarf down my food.

"Darius, don't just watch me. Eat your food."

"I must've zoned out."

"What's on your mind?"

"I like seeing you smile."

"Thank you for making me smile."

"I want you to be happy. You are my mate after all."

"Tell me more about that." Flashbacks of our intimate moments play in my mind. I touch my neck where he bit me, and I feel his want. My skin tingles. Darius asked me to be his mate and I agreed.

"That means you're mine."

"What exactly do you want from me?"

"I want you. The rest we will work out later."

"You said you were a wolf. What does that mean?"

"I'm a man and a wolf."

"A wolfman?" I ask.

"A wolf shifter. I can transform between human and wolf."

"What does a wolf shifter do in the real world?"

"I am alpha of a pack. Myself and my alpha brothers, Felix and Damien, are the most powerful wolves in the states."

"What do you do with your power?"

"I protect what's mine."

"Say that again."

"I protect what's mine."

"That's sexy."

He smirks. "There are dangers all around. My pack relies on me for protection, direction, and leadership. We thrive when we stick together. It's how we move."

"In packs?"

"Yes."

"What are these dangers?"

"When supernatural forces are involved, egos are inflated, and the thirst for power is inevitable. There's always someone who wants control, money, influence, you name it. There's always someone with something to prove. Packs look out for one another. The alpha decides what's best for the pack."

"You must be pretty important."

"Every member of the pack is important."

"How do you become a wolf shifter?"

"We are born this way. It's who we are. It's who our ancestors were, and we try to uphold their teachings and traditions."

"All of this goes on right under our noses."

"Our secret is not too hard to keep. You've been living amongst wolf shifters your whole life, and you never knew."

"How would someone like me fit into your world?"

"Perfectly. My mate is an important part of my pack and my life."

"I don't know how to be your mate. What if it's something I'm not capable of."

"Audrey, we already mated, and I have no intention of ever letting you go."

"But how can this work?"

"There's nothing to be afraid of. You are more than capable. I need you, just you. The question is, do you think that you could love someone like me?" he asks.

"Darius, that's a heavy question. We just met."

"But deep down, you know the answer. You feel it. Don't you?"

"I want to say yes, but I'm not even sure this is all real. How hard did I hit my head?"

"When we mated, you felt our bond. You feel it now. Our souls became one."

"And you're sure you want me to be your mate?"

"There's not a doubt in my mind."

"It all happened so fast. What are we supposed to do now?"

"I'm all in, Audrey. I'm all yours."

"Forever?" I ask.

"Yes, forever. We have a lot to discuss."

"I agree. I want to know more about you."

"Did you not find what you were looking for when you were going through my shit?"

"How could you accuse me of such a thing?"

"Don't insult my intelligence."

"I found some stuff. I still don't know how much you know about me."

"I did a background check."

"I still have some more searching to do, but I did find out that my alpha wolf mate is a botanist."

"I am."

"I thought you did something different. You look like you'd work with your hands."

"I do work very well with my hands. Maybe I should refresh your memory."

"I wouldn't mind that, but first, tell me about Alaria."

"You mean ora."

"Yes, ora. I searched for it, and I couldn't find it anywhere. I couldn't even find a photograph of it."

"That is because I created the ona. It is my special breed."

"It's an amazing creation. Do you have any idea what it does for my hair?" I ask.

"I did notice the difference. What made you use it in your hair?"

"They smell amazing. Most women love the scent of perfume. I'm obsessed with the scent of my hair. I didn't expect it to make my hair so soft and shiny."

"Come here," Darius beckons.

"What is it?"

"I want to smell your hair."

I put down my fork and sit in his lap.

His body is warm, and his arms are strong. He buries his nose in my hair. "Ummm," he purrs. His tongue finds my ear, and he whispers to me. "Are you nervous? You're trembling."

"I don't know what I am when you touch me." I close my eyes and listen to the soothing sound of his voice. His hands work their way under my shirt.

"You are safe when you're with me, always. I fought a bear for you, and I'd do it again. I'd take down an army for you, my love."

"You're just saying that."

"My feelings for you are strong and very real. I haven't confessed my love for a woman in a long time. It's not something I take lightly."

"Are you confessing your love for me now?"

"What do you think?" Darius asks. He licks my neck.

"I can't think right now," I whisper. He's growing beneath me, and as his dick thickens my body heats and my want for him grows. I grind against his erection. I kiss the side of his face.

He growls. "I'm going to fuck you until you know." He grabs my hair and pulls my head back.

"Wait," I say in between moans.

"Why?"

"Before we continue, I need to know who the woman is."

"There's no one but you." He unbuttons my jeans.

"Wait."

"Why?"

"I found a picture in your desk drawer."

Darius stops. I feel an instant shift in the air between us. His jaws tighten, and his body tenses.

I can feel his anger coursing through my body. "Darius, what's wrong?"

I swear I see steam rise from his ears as he glares at me with a mixture of sadness and rage.

This worries me. I don't like this. Is he still in love with her? "Tell me about her. What is her name?" I ask.

Darius abruptly stands. I slide from his lap and stumble as I try to stand in front of him. He doesn't look at me. He simply walks away.

"Darius, where are you going?"

I jump when the door slams behind him. "Unbelievable," I shout. I'm not letting him walk out without a word. I run to the door. He stomps down the path that leads deeper into the woods. I have to run to catch up to him. "Darius, you can't shut down on me. Seriously," I shout.

Darius turns around. "It's cold out here. Go back in the house."

"You're wearing a t-shirt. Come back inside with me. We need to talk."

"I'll be there in a minute."

"You need to talk to me now. I will not be your mate if you're stuck pining for another woman. I won't do it."

"You have no idea what you're talking about," Darius shouts.

"Then tell me. Who is she? What's her name? Tell me something."

Darius walks off.

I notice a greenhouse nearby. "Darius, did she dump you? Did she cheat on you? Did she leave you for someone else? Where is she?"

Darius turns back around heads for me like a raging bull. He stands in front of me and puts his finger in my face. "Don't you say those things about her."

"What did she do that has you like this? What?"

"She died," Darius shouts. His face turns red, and his chest heaves. "You happy now, Audrey? She died."

CHAPTER 8
Darius

I can't believe this is happening right now, and if she doesn't let this shit go, I'm going to lose it. I'm trying not to go off on her, but I have a feeling she won't let it go. I need space to collect my thoughts if I'm going to talk to her about this.

"I had no idea," Audrey says.

With every piece of restraint I have, I speak to her in a calm voice. "I know. Go in the house. I'll be back."

"Don't walk away from me, Darius."

"Can I just get a few fucking minutes?"

"Okay." She steps away and stands behind me.

"Alone," I shout.

"No," she says. "I won't begin this relationship this way. If you want me, you're going to have to talk to me. Look at me."

I turn around. "You don't tell me what to do, woman."

"You don't get to dictate how this works. I know your type. You're going to have to open up to me. I can't be with someone who shuts me out. I will leave, and I won't come back."

"Then how will you steal my plants?"

She stops to think.

"Don't kid yourself. You're not going anywhere." I'm not going to lie. Her saying she would leave really fucked me up inside.

She gives me a look that says try me. "No secrets," she says.

"I'm not trying to keep secrets. I have every intention of telling you about everything, including Sarah. We were having a nice meal, and you decided to hit me with that. Why?"

"I need to know who I'm dealing with too. These

72

feelings came out of nowhere, and this connection doesn't mean shit. I don't know you. You couldn't even sit at the table at the mention of her name. I think that means we need to talk about it right now."

"Listen to me, Audrey. If you want me, you're going to have to allow me to open up when I'm ready."

"Who said I wanted you?"

I growl as I slowly stalk toward her. She takes a step back. "Now you don't want me?" I ask. I lick my lips. "Huh? You don't want me?"

She stops walking. "I'm just saying."

"What are you saying?" I stop when our bodies touch, but I don't touch her, not yet.

"Don't try to distract me?"

"I'm not trying to distract you. I want you to know what I know. You want me. You crave me. I will give you what you need. I will open up to you, but you will not control me. You will not threaten me, and you will never talk about leaving me. Is that understood?"

"I'll do whatever the fuck I want."

My dick twitches. "Is that right woman?"

She looks up at me with her hands on her hips. "That's right."

"You talk big for such a little woman."

"I talk big, and I can back it up."

"I should fuck you right now, teach you how to submit."

Her eyes widen and she stops talking.

"Make you beg to be punished." I place my hand around her throat with just enough pressure to entice her. "I don't take orders, Audrey. I give them. See, I've been nice. You have no idea how feral I can be." I move my index finger to her lips.

I see her battle herself, but she can't fight my dominance. Deep down, she wants a man who won't back down to her. She licks my finger, swirls her tongue around it, then sucks.

"Shit, I fucking love that. That's a good mate." I sniff the air. "You can't hide your desire from me. You want to submit to me, don't you? You want me to rip these fucking clothes off you right now, bend you over, spank you, choke you, fuck you in every conceivable position, in every hole. You want to be dominated. You want me to show you who's alpha. And when I'm done punishing that pussy, and I cum all over your exhausted body, you'll thank me."

Her eyes are closed as she's hypnotized by my voice.

"Look at me, Audrey."

She opens her eyes.

"You're so fucking sexy. Do you know that?"

Her eyes shift. She's self-conscious.

"Audrey, listen to me. You are sexy and beautiful. I love every inch of your body, and I love your determination. I want you more than I've ever wanted anyone, and I would do anything to be with you, but none of that matters if you can't see it in yourself. The woman in the photo is not a threat to you, okay."

She nods.

"I asked you a question. Do you know you're fucking sexy?"

She nods.

"I couldn't hear you."

"Yes."

"Yes, what."

"I'm sexy."

I take her hand. "Walk with me."

"But I thought—"

"Come on. I'm still going to fuck you." I lead her into the forest.

"What about bears?" she asks clenching my hand.

"I'm not letting a bear get to this honey."

She smiles.

74

"I don't know where the hell that bear came from, but I doubt they'll be anymore."

"Okay."

I intertwine my fingers with hers and squeeze her hand. With a deep exhale, I begin. "Sarah was a teacher. I met her at career day at her school. She was smart, beautiful, and gentle. I fell in love with her, and everything about her, but she wasn't my fated mate."

"Fated mate?" Audrey questions.

"Shifters are fated to a special person, the one that completes them. I knew Sarah wasn't my fated one, but I wanted to be with her anyway. For a common man, this wouldn't be an issue, but I was part of a pack. I'm a shifter, and she was human. We were in a relationship for two years. She insisted that I go to church with her, and she wanted to get married. I saw her as this angel, and I couldn't show her the real me. She wouldn't understand. I knew she wanted to get married and have a family, and I struggled with what to do. Do I tell her who I am? Do I choose her? Should I take that chance on love and not wait for my fated mate?"

"That's a tough choice."

"It was. I would have to live a double life or give up my pack. I didn't want to keep lying to the woman I loved."

"You don't think she would've understood and accepted you?"

"I don't know. I was terrified that she'd think I was evil or something. She began to question my love for her, as she should have. She accused me of stringing her along. I don't know. Maybe I was a little guilty of that, but I knew that my feelings for her were genuine. I knew I had to choose, and I chose to be with her. I chose love. I was going to be with her and live a normal life."

Audrey squeezes my hand, and I squeeze hers.

"I planned it perfectly. I was going to surprise her and propose to her on Christmas Day. I was going to give her everything she wanted." I take a deep breath. "I bought a ring. I set the scene. I even bought us a house. It was a nice home in a suburban neighborhood, perfect for raising a family. She would've loved it. I sent her a message to meet me there. She never arrived."

There's a deafening silence as I try to keep my composure.

"She was on her way to see me. All I could imagine was the smile on her face when she saw the ring and the house, but she never stepped foot on the property. Some idiot was driving drunk, and, and—"

"She didn't make it," Audrey whispers.

"They say she died on impact."

"I'm sorry, Darius."

"Me too."

I hang my head as the thoughts that have haunted me for years replay in my mind. I imagine the crash, and Sarah's face as she screams when the car flips. I wonder if she called my name when I wasn't there to protect her. I wonder if she was rushing to get to me.

Audrey wraps her arms around me and holds me.

"It was my fault. I had to wait for the perfect time, on her favorite holiday to be romantic. I never gave her what she wanted, what she deserved, and she died so young, and she'll never have that."

"That's why you don't like Christmas," she says.

"Given what happened, it seems kind of stupid to wait for one day to show someone how much you love them, doesn't it?"

"It does. It wasn't your fault," she says.

I shrug.

"How do you cope?" she asks.

"I told myself that I wouldn't love again. I wouldn't marry, and I wouldn't mate. Then you came."

"Why me?"

"You are that one, my fated mate. I knew it the moment I saw you."

She stops walking. "Really?"

"Don't sound so surprised. You felt it too. It's nothing to be afraid of."

"Feeling something strong for someone you just met is terrifying."

"Imagine how I felt. I came outside to see who was on my land, and I got hit like a lightning bolt."

"You told me you never wanted to see me again."

"My goal has been not to complicate your life. I thought you deserved better."

"Better than you?"

"I tried to give you the chance for a normal life. You didn't ask to be mated to shifters."

"You decided to make that choice for me. Is that something you do a lot?"

"I don't know what you mean."

"You think you know what's best. You chose for her, and you tried to do it for me. You can't do that."

"That's not what I was doing."

"That's exactly what you did. What about these feelings I have? You thought I didn't deserve the chance to explore them. I thought I was obsessed, crazy, delusional. Is that what you wanted for me?"

"I had my reasons."

"You don't get to make decisions for me."

"I know."

"I don't think you do. I'm not an adolescent. This isn't a dictatorship. I control my life. Do you understand?"

I fold my arms over my chest. This woman will not run me.

"Darius, answer me."

"I understand."

"Are you sure you're ready for this?" she asks me.

"I'm ready."

"I don't know if I believe that. What about Sarah?"

"Sarah taught me how to love, and I'll never forget her, but this," I point between us, "is something different, something greater, and I can't ignore it anymore. The truth is, from the moment I saw you, I never stood a chance."

"Me either, but I'm not immortal, Darius. Are you?"

"No."

"I can't guarantee you a long, pain-free existence, no more than you can keep me shielded at all times. All we can do is live, and not waste the time we have together."

"I'm not perfect, and I've made mistakes. You have to know that all I wanted to do is protect you."

"You protected me, but I still got scratched, and I still got knocked down."

"I'm sorry."

"You don't need to be sorry. I'm just saying that you can't control everything. You need to understand that."

"Try not to be angry with me."

"I'm not angry. We're just talking. Why are you saying that?"

"I just—"

She interrupts me. "That stuff from earlier is irrelevant. Just don't shut down on me. Don't make decisions for me, and we'll be fine."

That's not what I was talking about, but I lose the nerve to tell her that. So I just say, "I won't."

We walk hand in hand.

"Promise me that you'll tell me the truth, and if your feelings change, promise me you'll tell me that too."

"We've only just begun, and you're worried that my feelings will change."

"All I'm saying is I would like for you to tell me if

they do."

"You don't have to worry about that."

"I'd like to believe that, but you never know."

"Tell me what happened. Who's the fool who changed his mind about you?"

"I don't want to talk about it."

"You wanted me to open up. You need to do the same." I put my arm around her, letting her know it's okay.

"My ex and I were together for four years. I thought everything was great between us. We were in love. I thought we had a good friendship and we were solid, so when I did a little self-reflection and decided I wanted to wear my hair natural, I didn't think he would mind. So I did the big chop."

"What's that?"

"My hair used to be relaxed, you know, chemically straightened. It did a number on my hair. I cut off all the straight hair and only left the unprocessed hair."

"Oh."

"It was short."

"I see."

"The initial look on his face told me everything, but I ignored my instincts. He asked me why I did it, and I told him I wanted to be my authentic self. He said okay, and we carried on. I thought we were fine, and then things changed. He started picking fights with me, and he just acted indifferent. Suddenly, he had new friends, and he was too busy for me. A month later, he broke up with me."

"Fucking idiot."

"And it was because I cut my hair."

"Did he say that?"

"I always thought it, but he never said it. He said he felt like we had grown apart. After we broke up, he started dating my cousin who is the complete opposite of me, tall, long hair, and beautiful. He proposed to her six months later. They're still together now."

"I'm sorry that happened."

"I'm not. He was no longer the guy I dated. He was always ambitious, but he became all about money and status, almost as if nothing else mattered. If he's not at work, he's at a work function, at the gym, or traveling for work. His relationship with Michelle is different than ours was. They both like to show off, but they're never together. He's always missing in action with no explanation, and when he's around, he's on his phone or distracted. Our breakup taught me to trust my instincts."

"That's a good lesson to learn."

"My instincts told me that you wouldn't hurt me."

"Did they?"

"And I knew you wouldn't call the police on me. Somehow I knew that you felt what I was feeling."

"You did."

"The day I met you he showed up at my house out of the blue."

"Did he?" I remain calm and hide my anger.

"I told him to admit that he dumped me because I cut my hair, and he did. He said it out loud for the first time."

"What you do to your hair is your business. It's your head."

"I thought so too, but I was wrong."

"Bullshit. Did he fall in love with you or your hair?"

"That's what I asked myself many times, but it doesn't matter now. I'm glad I know the truth."

"What else happened when he showed up at your house?"

"Nothing."

"Don't lie to me."

"We talked. I got closure. He said he made a

mistake."

"And, did he try anything?"

She hesitates. "He kissed me."

I ball my fist. I will hunt him down and kill him. "Did you want him to?" I ask.

"No. Before he showed up I was thinking about you."

"Did anything else happen?"

"That was it. I put a stop to it and told him to leave."

"If he comes near you again, you let me know."

"Why?"

"Just let me know."

"There's nothing to worry about. He's not a threat. I think I found something better."

"You think?"

She smiles. "I hope so. Only time will tell."

"I'll give you something to think about."

We stop walking when we reach the lake. I thought she might like the view. It looks like it was carved out of a dream, surrounded by trees and a dirt path. The water sparkles like her eyes. The sun will be setting soon, and the sky is a mixture of red, orange, gold, and pink.

"It's so beautiful out here," she says.

My heart warms when she snuggles against my body. "Do you want to sit for a minute?" I ask.

"Sure."

We sit with her between my legs. I rest my head on her shoulder and wrap her in my body.

"It's so calm out here," she says.

"I love it here."

"Do you come out here often?"

"I usually go for runs a couple of times a week."

"Just because you run don't make you better than me."

"I didn't say that."

"I was just playing with you. Loosen up, Darius."

"I'll try."

"So, you like to exercise?" she asks.

"I guess."

"I don't," she says. "Are you okay with that?"

"I'm okay with whatever makes you happy."

"So what did your background check say about me?"

"Typical stuff. You're the middle child of three. You have a younger brother and an older sister. You're a licensed cosmetologist with a degree in English. I'm curious about how those things go together. You own a hair salon, and you're a content creator. You created a haircare line. You have good credit and no arrest record."

"Wouldn't it have been better to find out those things in a conversation?"

"I never planned on talking to you."

"Deep down you planned on something. Why else would you do that research?"

"Maybe you're right."

"Tell me about yourself."

"There's not much to tell. What do you want to know?"

"I don't know. Let's get personal since we're mates. Who is your favorite person?"

"You mean besides you."

"Obviously."

"I guess I'd say, my father."

"Are you two close?"

"We're as close as we can be. He's different. He's quiet. He doesn't let anyone in."

"He sounds exactly like you."

I laugh. You may be right. He raised me. Everything I am is because of him. I learned from him. I act like him. I look like him. He's strong, formidable, and very

82

smart, but he's a lone wolf."

"What's that?"

"He doesn't belong to a pack. It's rare for wolves to survive on their own, but that's what he does. He lives in the woods, he doesn't need many things, and he keeps to himself. He left his pack when my mother was killed by rivals. Because of that, he chooses not to depend on anyone, and I don't blame him. He's carried her in his heart all these years. Every once in a while, I can scent a woman on him, but it's not often."

"I understand you better now."

"Once I became an adult, he sent me out into the world. He told me that we weren't meant to be alone. It was his choice, but it didn't have to be mine. I'm grateful that he always stayed close. I like that he lives in my woods now. He's the only family I have."

"You can have my family."

"You don't mean that."

"Sure I do. Except for my grandpa. He's mine."

"Tell me about your grandpa."

She smiles when she thinks of him. "He's the only one in my family that truly sees me. I think I'm so lucky to have him. He accepts me for who I am. He encourages me to be myself. He's just a good man. I always say I want to marry a man like him."

"Do I measure up?" I ask.

"You've exceeded my expectations so far. I think he'll like you. He always told me that the perfect man was preparing for me."

"He sounds wise."

"He is. Tell me what made you become a botanist?"

"My father and I spent a lot of time in the woods. He taught me how to survive and how to hunt. While I was learning the rules of nature, I discovered a love for plants."

"You must be really smart," she says.

"I'm done talking. Take your clothes off," I command. My hands venture beneath her shirt. I can feel the tremble of her skin. "I don't like to repeat myself," I inform her.

She slips her arms through her shirt and lifts it over her head.

"Pants off."

She stands and unzips her jeans and slides them off along with her shoes. She's wearing a black thong, and I don't resist the urge to squeeze her plump ass before I rip it from her body.

"What about your clothes?" she asks. She faces me, holding my gaze as she tugs at my shirt.

"Did I tell you to touch that?"

"No."

I grab her throat and pull her slowly to the ground. I climb on top of her and I lift her hand over her head and hold it in place in the grass. "Give me your other hand." I hold both of her wrists together.

Her eyes sparkle. "Growl," she says.

I raise an eyebrow. "That's what you like, isn't it? You want the animal."

"Yes."

"What will you do for me?"

"I'll be your mate."

"You're already my mate."

"I'll cook for you."

"Naked."

"Fine, naked."

I stand her up. "Take my clothes off."

She removes my shirt and pants.

"Face the tree," I say. I back away from her quietly.

She turns her head slightly.

I reach out to her through my mind. *I told you to face the tree.*

She jumps.

The animal wants you too. I need to tame him. Do you understand?

She nods yes. *Hurry up. It's cold.*

I run as fast as I can, away from her. My wolf is eager, panting to break free. With my enhanced speed, I'm a mile away in two minutes. I shift. My wolf howls, and I feel Audrey's excitement and nervousness from this distance. I communicate to the wolf to hold back his aggression or I won't let him near her again. He agrees to behave and takes off running toward her scent. My desire for Audrey can never be quenched. I growl as I make my way back to her. Her want is strong, and so is mine. I spot her obediently facing the tree where I left her. I'm close, clawing at the dirt as I approach.

When I reach the tree, I know she can feel me. I charge for her and leap on my hind legs. She shouts with surprise as my body and my fur cover her. She calms underneath me.

"Darius," she moans.

My mate. I say through my mind link. I growl in her ear.

"Yes," she moans.

I lick her neck and growl into her skin. I can't get enough of her scent. I gently graze her skin with my canines and my tongue. *You may turn around.*

She slowly turns and we're eye to eye. Her eyes are kind, gentle, curious, and beautiful. I love her, and I will protect her with everything in me. I hope she can see it in my eyes.

CHAPTER 9

Audrey

I've never felt so safe in my entire life. This sexy ass wolf is driving me crazy. He cares for me, and I can feel it, just like when he fought that bear. He's a ferocious beast, but with me, he's a lamb. I run my fingers through his fur. He whimpers at my touch, and that makes me feel powerful. I'm not afraid of him. I'm only afraid for anyone who tries to come between us.

He lowers himself on all fours and looks at the lake. I can hear him in my head. *There's so much you don't know.*

"I understand that. What's wrong, Darius? Why are you worried?" I think that's what I'm sensing.

I want you all to myself.

"You have me, and there's no one here but you and me."

That will change.

"What are you saying? I thought this was for life."

It is. I'll always be yours.

"Your fear is the same as mine, that I'll change my mind," I say out loud.

The wolf nods.

"I won't."

We still have a lot to discuss, but for now, let's live in the moment. He turns to face me with determination in his eyes.

His gaze is so powerful I want to back away, but I stand my ground. He growls as he approaches. He's big, powerful, and he's mine.

Lie down. He commands.

I look around and lie in the grass face up. He walks over to me. His paws are at my sides. He sniffs his way up my body. I'm wetter than that lake over there. My chest heaves with anticipation. I feel his snout against my skin, then his tongue. My body heats. He circles my belly button. I grab his fur and close my eyes. He licks my stomach and then my breast, lapping over my nipple. My back arches and my hips lift off the ground, reaching for him. He licks his way up and growls in my face.

"Darius," I moan.

He works his way down my body and pauses when he reaches my pussy. I bend my knees and open my legs. I push his head down. He growls against me, and I'm certain I'm about to cum. He changes into himself, and I smile as he hovers over me.

"Don't tease me like that," I say.

"I don't want to move too fast," he says.

I wrap my legs around him and pull his body to mine. "Then go slow." I reach between our bodies and grab his thick, long, pulsing dick.

He growls.

I gasp when he slides inside me, slowly stretching me, filling me, giving me a satisfaction I can only get from him. He takes my lips, slowly, just like he takes my body. I give myself to him fully aware of what we are. We are mates, the human and the wolf shifter.

I thrust my hips to meet his. The agony and intensity build between us. I hold on to him with every part of my body, including my pussy. He grunts when I grip his dick, and I love it.

I cry out his name as I cum. I dig my fingers into his skin. His hips move at a steady rhythm, driving deeper into me. He pulls me up to a seated position with my legs around his waist. We stare into one another's eyes as I secure myself on his lap. His hands roam my back, heating my skin with every touch. Our lips stay connected while I slide up and down his dick.

His head rolls back while he sinks his fingers into my ass. He kisses my neck and whispers in my ear.

"Ride this dick, Audrey."

His hypnotizing voice drives me insane. With little effort, he guides my body up and down his shaft until I take over, losing control, taking him for myself. He grunts and growls, and scratches. I'm on the edge, about to cum. Suddenly, he stops. He looks panicked.

"What's wrong?" I ask.

"Promise me something."

"Anything." I kiss him.

"No matter how angry you get with me, I need you to listen to me. I wouldn't do anything to hurt you. Can you feel how much I mean that?"

"Yes."

"Promise me you'll trust me."

I touch his cheek. "I trust you, Darius."

Without a word, he flips me onto my back. The lamb is gone, and the beast in him takes over, showing my body no mercy. He takes me hard and fast, and I cum again and again. He's relentless, and I love it, but I swear something is driving him.

A loud voice booms through the forest. "Darius, what have you done?" I look up and two guys are marching toward us.

I scream. My mind flashes. I have a brief vision. I see three white wolves surrounding me as I lay in the grass.

Darius squeezes me tight as I try to get away. "It's okay," he says. "They won't hurt you. Close your eyes."

I look at him puzzled. "Trust me," he says. He kisses me, and I close my eyes. He crashes into me with more fury. We sink into the grass.

I see another vision. I'm naked with three men touching me. One of them is Darius. One of them kisses my lips and another my neck. I didn't get a good look at the two coming this way, but I think it's them.

My pleasure spikes to heights I didn't know existed. The things I'm seeing are scandalous. Darius goes hard, bringing me back to the moment with him.

I hear his voice in my head. *Cum with me.*

He lifts my leg over his shoulder and roars as he cums, pulsing into me while I scream his name. He sinks his claws into my shaking leg and I come so hard, I think I'm going to pass out.

I hear the voice again. "Darius, you son of a bitch."

He collapses on top of me, and I sink my teeth into his shoulder. I can't move. I'm spent.

"What the fuck did you do?" the man shouts.

I spring forward and Darius sits up. "Darius, what's happening?" I shout. I try to scoot my body away.

Darius stands and pulls me up. I cover my body with my hands. "You're safe," he says. "I need you to listen to me."

I back away as Darius holds my hand and blocks me with his body. I look around him to see the two men advancing. "Who are they?"

The two guys are almost as tall as Darius. They look strong. They're big. They're sexy as fuck. One of them has brown skin and long dreadlocks. His eyes are blue. When he looks into my eyes, I am speechless. The other is darker with grey eyes and just as fine. He licks his lips when he looks into my eyes. The corner of his lips curl, and I'm tempted to walk toward him. I feel something familiar with them both. Like I know them. Like I feeel with Darius, but I'm terrified, and I'm alone and naked with three strange men.

Darius turns around and kisses my cheek.

I flinch. "Who are they?"

"I know you're confused, and I know you feel something, and it's okay."

The man with the dreads scolds Darius. "I can't believe you did this?" His voice is the one I heard from the distance.

"I know you're upset."

"Upset. I'm beyond upset. I want to rip your fucking throat out."

"Do that, and she'll never trust you."

He wrestles with himself. He turns around and paces back and forth.

"I understand you're upset. We can talk about this."

"You lied to us." The other man finally speaks. His voice is deep and smoky.

"I know."

"Why? You didn't have to. I would've understood."

The other man stops pacing. "I don't. This is unforgivable."

I clench Darius. "Stop this." I can feel the anger from the man with the dreads.

"It's okay, baby."

"This is not okay. Make them go away."

"I can't do that."

"Why not?" I look around for a way out. I'm getting away.

"Don't run." Darius grabs my hand. He guides me to his side. "I didn't want you to meet like this."

"How did you want us to meet?" The man with the dreads shouts.

I clutch Darius's arm.

"You're scaring her. Is that what you want?" He points to the man with the dreads. "This is Felix." He points to the man with the fade. "This is Damien. I told you about them."

"What are they doing here?" I ask.

"Did you think you could get away with it? You know we're connected. Did you think we wouldn't feel it? This is unforgivable," Felix shouts.

Darius looks at me. "They know."

"They know what?"

"We know you mated," Damien says. He's calmer than Felix. He puts me at ease. "I apologize. His anger

90

is directed at Darius. It's not about you."

I look at Darius for answers. "The three of us are connected. Like I told you. I didn't tell you we were connected to you as well. Not only are you my mate, you're theirs too."

My jaw drops. "I don't understand."

"Damien, Felix, this is Audrey."

"Audrey, Damien, and Felix are alpha wolf shifters like me. They're leaders in my pack, and they're also your mates."

"Audrey, you're more beautiful than I could've imagined," Damien says.

"I suppose you'll do," Felix says.

Their eyes are glued to me and they step closer to me in slow motion. They're both wearing t-shirts and they both have muscular bodies and handsome faces, one more serious than the other. I'm overcome with lust. I imagine what they look like naked.

Darius moves me in front of his body, and he holds on to my waist. He whispers in my ear. "I know you want them. I can feel your desire, and it's okay, love." He kisses my neck and grabs my breasts. He squeezes and rubs as I moan.

I want to talk, but I can't. My senses are in overdrive. I thought Darius had taken all my body could give, but I'm rejuvenated looking at these two.

Felix and Damien stand in front of me. Felix takes my hand. I feel a static connection. He turns me slightly and inspects my body in a very mechanical way. I try to pull my hand back, but he tightens his grip. With his other hand, he grabs my breast and squeezes. I try to contain my moan because I'm curious as to what he's doing. His touches are not at all romantic, but they scare me and excite me. I want him desperately. Darius kisses my neck as Felix continues his inspection. Both his hands are on my body, touching my skin. He kisses my forehead, and I feel a spark crackle through my body. He looks over my naked body like he wants to devour me.

"What's happening?" I ask Darius.

"He's getting to know you."

Felix touches me between my legs. I twitch. Darius was just inside me. His cum sticky between my legs. The thought makes me uneasy, but Felix is unfazed.

"It's okay," Darius assures me.

Felix slips his finger inside me, and I tremble. I hold on to his shoulders as he finds my g spot with expert precision. He slips another finger inside me and I'm embarrassed. It feels good. The desire in his blue eyes makes me want to submit to his will. He howls. My head leans back against Darius's chest as my body clutches Felix's fingers. I groan and grunt as he growls until I cum. He bites his lip, and his fingers move faster inside me, controlling me. I want more of him. I sink my fingers into his shoulders as he slows down with me until I close my eyes panting to catch my breath. Felix moves to my side and takes my hand. He kisses my fingers and works his way up my arm.

Damien takes my free hand. The spark intensifies. He brings his face close to mine and I stare into his grey eyes.

The three of them touching me makes me weak in the knees.

"Darius," I manage to whisper.

Darius talks in between kissing and sucking my neck. "It's okay. You can do whatever you want. Do you like Damien?"

I gulp. I can't seriously answer that question.

"Don't be afraid. You're fated to him just as you are to me."

Three bodies are pressed into mine. Maybe this is a dream. If it is, it's the best fucking dream I've ever had.

Damien's face is waiting. He licks his lips. I move my head toward him less than an inch. I don't want him to know I want him, but I feel this pull. He inches closer. I can't resist. I poke my lips out and his lips meet mine. They're soft and the kiss is sweet. I don't know what's going on with me. I want more, but I sense that Damien won't budge more than I budge. He wants me to want him. I lean in and give him another peck. This one lasts longer. As our lips linger, I part my lips. He slips his tongue into my mouth and he presses his body against mine.

I can feel Darius behind me, Damien in front of me, and Felix at my side, stroking my arm. Damien grabs my waist and deepens our kiss. I moan into his mouth. We kiss like no one is watching. He softly pecks down my neck and Felix kisses my cheek. He growls in my ear and I shiver. I turn my head to catch his mouth, and our kiss is passionate and hungry. There is a primal urge that radiates between us.

All these strong hands are touching me, caressing me. Damien slips his hand between my legs. I love this feeling so I don't object. I spread them slightly. Felix sucks my nipple and Damien explores me with his fingers. He rubs my clit, and sucks my other nipple. My head rolls back and Darius captures my lips.

I turn to Darius and pull him closer. His naked skin sticks to mine. His dick is hard again, and his hands grip my waist. Felix moves behind me. I can feel his dreads against my back. He kisses down my spine. I hear his pants unzip, and I feel his dick pressed against me. My ears are invaded with whispers of wanting me, needing me, craving me, and fucking me. I look behind Darius, and Damien smirks at me as he removes his clothes.

I can't believe this is happening. I feel their want. It's a force. Felix turns me around and picks me up. His clothes are in a pile beneath him. I wrap my legs around his waist. His dick is pressed against me as he sucks my neck. "Let me fuck you, beautiful. I'm going to claim you, mark you, and make you mine."

I touch his hair and run it through my fingers. He smells so good, and he's so close to being inside me. Everything in me screams yes. I bite my lip. A slight move of my hips is all it will take. I can tell he's well endowed, and I want to slide down his pole so desperately.

"Say yes," he whispers in a deep, raspy voice.

"I want to," I whisper. I have a flash of the three of them. One behind me. One underneath me, and one in my mouth. I gasp.

"Embrace it," Felix says.

They growl.

"I saw that," Darius says.

"Felix," I whisper.

"Yes, Audrey. Say my name just like that."

Damien is pressed against my back. His hand travels down my ass and his dick pokes between my but cheeks.

Felix kisses my lips, and Damien lifts my hair and kisses my neck.

There's a one-second window where everything that happened comes to me. "What am I doing?" I shake my head as I climb down Felix's body.

"Audrey, please," Felix pleads in a whisper.

"Darius, what's going on? You said we were mates." My head spins.

Darius steadies me and holds my hands. "We are. The three of us are a triad. It's rare just like our white wolves. We have a special bond, and that bond extends to a mate. Most wolves are fated to one. The three of us are fated to you."

"I trusted you. You lied to me."

"You betrayed us," Felix says to Darius.

I turn around. "I need to talk to Darius."

"I was going to tell you," Darius says.

"I can't believe anything you say." I snatch my hands from his.

"Believe what you feel."

"What I feel is confused and stupid. What was this? Some game you came up with so you could pass me around to your friends? You didn't waste any time. Did you?" I search for my clothes. Darius hands me my shirt and pants, and I struggle to put them on. I don't know which way is up at this point. My head is spinning. I almost let all three of these guys fuck me.

He and the other guys get dressed.

"I can explain," Darius says.

"There's no explanation for this," I shout.

"I would never disrespect you by passing you around. I kept the truth from them as well. That's on me. You all are right to be angry, but if we can talk about this you'll understand."

"You're sick." I struggle to pull up my pants, and I almost fall. "What kind of woman do you think I am?"

"You are the woman of my dreams," he says. I feel his sincerity, but I don't know if I can trust myself anymore, or him.

"And mine."

"And mine."

I look at the three of them.

"I'm sure we'd all rather have you to ourselves," Darius says.

"You've proven that," Felix snaps.

"There's nothing to be afraid of," Damien says. "I know this is a fucked up situation, and Darius fucked up for not preparing you or us. We don't want to harm you. We would never disrespect you. We're respectable men. Our reaction to you is pure animal instinct. Our wolves were pushing us. Our desire for you is intense, and we got caught up in the moment. Can you forgive us?"

"I don't know what to say to that." I'm agitated because I like this guy. He's genuine, and I'm horny as fuck, but I don't know how to process this.

"I'd love to talk to you, please," Felix says.

"Look, why don't we all just go to my cabin? We can talk there."

"I don't know."

Despite everything, you know this is real. How else can you hear my voice? We're connected and our minds are linked.

I don't know anything anymore, Darius. I feel stupid.

You promised to trust me.

And you tricked me.

"I'll make it up to you," he says.

"I don't think you can."

"Just let me explain." Darius looks around. "All of you. I owe you all an explanation. Let's go, baby." He reaches for my hand.

I look him up and down and walk past him.

Three mates. Is this fool crazy? He must be.

As we all walk to the cabin, I don't know what to say. I try to distance myself from the three of them. I hear grunts and growls between them, and I wonder if they're communicating amongst one another.

Once we reach the cabin, I step inside and think about why I'm still here. Why didn't I run? The answer is I don't know. I'm pissed at Darius, but the thought of walking away from him fills me with sorrow. Still, I don't think there's anything he can say to me.

"Let's all sit," Darius says.

CHAPTER 10

Darius

I'm not particularly good with words, but I have to try with everything in me to keep our mate from walking away. This is what I was afraid of, and I'm afraid of what comes next.

"Talk," Audrey says to me.

Damn, my palms sweat, and our futures hang in the balance. "I know that I was wrong."

"Why did you lie?" Felix asks.

"I was one hundred percent selfish. I haven't been happy in so long, and I thought I'd never be happy again. I discovered Audrey months ago, and not only did I try to keep her from you two. I tried to keep her from myself. I thought I knew what was best for her." I look at Audrey. "I thought she deserved more. I already lost one love. I didn't want to lose another so I made the choice for all of us that Audrey would be left alone."

"You had no right."

"Once I came face to face with her, I couldn't resist her, and once I kissed her, I wanted her to myself, even if it was brief."

"You shouldn't have mated her. You've ruined everything. You're not sorry. You knew exactly what you were doing. Now, she's bound to you. What does that mean for us? She's our mate too."

"I know, Felix. I thought we could fix it later. I was going to tell you."

"When were you going to tell me?" Audrey shouts.

"Today. I promise."

"Your promises don't mean shit."

"You're supposed to be our leader and our brother. We trusted you. If we lose Audrey, I'll never forgive you."

Damien hasn't said much. I think he wants Audrey

more than he's angry at me. He addresses Felix. "Cut Darius some slack. You've watched him all these years. He's been a shell of his former self." He looks at me. "I'm angrier that you didn't trust us, but I understand. I want to see you happy, brother. I just wish you hadn't kept this from us."

"What about me?" Audrey shouts. "Why am I even here?" She stands. "Maybe I should let you three work through your issues. I'll leave."

"NO!" We all shout. She jumps.

"Please, you accepted me. Do you think you can accept us all?"

"What are you? I don't understand this thing you're talking about. Are you all friends? Are you lovers? Are you both? How do I fit in this situation?"

"We are not lovers. As our mate, you will be bound to all of us. You may love all of us. We'll all take care of you."

"I don't need anyone to take care of me."

"I know you don't, but we can try."

"And what? I'll have sex with all of you? Who does that?"

"We will do whatever it takes to please you, Audrey, you and your entire, sexy, voluptuous body," Damien says.

I can sense her desire, and I know they can too. Their wolves growl, and Audrey's cheeks are flush.

Damien stands in front of her. He takes her hand in his. "We don't want to use you, Audrey. It's not about our pleasure or some fucked up fantasy. It's about you. You need to understand that."

Damien is an alpha wolf, but in our pack, he's the omega. He is the epitome of balance. Brute strength and understanding. He knows how to reach people on an emotional level. Felix, on the other hand, deals best with facts and logic. I'm the protector.

"Why would three good-looking men who can have any woman they wanted, want to share a mate?" Audrey asks.

"You're special. You were made for us to love and protect. You will bear our children, and they'll be more powerful than we are. The elders have declared it," Felix says.

"What elders?"

"We trekked the Himalayas to have an audience with the elders, the oldest and wisest wolf shifters in the world. They know things. They told us of our fate, that we are a strong triad, and that our seed would be stronger. They will be born to one mate, and they'll continue our legacy to maintain the balance between shifters and humans. They will save humankind from destruction. You see, Audrey, this is bigger than all of us. You're an important part of our legacy."

"This is about me having kids? For all of you?"

"Yes," Felix says.

Damien gives Felix a look and tells him to be quiet through our mind link.

"You must be crazy," Audrey says.

"It's more than that," Damien assures her. "We value you as a woman and as our mate. Our pack will cherish you, and we will treat you like a queen."

"You all want to share me. How does that work?"

"How would you like it to work?" I ask. "You're in a position of power here. You call the shots."

"I can't even fathom what you're talking about. I wouldn't know the first thing about navigating this lifestyle. I want to get married someday. I want a normal life."

"You can still get married."

"How? It's illegal to have three husbands."

"You can marry me," Damien says.

"Or me."

"Or me."

I see a hint of a smile on her face.

"Slow down guys. Don't you all want your own mates?"

"We are willing to adjust."

"What about monogamy? Is it fair to you that I can sleep with all of you, have all your children, and you have to share me? How can I realistically please all of you? It's too much pressure."

"There is no pressure. We can determine what works for us and most importantly what works for you."

I hold her hand. "Please give us a chance."

She stands. "I can't. I have to go. I don't know. I, I'm sorry." She looks around frantic. She's overwhelmed. "Where are my keys?"

The three of us feel the deep pang of rejection.

"They're on the table by the door."

Audrey looks into my eyes. She's confused. I can tell she doesn't know what to say. I don't either.

"I have to go."

"I understand." My heart breaks.

She opens the door.

"Wait," I shout. I hug her and wait for her to hug me back. "I'm so sorry." I kiss her lips for maybe the last time.

"I just. I can't."

Felix and Damien walk to the door.

"Can I hug you before you go?" Damien asks.

"I guess that's okay."

He embraces her and kisses her forehead. "It's okay, Audrey. It was nice to meet you. I only wish it were under better circumstances. I hope someday we can at least be friends. Would it be okay if I checked on you later this week?"

"I don't know."

"I'm not going to pressure you, luna."

"What's a luna?"

"In our world, a luna is a woman who gets the utmost respect. She knows her power, beauty, and intelligence. Many men desire her, and she is a force to be reckoned with. A luna such as yourself could rule me any day."

"And you'd obey me?"

"Without question."

She has a big grin on her face. "That's how you think of me."

He flashes a devilish smile, and his eyes glow. "Hell yeah."

"Why?"

I smile to myself. Damien has worked his charm on her.

"So, luna, is it okay if I check on you, just to say hi."

Audrey looks at me with confusion and a little intrigue. I nod slightly.

She shrugs. "I guess so."

Damien rubs her arm in a friendly manner, and she's comfortable with his touch without realizing that his hand slowly moves down her arm. She catches her breath as his finger lingers, barely tracing her skin until he holds her hand and gifts her with a gentle kiss on the wrist.

"Just so you know, you're not as irresistible as you think you are."

Damien smirks. "Oh, I'm not?" he asks.

The grin on her face says otherwise. "No."

"Challenge accepted, luna. Challenge accepted."

"That wasn't a challenge."

"It absolutely was." Damien walks away, and Audrey watches him.

Felix holds his arms open. She reluctantly hugs him. "This isn't something you can walk away from," he says.

Audrey tenses and backs away. "Goodbye," she says as she closes the door.

Damien reprimands Felix. "Why would you say that shit to her?"

"I was just letting her know what to expect. I'm not the bad guy here. Darius is the one you should be mad at. If you had handled this situation correctly, we wouldn't be in this predicament."

"I know, but we can't dwell on that now."

"Darius is right."

Felix shakes his head.

I address them. "We need to come up with a plan. There's no way we're letting our mate get away."

"Your last plan worked so well. I can't wait to hear what you come up with next," Felix says.

"I know you're mad bro, but come on. Can we work together to figure this out?" I ask.

Damien's mind is working as he paces. "We need to divide and conquer, we each need to connect with her and show her what life would be like as our mate."

"How do we get her to talk to us?" Felix asks.

"I can handle that," I say.

"You're the one that fucked all of this up," Felix reminds me yet again.

"I'll fix it. I'll go visit her tonight."

"You mean you'll go fuck her tonight, again."

"Felix, I get it. You're pissed, but that's enough. I'll do whatever it takes. You know it's our best option. She's already connected to me, and I have the best chance of reaching her."

"I hate this," Felix says.

Damien asks, "How are we supposed to claim her now that you've mated?"

"The ritual isn't complete without all of us. We can all still claim her during the next full moon," I say.

"Are you sure, or is that just what you told yourself?" Felix asks.

"I'm sure."

"The next full moon is New Year's Eve," Felix says.

"Then we have until then. I'll lay the groundwork tonight."

"It'll be alright," Damien says. If anyone can get through to her, it's Darius."

"If you fuck this up, I won't forgive you."

"What are you prepared to do about it, Felix?"

"For this, I could kill you."

"I'd like to see you try. I'm sick of your comments, and there's only so much I'm willing to tolerate."

"I could take this to the pack, tell them how you betrayed us and cost them their luna."

"I wish you would try. You don't want to start a war with me."

"Both of you need to calm down. Put your egos aside. The only thing that matters is Audrey. If we fight amongst ourselves, she'll never accept all of us. Stop acting like children. We're brothers and brothers forgive, Felix. Darius made a mistake, but he's always been there for you."

"Whatever, you don't have to cry about it."

"I'm going to talk to Audrey like I should have before all this happened. Let me get through to her tonight and you two can visit her tomorrow."

"Are you sure?" Damien asks.

"Yes, you're going to have to help her see the benefits of multiple mates. You saw her outside. She was on the verge of succumbing to all of us. The attraction is there, you have to make her comfortable."

"How did you make her comfortable?" Felix asks.

"She's special. She looks through you and she will see you for who you are. If you want to connect with her, you'll have to open up, Felix. Don't focus on facts and statistics about compatibility."

"Sure," Felix says.

"Damien, while it's clear that your charm works, you can't treat her like the average woman you try to hook up with. Both of you need to show her the real you. Be vulnerable, but don't be pussies. She likes it when men take charge even if she doesn't listen."

"Good looking out," Damien says.

"Do you two want a drink?"

"No," Felix says.

"Yes," Damien says.

I go to the kitchen and get three snifters. I pull out Felix's favorite cognac and pour doubles for all of us. "Sit, fellas."

They sit, and we all sip.

"Tell us about her," Damien says.

"She's a good woman. She works hard, she's feisty, and she's smart."

"How did you meet her?"

I tell Felix and Damien about how I discovered her picking my plants and our first confrontation.

"So you threatened to call the police on her, and in a matter of days you managed to mate her?" Felix asks.

Damien nods. "That's skill."

"I don't know about all that."

We sip and talk as I tell them everything I know about our mate. Felix is stubborn, but I think I'm making progress. I've only accepted his attitude because I fucked up. I can only apologize so many times. If he doesn't let this go, we'll have to fight it out.

Once I say goodnight to them I prepare myself to see Audrey. We're still mates and my wolf and I long for her as much as she longs for us.

I try to come up with something to say as I drive to her house, but nothing sounds good. When I pull into her driveway, I'm pissed. I scent male pheromones and

I hear voices. She's telling him to go away, and he won't listen. When I hear her say let go of me, I determine that whoever he is, he's a dead man. I'm not even sure if I put the truck in park when I jump out and run to her.

"Audrey, are you okay?" I ask as I push the man she's talking to out of the way. I hold him against the wall while he struggles to break free.

"I'm fine." Her heart is racing. I don't believe she's fine. I smell fear.

"We're fine," he says.

"What's going on here?"

"Nothing's going on. He was just leaving."

"Get off me," he shouts.

I slam his head into the wall with a growl. "You touched my mate. I should kill you."

"What have you done, Audrey?" he asks.

"None of your business," she shouts from behind me.

"Who is this?" he shouts.

"You can address me. Audrey, go inside."

"Just let him go," she says.

"I've been looking for you for days. Is this who you've been with? You're that desperate that you had to whore yourself out."

"What?" Audrey shouts.

I push him away from the door and into the front lawn. He shouts Audrey's name, telling her to get me to back off, but I'm not backing off. I punch him in the face, and while he recovers I continue to punch. His blood covers my knuckles. I faintly hear Audrey begging me to stop, shouting that I'm going to kill him, but the rage in me and my wolf won't let me stop.

The man begs me to stop as well, but I only see red. He insulted my mate. I feel a tug on my arm. I push before I realize it's Audrey trying to hold me back. She tells me to stop through our mind link. I grab her before she can fall, and I hold her in my arms. I find myself apologizing to her once again, but I'm hopeful because she's holding on to me. She's more concerned with me than she is angry at me right now. As much as I want to enjoy her embrace, I can't forget about my opponent. I position Audrey behind me.

"Who is this?" I ask her.

"My ex," she says.

"The same ex who's engaged to your cousin?" I ask.

"Yes."

"The same ex who kissed my mate." I ball my fists.

He spits blood. "She wanted it."

"Darius, don't do it. He's not worth it."

I grab Audrey by the waist. I don't want her to be afraid of me so I decide to stop. "Get out of here."

"Fuck this bitch," he says as he walks away.

I growl.

"Fuck you, Andre," Audrey shouts.

He holds up his middle finger as he gets into his car. "Nobody wants a fucking whore." He drives off.

"What was he doing here?" I shout.

"I don't know. I certainly didn't invite him. He said he was checking on me."

"For what reason?"

"He's been acting strange. I don't know what's wrong with him."

"I'd better not see his face again."

"I don't want to see him again either. Thanks for stepping in."

"I'll always protect you, Audrey, even if you hate me. Tell me you don't hate me."

"I can't deal with that right now."

"We'll talk about you and me after you tell me what he did to scare you."

"I've never seen him act like that before. Even before

106

you got here, he was talking crazy, calling me a whore." She starts to cry. "I don't even understand this. There hasn't been anything between us in years. Why would he say those things about me?"

I comfort my mate as she buries her head in my chest. I guide her inside her house and close the door. Her house smells like ora. I sit her on the couch and squeeze her tight. "He's jealous. If I had to guess, I'd say you're a hard woman to get over."

"But he broke up with me."

"Men do stupid things for stupid reasons, and once you turned him down, it must've driven him crazy. Seeing him drove me crazy. I don't want anyone messing with my mate."

She sits up. "Oh yeah, I'm mated. This is so messed up. All I wanted was some flowers, and now I'm in a situation I don't know how to get out of."

"You want to get out of this," I say quietly. I hang my head at the thought that she doesn't want to be mated to me. My wolf whimpers. My heart breaks, and I want to cry. This is harder than I thought it would be. I clear my throat, and I almost choke on my words. "I have to go." I stand.

"Darius, wait. What are you doing?"

I pretend I don't hear her and keep walking. My wolf is pressing me to go back, but I can't. I should've followed my instincts and kept her at a distance.

"Darius," she shouts.

I hold the door handle in my hand. I can't bring myself to look at her as I step outside and walk to my truck.

CHAPTER 11

Audrey

One minute he was holding me, and before I could blink he turned cold. I stare out the window and watch him get into his truck. My emotions are all over the place. I was angry with him and sad because for a moment I thought we had something beautiful. I was grateful when he showed up at my house because Andre was starting to scare me. I felt comfort and safety when he held me a few minutes ago, and now I feel guilt.

The amount of pain that radiates from him makes me feel sick, and being the one that hurt him with a few simple words makes me feel worse. This isn't fair. I'm the one who was lied to. I don't even know what he was trying to get me into. Now, tears are welling up in my eyes. The look on his face destroyed me. He's so big and powerful. I swear he's a big ass baby, but still, he's mine. Damn.

I walk outside and knock on his passenger side window. He lowers it.

"What the hell is wrong with you?" I ask.

"You don't want to be my mate," he says.

"That's not fair."

"I know. I didn't mean it like that. You're entitled to be angry with me. I'll be fine."

"Will you really be fine? Why do I feel like I was stabbed in the heart?"

"I guess that's my fault."

"Can you please stop feeling sorry for yourself? What happened to my big, strong, alpha?"

"Go back inside. Don't worry about me. I've put you through enough."

I open the door and as I attempt to sit down. I recognize my basket in his seat. In addition to my glasses, it's filled with plants that I normally pick in the forest and the flowers that I love and need. I pick up the basket and put it in the back seat after I sit next to him. "You brought those for me."

"I know you use them in your hair products, so I gathered some for you."

"Thank you. That's really sweet."

"You're welcome."

There's an awkward silence. I peek at him, but he continues to look straight ahead or out his window. After a few minutes, I speak up. "Why are you still sitting out here?"

"I have to make sure he doesn't come back."

"I'll be fine."

"I have to make sure," he says with a stern voice.

"How long do you plan to stay here?"

"All night."

"You're impossible," I say.

"You don't have to stay out here. Go in the house."

"You're so —"

He finally looks at me. There's a question in his eyes.

"I mean I just want to stay mad at you, but you make it impossible," I say.

"I ruined everything, and I don't know if it can be fixed. I may have ruined your life, and I'm sorry about that. I ruined my relationship with the triad. The fate of the world and the future of both our kinds are at stake, and it's my fault. This is so much bigger than me. I lost sight of everything."

"Wolves mate for life because of the importance of parental relationships. I read that online."

"Yeah but that's not all this is," he says.

"And I'm supposed to have children for all of you for the purpose of saving the world?"

"Amongst other things."

"Do you believe that?"

"Yes, I do."

"What am I supposed to do with three mates?"

"You don't have to figure that out right now or at all. Maybe we can—" He pauses.

"Maybe you can what?"

He's in agony. "Maybe we can find another mate."

"Why would you say something like that?"

"We may not have a choice. I have to think about our future. I can't be selfish anymore. We don't have a lot of time. I may have to sever our bond and find another mate for us. I'll have to choose someone who understands our purpose and our ways."

"You'll have to choose someone?"

He nods.

"Who will you choose?"

"I don't know."

"What you do know is you need someone better. Someone more suitable than me."

"Audrey, all I need is you. There's no one better, no one more suitable. I don't want anyone else, but I won't have a choice. I may have to settle. My pack put their faith in me as their leader. They trust me. I have to fix this.

"So I lose you. I lose my mate."

"I didn't think you wanted me."

"I accepted you, didn't I. I said I wanted you and only you. You didn't tell me about anyone else." Tears stream from my eyes.

"I know." He looks out his window.

"How is this fair?"

"It's not, but I can't think about myself. Our bond has to be sealed by the next full moon. All of us. If not I have to make a decision." We sit in silence, and then I hear a sniffle.

"Darius?"

"I'm sorry."

"Darius, look at me."

"Go inside, Audrey."

"Look at me," I shout.

He turns around. His eyes are red and filled to the brim with tears he's desperately trying to hold back. The moment our eyes meet, tears fall from his eyes.

I wipe his eyes and hold his cheek in my palm. We stare at one another for what feels like an eternity and I reach over and hug him.

"I don't think I can survive this if you don't forgive me. I'm sorry, Audrey. I'm so sorry."

I know he's sincere, and he feels terrible. "It's okay. I can forgive you."

"I don't deserve you."

I rest my head on his chest and he kisses the top of my head. This feeling is one I don't want to lose. I kiss his hand and he shuffles in his seat. I can see why when my eyes avert between his legs. I see a bulge hardening in the center of his lap. My mouth waters. I can't resist rubbing my palm against it. "Is that all you think about?" I ask.

He rubs my hair. "It's kind of hard to stay soft around you."

I rub his pants more furiously.

"If you don't stop I won't be able to control myself."

"Then don't control yourself. Unleash."

He grabs a fist full of my hair and growls. He can't stay soft around me, and I can't stay dry around him. "Woman, don't play with me."

I unzip his jeans, and his heartbeat quickens. He takes a deep breath as I unbuckle his pants. He's not wearing any underwear, and his perfect appendage rises and stares at me eye to eye. The smooth curve of its head beckons to be licked. I must admit I'm pretty nervous. It's been a while since I sucked a dick, but if my memory and my pride serve me correctly, I was pretty good at it. Who am I to deny such a beautiful thing what it wants? I want to go straight for the head, but I want to play first. I lick up his shaft and swirl my tongue around the tip. Then I suction the tip between my lips. His neck slams against his seat, and he sucks in air. I peek up at him. His eyes are closed and he licks his lips. He moans his delight as I open my mouth and take him in halfway. My hand grips the other half of his shaft and I work them together swirling my tongue as I suck. His hips lift off his seat, pushing him further into my mouth. I move my hand to play with his balls as I take him all in, rhythmically working my head from left to right as I move up and down. The harder he grabs my hair, the more I feel his enjoyment, and the more I push myself to give him more. I open wide until the tip of his head reaches the back of my throat, and I bob my head.

"Fuck, Audrey," he moans.

I spit on his dick. He hisses. I repeat bobbing my head, telling myself to breathe through my nose as my pleasure soars from watching him lose control. I kiss my way down and work him with my hand as I suck his balls. I lose myself in his pleasure. I forget about technique and perfection and just enjoy the masterpiece that is his dick. I taste it, tease it, suck it, lick it. I don't have to look at him to know he's enjoying every moment. I roam my hand underneath his shirt and rub his chest. When I find his nipple, I run my fingers over it and squeeze. He can no longer contain himself. He pushes my head down and fucks my mouth with intensity. I keep up the best I can. I will not be defeated by the dick. My head works in tandem with his hips as he announces he's about to cum. He strokes himself as I watch hungrily, waiting for the eruption.

"Cum for me." I lick my lips. "Cum in my mouth." I want to see him lose it. "Cum on my face. I tweak his nipple and he grunts. I suck his tip. His body jerks. He's close. I replace his hand with my mouth, taking him all in. He howls and I growl. He slams my head down and he grunts and groans and pushes my head as he erupts in my mouth. His cum fills my mouth. I swallow as much as I can. His body convulses as I suck. He pumps against my face, and I take it all until his body relaxes and he struggles to catch his breath. I suck one last time and kiss his tip with a smile. His body quakes one final time.

"Fuuuck," is all he can say as he strokes his dick.

I wonder if it was the best head he's ever had because I put in work. I lay my head on his chest and he puts his arm around my shoulder.

"Girl, that was just… damn."

I smile to myself. My eyes are glued to his dick. He has not gone soft, and my pussy is dripping for him. He gently lifts me off his chest and opens his car door.

"What are you doing?" I ask.

He doesn't reply. He only steps out of the truck and walks around to my side. It's dark outside, but I'm appalled that his pants are still unzipped and his dick is poking straight out. He opens my door. "Get out of the truck."

I obey.

He opens the rear passenger door. "You left your basket. Get it."

I'm confused. He's all serious, and I'm trying to figure out why he's worried about this stupid basket when I just want to fuck.

"Get your basket," he commands interrupting my thoughts.

I jump slightly. "Why?"

"Don't ask me no fucking questions. Do what I said?"

"You know what? You sure are right. Let me get this

fucking basket so I can take my ass in the house."

"Yeah, that's what you'd better do."

I'm angry, but I don't want to get into it with him. It's probably best that I end this now. I bend over the seat to get my basket. While I reach I feel a poke on my ass cheek. "What the —"

"Hurry up."

"That's it," I shout. I'm pissed.

Before I can say anything else his body is pressed against mine. He pops my ass with his palm. I wince. I turn my head and swat at his hand, but he's too quick. I reach for my basket and he pushes against me. I try to turn around and swing at him but he holds me in place. I wiggle against him, but he doesn't budge, and he won't allow me to budge either. I try to elbow him in the stomach, but he catches me before I can do anything. I'm exhausted from my attempts to outmaneuver him.

"Get your basket he says." I bend over for one final attempt to retrieve my basket. He pops me one more time and caresses my ass.

"What's wrong with you?" I shout.

He doesn't say anything. He swiftly unbuttons my jeans and pulls my pants down.

My body stiffens. I see what he's doing.

I try to turn around and he grabs my hands and holds them together behind my back. I wiggle to break free. The struggle only adds to my excitement. With his free hand, he tugs my jeans down over my hips. They rest slightly below my ass. He reaches between my legs and plays with my pussy. I moan at his touch.

"Listen to me, Audrey."

"What?"

He pops my ass and rubs the sting. "I said listen. Don't talk. Do you understand?"

I nod yes.

He whispers in my ear, and I shiver from the vibration of his deep voice. "I'm going to fuck you now, and I'm not going to hold back. Do you understand?"

"Yes." My body tingles with excitement.

He pops my ass.

"Sorry," I say.

Another pop.

I muffle my yell and wait quietly for him to speak.

"I'm not going to hold back, but you have to unless you want all your neighbors to know what you're doing."

My eyes widen. We're not in the forest anymore. I forgot we were in my driveway.

"You're not afraid, are you?"

I shake my head no. I'm horny as fuck.

"That's a good mate. You want this dick, don't you?"

I nod.

"I know you do. I'm going to fuck you hard, and you're going to take every inch of my dick, and you're not going to make a sound. Do you understand?"

I nod.

He slips his finger inside me from behind and slips in and out. "My pussy," he says. "You stay wet for me. I like that shit." He removes his finger and before I can respond he slams into me.

I shout, and he covers my mouth with his hand. He slides in and out of my pussy, and my eyes roll back in my head.

"I told you to be quiet, Audrey."

With every thrust, I shout into his palm. He doesn't give me a second to think. He savagely pounds me, sending vibrations of excruciating pleasure through my body. I lose my mind as I claw into the seats and arch my back.

I moan. I want to scream his name for everyone in

the neighborhood, but I can't form words.

Darius releases my mouth and hands, sinking his fingers into my hips on both sides. "This is my pussy."

I swear I'm high off his dick. He makes me cum. I try my best to stifle my cries, but I can't. He grabs my throat and squeezes. That works. I can barely form sounds other than gasping for air, but my orgasm intensifies and a tear rolls down my face. He pulls my body upright and leans me against the open door. He pulls my hips slightly against his and he circles his hips as he moves inside me. He bites my neck and slips his finger inside my mouth. I suck hard to keep myself from shouting as he pounds into me against the door. I'm afraid he's going to break it with all the force he uses. My hips meet his thrust for thrust and I cum again with the side of my face pressed against the window. My breath steams the glass."

"Tell me this pussy is mine."

"It's yours. It's yours. Yes, it's yours," I cry out.

His hands roam my back and my ass. He spreads my juices with his thumb and slides it into my ass. I whimper as he pleasures both my holes. I bend over and push my ass into his finger. I grunt and groan as the intensity builds in my body. I'm going to cum, but I know it's going to be loud.

"Darius," I cry.

"Yes, love."

"I can't hold back," I manage to say in between thrusts.

"And why should you, my love?"

"But."

"Fuck what people think."

"But."

"You need to stop worrying about other people and focus on your happiness. Do you want to cum, my love?"

I nod.

"Doesn't this dick feel good?"

"Yes."

"Do you want to hold back?" He growls. "Or do you want to enjoy every drop of pleasure? Do you want to feel free?"

"Yes."

"Then cum for me, my love. You don't have to hold back. I'll always be here to protect you." He growls and his thrusts become deliberate, powerful, and penetrating.

I clench his dick and thumb, and pressure builds inside me. My hips buck wildly, and I cry out to the heavens as he fucks me like a beast. He replaces his thumb with two fingers, and I feel another wave of pleasure. I'm so fucking loud, and I don't care.

He cums with me, releasing into me as our bodies move together, soaking up one another's passion until our tongues meet in an exhausted kiss.

I can barely move. Darius holds me steady as he closes the doors to his truck. He picks me up and carries me into the house where he draws a bath for us. My garden tub is hardly big enough for him, but he doesn't seem worried. He kisses me as he bathes me and I bathe him. We retire to my bedroom naked and he holds me while I fall asleep.

CHAPTER 12

Darius

I lie in bed with Audrey staring at the ceiling. Audrey wakes up after a brief nap. She instinctively hugs me. That would normally make me smile, but my mind is preoccupied.

"I don't want to lose you," she says.

"Me either."

"And I don't want you to mate someone else."

"I don't want that either."

"Can't we just run away together?"

"I can't run away from my problems, and I don't think you can either. Your life is here."

"I know"

"Can't you just try?" I ask.

"Try what?"

"Are you going to deny that you're attracted to Felix and Damien?"

"No, but Felix is kind of strange."

"You still wanted them. You liked their touch. You had thoughts about them, didn't you? As a matter of fact you're thinking about them right now. The idea of being fucked by all of us excites you. I can feel it, and you can have either of us whenever you want."

She stirs uncomfortably.

"I just can't fathom being with three men."

"If you're worried about our relationship, we'll be fine. You don't have to choose. You can enjoy all of us to your heart and your body's content."

"It's just weird."

"It'll be an adjustment for me, too, but it doesn't have to be complicated. I made it that way when I didn't tell you everything upfront. Don't close the door on this. Your fulfillment is at stake. I don't want to find another mate. I don't want anyone else."

"So it's all or nothing."

"I don't see any other way."

"This is so unfair."

"I need you to do something for me."

"What is it?"

"I need you to give them a chance. I need you to try."

"I can't do that."

"You can get to know them. You can see what they have to offer."

"That's a huge ask."

"I know. What I'm about to say pains me more than it will pain you."

"What are you about to say?"

"I have to back off."

"From what? From me?"

"I have to. I need you to spend time with Damien and Felix, and I can't interfere."

"No."

"I can't see you."

"No."

"I'm sorry."

"Stop it."

"I have to do this, Audrey. I can't see you again until you at least try."

"You're leaving me."

"I hope not. I'm giving them a chance that I stole from them and you. You're all important to me, and I need to make this right."

"Don't do that to me."

"Listen to me, Audrey. If you try, I mean really try, and you can't accept all of us, I'll understand and you and I can have a night to say goodbye, but if you don't give them a chance I can't see you again." My heart breaks as much as hers.

"That's not fair."

"It's not, but it's necessary. You and I have tonight. You can think about it, but we don't have much time. Hard decisions have to be made, and as alpha in charge, they have to be made by me."

"Fuck you," she shouts. She hits my chest.

I grab her hands. "Listen to me. I hope this isn't the end for us, but I know I fucked up. If you refuse, I don't blame you. I know it's too soon to say this, but I love you, Audrey, and I want to see you again. I want to wake up next to you every morning and fall asleep with you in my arms every night. Please just try."

She moves away from me and rests her head on the headboard with her arms folded over her chest.

I twirl a lock of her hair in my finger, and she jerks away from me. "Do you want to spend this time angry at me or making love to me?"

"Angry. You can go to hell."

"Life without you is hell."

"Yet every time you get the chance, you try to push me away."

"I'm trying to keep you forever."

"Don't do this."

"I have to."

"I won't give them a chance, and I don't like you trying to control every aspect of this. You're doing it again, trying to make decisions for me."

"Baby, I'm giving you a choice."

"You're backing me into a corner. I don't like that," she says.

I move my hand up her thigh. "But you like me."

"Not anymore."

"You love me."

"I won't forgive you this time. I won't forgive you if you abandon me."

"I won't forgive myself if we lose you. They need you as much as I do, and you don't know it yet, but you need them."

"I don't need any of this. I was fine before you, and I'll be fine without you."

I feel between her legs. "The body doesn't lie," I inform her.

"But men do."

"Our wolves don't. They have no reason to. They are aware, unafraid, and loyal. I saw your vision. You saw all of us, the way we were meant to be, protecting you, comforting you, adoring you. That's not a lie, and deep down, you know it. Look at me, Audrey."

She reluctantly looks into my eyes. "I've never begged for anything in my life, and I'm begging you to give us a chance."

"I can't."

"I have no choice but to respect that. Do you want me to leave now?"

"No."

"What do you want?"

"I want you to tell me we can be together. I want you to tell me I'm worth it. I want you to say you want me for yourself."

I press my forehead against hers. "I want you for myself, baby. I really do. I'd rather die than lose you." Tears fall from her eyes. "I'm sorry I caused you pain. I'll do it. I'll give it up for you."

"Don't just say what I want to hear."

"You're worth it, and you and I will have the strongest offspring anyway. Our child will be the next alpha. We can do it. Fuck it."

"You're saying yes?" she asks.

"I'm saying yes to you and me forever."

"Forever," she whispers.

"My mate," I say.

"Yes."

"Kiss me."

She wraps her arms around my neck and presses her lips against mine. I feel her joy and relief. "Thank you," she says.

"I love you, Audrey."

"Make love to me," she says.

I lay her on the bed and look in her face as I climb on top of her. I want to remember her just like his. Her natural beauty and radiant skin make my body tingle. The grateful look in her eyes mixed with lust seduces me. We make love through the night until we're both exhausted. It's so tender and beautiful. Our connection is electric. I know I won't get that from anyone else. I love the way she holds on to me with every part of her body. I can't get enough of her touch, her scent, and her voice, panting my name as I fuck her to ecstasy. She's my drug. I hope we'll have many more nights like this one. As she cums for the last time I remind her that I'm hers and she's mine, always. This time when she sleeps, she's out for the night.

I don't want to sleep. I want to listen to her heartbeat. I want to smell her scent before I say goodbye. I'm going to miss her. We had a short amount of time together, and I'll cherish her forever.

I watch her as the sun rises. I kiss her lips while she sleeps. I promise her that my heart will always belong to her. Once I'm dressed, I retrieve her basket from my truck and sit it on her nightstand. For the time being, I'll make sure she gets all the plants she needs, but I sure am going to miss watching her pick them from my forest. I attempt to calm my wolf and let him know this is temporary. I have faith in our mate. She'll come back to us.

I call Felix from the road. He gives me attitude when he picks up the phone.

"I've called to make amends."

"I don't see how you can," Felix snaps.

"Audrey is still uneasy about having three mates. You have to be understanding with her."

"That's if I get the opportunity."

"I know you well. You won't give up on her. You can't afford to."

"What do you want?"

"I told Audrey I couldn't see her anymore."

"You can't help fucking us over, can you? This is unbelievable."

"Listen Felix. I told her I can't see her again unless she gives you and Damien a fair chance."

He takes his time responding. "You did that for us."

"Not just for you, for all of us. She's going to be angry with me, but I've done all I could. The rest is up to you."

"How do we proceed?"

"Without me in the way. Promise me you'll make her happy."

"I promise."

"You have to take care of her. I'm trusting you and Damien with her safety and her heart." I tell him about her ex showing up at her house and his behavior.

"You know we'll protect our mate with our lives. Thank you for this. I understand this is a big sacrifice for you."

"I owed you one."

"I appreciate it."

"I'm sending you her contact information now and everything I have on her. I'm counting on you."

"You can trust us."

I hang up the phone as I pull up to my cabin. The boarded window haunts me. As I walk through the door, the scent of my mate on my body and in my home haunts me. I sit in my favorite chair and think. Did I make a huge mistake? It sure as hell feels like it. My mind is tortured. My wolf is sad and angry. Heavy with grief, I howl my despair.

This is the time we should be bonding, getting to know one another, talking about our future, celebrating with the pack, and because Audrey loves the holidays, making Christmas plans. The tree that I bought for her sits empty, in desperate need of her feminine touch. The food we were in the middle of eating still sits on the table. I walk into my bedroom expecting to see tousled sheets from the love we made. As I approach the door, my room smells like her.

I smile as I stand in the doorway. She changed the sheets and made the bed. She's fucking perfect. I desperately want this to be her home. I need to do something. I go to the only place that brings me comfort, my greenhouse.

I'm working on a couple of projects that'll keep me occupied. The tags on my current works in progress look like a sea of paper. I can't focus on anything except Audrey's face in my mind. I howl and try to resist the urge to fall to my knees. All I can do is take deep breaths and try to focus on the flowers. I've been working on a special breed for months now, but I can't seem to get it right. My best rose comes into focus, and I walk toward it. Something is missing, but what? To anyone else, I'm sure it looks perfect, but it doesn't speak to me like I need it to.

"I thought I'd find you in here."

"Dad, what are you doing here?"

"I heard you crying."

"I wasn't crying."

"You may as well be. What's wrong, son?"

"You don't want to know."

"Let me guess. You mated that young woman, and you fucked everything up."

"And you're going to tell me I'm stupid for not heeding your advice."

"I'm not going to do that."

"You're not."

"I'm sure you feel bad enough."

"I was blissfully happy for a moment."

I tell my father about the bear, mating, Sarah, and getting caught by Damien and Felix.

"Damn, son. Where's your honor? Your integrity?"

"I know. I'm trying to make things right. I told Audrey I couldn't see her anymore."

"What does that fix?"

"She needs to give Felix and Damien a chance. What I did to them was wrong, and I know that."

"How does she feel about that?"

"She wasn't trying to hear it, so I told her what she wanted to hear before I left. If she doesn't accept us all, I'll have to find us a mate, and I'll lose her."

"I'm sorry, son."

"She begged me to choose her. She begged me to be with her and I lied to her, but deep down, I wanted to give it all up for her."

"But you know why you can't do that."

"I came to my senses. I can't betray my pack and live with myself."

"You're a good man."

"She's going to hate me."

"She'll come around."

"I hope you're right."

"What are you going to do now?"

"I'm going to allow her to build a relationship with the rest of the triad, and I have to prepare in case she doesn't change her mind."

"Meaning?"

"I need to find a mate for us. If Audrey refuses, and she has every right to refuse, we still have to move forward. Come New Year's Eve, we will claim Audrey, or I'll sever our bond, and we'll claim another."

"Who would that be?"

"I have to find someone. While they're wooing Audrey, I'll be looking for a replacement."

"Damn, that's brutal."

Saying the words made me sick to my stomach. "I know."

CHAPTER 13

Audrey

I'm angry. I'm more than angry. Three days ago, Darius slipped away in the middle of the night after telling me we'd be together. After spending two gut-wrenching days crying and trying to connect with him, I've decided that it's time to get on with my life. I want to drive to his cabin and force him to face me, but fuck a fated mate. I don't need him. I lost focus on what's important, my career. I need to create some new content. I need to get ready for the launch of my new haircare line. I need to act like the past week never happened. I cannot let this ruin my Christmas. I realize I was foolishly looking forward to spending Christmas with a man I barely know. I was sidetracked by the desire to avoid spending another holiday alone. I thought I had found the one.

My phone rings. It's my mom. I haven't talked to her in almost a week, and I don't know if I want to talk to her now, but I decide to answer.

"Hello."

"Hey, baby. Mama hadn't heard from you. I was just calling to check on you."

"I'm fine."

"You sure?"

"Yes ma'am."

"Alright. What have you been up to?"

"Nothing much. Same old, same old."

"Well, you missed Christmas shopping and dinner last weekend."

"I didn't think you noticed."

"Girl, what are you talking about."

"Nobody cared enough to check on me. I could've been dead in a ditch somewhere and you wouldn't have known."

"Well, missy, I was just giving you space like you asked."

"What are you talking about mom? When did I ever ask you to give me space?"

"Your cousin said y'all talked and you told her you weren't coming this weekend."

"Which cousin?"

"Your cousin Michelle. She said you told her you needed some time and you had to work."

"Michelle is a real piece of work. She straight up lied to you."

"Honey, please don't start."

"Mom, she lied. I didn't talk to her. I planned to go shopping with you guys. I look forward to it every year. Michelle and I don't even talk like that."

"Maybe she misunderstood."

"There was nothing to misunderstand. The conversation never took place."

"Why would she say you did if you didn't?"

I sigh. "I don't know mama." It's pointless trying to get my mom to see Michelle for who she is. I give up.

While she talks I grab a pen and notebook from my nightstand. I want to write down some ideas for new videos for my channel before I forget. I'll be launching the Alaria Haircare line after the New Year, and I need to do a wash and go and a twist out with the new product line. I may have to change my plan since Darius and I are done, and everything is messed up. I don't know what will happen with the new line. Maybe I can make it a limited edition and use what I have for the supply. Maybe I can find another exotic plant bred by a botanist that works miracles.

My phone starts beeping. When I look at the screen, it's a call from a number I don't recognize so I ignore it. The person calls back, and I'm curious. I get a dreadful feeling in the pit of my stomach. I ask my mom to hold while I click over.

It's a woman's voice. "Audrey Stafford?" she asks.

"This is she." The woman calling is from the police station. The alarm at my hair salon was triggered, and the salon was vandalized. Her words fade in the distance. My head starts spinning.

"Is this a mistake?" I ask. "My salon is Regal Haircare."

"Unfortunately, it's not a mistake. Officers are on the scene as we speak."

I start to panic. My heart races. I have to try to control my breathing. "I'll be right there." I switch lines and inform my mother. "Mom, someone broke into my shop."

"What?"

"It sounds like they trashed it. The police are there." I look around the room for my keys. Everything is blurry. My legs feel like jelly. "I have to go. Where are my keys? Where's my purse?" I look around frantic.

"Calm down, Audrey."

"I can't. I can't. I have to see get down there, and I can't find my keys."

"Audrey, take deep breaths baby. Don't get too excited. Everything will be okay."

"It's not okay. This is my life."

"You have insurance, don't you?"

"Of course, I do."

"It'll be fine then. It's just a beauty shop."

"It's not just a beauty shop. It's all my work. It's something I created. It's the only thing in this world I'm proud of."

"If you had kids and a husband, your whole existence wouldn't be tied up into this little project."

My mother has said some fucked up things to me, but this is the first time I've really, really wanted to curse her out. "Found them. I have to go." I hang up the

129

phone because I don't want to have this debate with her, and I don't want to disrespect her. I'm not going to lie, that hurt like hell.

I get into my car and realize I don't have a husband to call on. I don't have anyone to turn to. I want to call Darius. I need him, but he's gone. I have no one. I call the one person I can talk to. "Hey, Papa."

"Sweet pea. You sound so sad. What's wrong?"

"My shop has been vandalized." I start to cry thinking about who would do this and why. I have no idea what the damage is. I don't even know what steps to take next.

"Sweet pea. You stop that crying okay. Everything is going to be alright. You hear me?"

"Yes."

"Where are you now?"

"I'm in the car on the way to the shop. Papa, everything is there. All my product, everything."

"It's going to be alright. We'll figure this out. You can't panic. You need to stay safe while you on the road, so pull yourself together."

"Yes sir." I try to stop crying and breathe. I do as he say and concentrate on the road.

"Take it one step at a time. The first thing you need to do is see what's going on. Don't assume the worst. Wait until you get there to judge the damage."

"Right. You're absolutely right. It may not be that bad."

After some soothing words from my grandfather, I'm in a better headspace. I can handle this. When I pull up to the shop I see I was wrong. I can't handle this. My beautiful building has been destroyed, and I haven't even walked inside yet.

The ground outside the front entrance is covered in glass. The front windows have been shattered. I picked this building because of all the windows. I loved how

130

you could see the chairs and the Regal Haircare display from outside. It's ruined. I don't even want to know what to expect next.

As I stand in shattered glass looking inside at flipped over chairs, broken mirrors, red spray paint on the walls, product destroyed, and supplies damaged, I'm in disbelief.

"Excuse me miss. I need you to back away. This is a crime scene." An officer approaches me.

I feel like I'm outside of my body. I can't talk. I just stare, hoping that I'm dreaming.

The officer taps me on the shoulder. "Miss, miss. I have to ask you to leave."

I realize this isn't a dream. I take a deep breath. My voice comes out barely above a whisper. I clear my throat and try to speak again. "I'm Audrey Stafford. This is my salon."

"Miss Stafford. I'm Detective Harry Lewis. I'm sorry this happened."

I turn to look at the tall, handsome officer. His badge hangs from a lanyard on his neck. Our eyes meet. He gives me a sincere look of concern. "What happened?" I ask.

"The alarm was triggered at 0347 hours. It was a busy night, and when we arrived on the scene this morning, this is what we found."

"Who would do something like this?" I ask.

"That's what we'd like to ask you. Can you think of anyone who'd want to hurt you?"

"I haven't done anything to anyone. I keep to myself."

"I need you to think Miss Stafford. This looks personal. You need to do a walkthrough to be sure, but it doesn't seem as if anything was stolen. We think someone is after you. Come with me." Detective Lewis leads me inside. He takes me to a station that sits untouched. The only station that hasn't been trashed. It sends a chill down my spine. I look in the mirror, and written in red spray paint are the words DIE WHORE.

I gasp. "This is my station."

"I'll ask you again. Can you think of anyone who'd want to hurt you?"

"No. I don't know of anyone."

"We notice that you have security cameras, which is smart, but the power was cut off when we arrived. We can try to see if the cameras caught anything, but chances are we won't have anything to go on."

"How are we supposed to find out who did this?" I ask.

"We're going to work on it, Miss Stafford. I'm going to file a report. You need to contact your insurance. We're gathering any evidence we can, and I'll keep you informed. Here is my card. You can contact me anytime." He touches my hand. "I mean that."

"Thank you."

Detective Lewis shows me around and talks me through the next steps as officers take pictures and I take pictures with my phone as well. The detective is really nice and helpful. He puts his hand on my shoulder as I sit in my chair defeated.

"Audrey I need you to make a list of anyone who might hold a grudge. It will help us."

"I can't think of anyone," I say.

"What about your ex?"

I look up. Felix and Damien are walking toward me. I gasp. "What are you doing here?"

Felix ignores my question. "Did you tell them that your ex visited you? He was aggressive." Felix looks at the officer.

"Can I help you?" Officer Lewis asks.

"We're here for her," Felix says.

"Who is this?" Detective Lewis asks.

I can't respond. I'm still in shock. Felix looks like a GQ model in his black suit, and Damien looks like a snack in a red sweater and jeans.

"We're friends of Audrey's," Damien says.

The detective looks at me.

Damien rushes to my side. He kisses me on the cheek, and I'm so shocked I don't move, but I do feel comforted. "Are you okay?" he asks me.

I shrug.

"I know this is a lot. Let us take care of you."

Nobody takes care of me. I don't think I know how to do that. Felix and the officer walk away. I don't know what they're talking about at this point.

"I'll be right back okay," Damien rubs my shoulder.

I nod.

He follows the detective and Felix as I sit and stare. Soon after, people start clearing out. Detective Lewis waves goodby from the door, but he doesn't say anything else to me. What happened? I don't have the energy to care. My mind is in overdrive trying to figure out what I'm going to do. The damage is overwhelming. I wouldn't know where to begin to fix it. I have to alert the staff. I have to call the insurance company. I have to make an enemies list. I rest my face in my palms. All I want to do is curl up in a corner and forget this.

"Audrey, do you think Andre did this?"

I look up and stare at Felix and Damien.

Damien speaks before I can. "What he means is what do you need?"

"I don't know. I don't know what to do. What are you two doing here? Why are you here now?"

"We've been keeping tabs on you," Felix says.

"How?"

"We heard about Andre so we hired security to watch your back."

"Why?"

"We wanted to make sure you were safe. They're going to keep an eye on you."

"No. What are you talking about? You can't do that."

"This says otherwise." Felix points at the writing on my mirror. "I'm not going to risk you getting hurt."

"It's not your responsibility."

"It's our pleasure," Damien says with a smile. "It's the least we can do." His grey eyes sparkle. "Please allow us to help."

"There's nothing you can do. This is a disaster. I don't even know where to begin."

"I do," Felix says. I'll be back. He walks away before I can respond.

I look at Damien. "What's he doing?"

"Come here, luna," he says. He pulls me out of my chair and smothers me in the warmth of his embrace.

I'm reluctant at first, but this feels good. My body warms from his touch.

He squeezes me. "I'm not letting go until you hug me back."

I give him a quick hug.

He holds me tighter. One of his hands rests in my hair and the other around my back. I'm torn between the familiar comforting feeling that I don't want to lose and the fact that I don't know this man. I choose the familiar feeling. I wrap my arms around him and hold on tight. He rests his head on top of mine, and we stand in the middle of the floor in an embrace I didn't know I needed.

"Don't let go yet," I whisper. I don't know if he can hear me.

"I won't," he says. He kisses my forehead, and I hold him tighter.

"I don't want you to worry, baby. I'm here for you."

I loosen my grip and look into his eyes. He's saying everything I need to hear, but I don't think there's anything he can realistically do. I'm in this alone. It's nice to be comforted though, and it's even nicer that it's by someone so strong and handsome. "Thank you for checking on me, but I need to figure this out right now."

"You don't have to do that alone."

"I do. It's okay. I'm used to doing things alone."

"Those days are over." He touches my cheek. I close my eyes.

"Damien, I don't have time for this."

"Don't be afraid, luna, and don't worry. You can trust us."

"I'd really like to trust someone, but I can't be distracted right now."

"Life is about distractions, beautiful. One day everything is perfect, then something happens that shakes you to your core, and you have to figure out how to deal with it. That's just life. One day you're going about business as usual and someone comes along and takes your breath away. You stay awake at night thinking about them. You want to know more about them. You want to hold them, touch them, love them. Suddenly life becomes about the distraction and the fact that you can't think about anything else."

"Am I a distraction to you?"

"The best kind."

"Why do I have a feeling you're going to be a distraction for me?"

"I'd be lucky to occupy any space in that beautiful head of yours."

I've thought about them both occasionally over the past few days, and my nights have been filled with dreams about them, all three of them taking me at once and separately. "If you keep talking to me like that." I blush.

"Then what?"

"I don't know."

Damien licks his lips. "You know. My luna is brave and fierce, and she knows exactly what she wants. Don't you? Don't you, Audrey?"

I nod.

We stare at one another. Our faces slowly come together. I want to kiss him, and the attraction I feel to him is intense. My heart races. Our lips are centimeters apart.

"I don't want you like this," he says. He moves his head back.

I'm embarrassed. I let go of him and try to hide my face.

He's still holding me. "Look at me."

I look up.

"I want you happy. I want you whole, and I want you to tell me how much you want me, too. Can you do that right now?"

I gulp.

"I can be patient." He plays with a lock of my hair.

I stand on my tiptoes. "I, I—"

There's a hopeful look in his eyes as he moves his head closer to mine. If he's going to kiss me, I'm okay with that.

"What the hell is going on in here?"

The moment passes.

"Papa, what are you doing here?"

"I came to make sure you're alright."

I run to hug him. I want to cry. "I can't believe you came all the way down here."

"I didn't want you to be alone, but I see that you have company. Who's this young man?"

"My name is Damien, sir."

"And what are you doing here?"

Damien stands in front of him and looks him square in the eyes. "I'm trying to win this lady's heart, but I'm having a little trouble. A special woman like her is highly desired. In the meantime, I heard about what happened, and I wanted to be here for her."

"I see," my grandfather says. He looks at me with an impressed nod.

"How exactly do you plan to be here for her?"

"I'm going to make sure she doesn't have to worry about anything, and I don't want you to worry about her. I imagine this situation is scary. Rest assured I'll do everything I can to keep Audrey safe."

"And what do you want from her in return?"

"I want to see her smile."

"I've got my eye on you," my grandfather says.

"I'd expect nothing less."

I smile at the exchange between the two. I think my grandfather likes him. He seems like a decent enough guy, but I can't help but wonder what my grandfather would think of Darius if he met him. Then I get a little sad thinking about Darius.

Damien squeezes my hand. Does he know? I wonder.

Felix walks into the room holding a push broom. He took off his suit jacket and shirt and tie. He's wearing a t-shirt over his pants. His biceps bulge against the thin fabric and he wears a serious expression. I think that's the only expression he has.

"Audrey, why don't you go home, and let us take care of this."

"This is all too much, and it's not your problem. I'm glad you two stopped by to check on me, but you can leave. I have a lot to figure out. I don't think this can be salvaged and it would be unfair for me to drag you into it."

Felix nods. "Fine." He doesn't say anything else. He

stares at me. His expression is unreadable.

"Okay then." I breathe a sigh of relief.

Felix walks toward me, and I watch as he passes me and picks up a chair behind me. He sits it up straight on the floor. He pushes the broom across the floor, moving some glass out of the way, and picks up another chair. Damien walks past me and begins to pick up furniture as well. I look at my grandfather. He shrugs. He watches the two men with his arms folded and a smile on his face. Then he walks past me, too. He makes his way over to Damien and helps him pick up a chair and moves it to a back wall.

I watch in awe. While they're moving stuff, I step away to call the insurance company. Once I get everything squared away I come back to find them still working. The guys laugh and joke with my grandfather as I watch. I guess I was wrong. Maybe I'm not alone. If he likes them, they might be okay guys, but if he knew what they wanted from me, would he still think so.

I grab a broom while I contemplate. I quietly work as I listen to the three of them. Every once in a while my eye catches Felix's, or my shoulder brushes against Damien. I'm not going to lie, they both take my breath away. There's only one thing missing.

Felix ordered lunch while no one was paying attention, and we sit down in the chairs against the wall to eat.

"Alright. This old man needs to get on home. I see my sweet pea is in good hands."

"Grandpa, please don't go."

"Your grandmother must be worried sick, and I'm getting tired."

"Why don't you sit and eat?"

"I can't do that. Pearl will kill me if I don't eat the meal she prepared. You know how she is."

"Well, let me walk you out."

I hook my arm in his as I walk him to his car. "I can't believe you're leaving me here with strangers."

He unlocks his car doors. "They're good men. You know I wouldn't leave unless I knew for sure you were in good hands. Now is the time for you to navigate this on your own. Don't be afraid."

"What exactly do you think I'm afraid of?"

"You're afraid of life's choices, but you're young and beautiful. You don't have to choose."

He has no idea what he's saying. My eyes widen. "If you only knew," I say.

"This is the time for you to take chances. It's okay."

Wait. Does he know? I don't even want to ask. "Papa, it's not that easy."

"Only you can uncomplicate it. Papa's gotta go." He kisses me on the cheek and gets into his car before I can ask follow up questions.

I think about what he said as I go back inside. I politely smile at Damien and Felix as I make my way back to my chair while they stare at me with lust in their eyes.

"You've been quiet," Damien says.

My nerves get the better of me and I chuckle.

"What's wrong with you?" Felix asks.

I try not to feel like an idiot. "Nothing. I do want to say thank you to the two of you for everything you've done."

"You're welcome," Damien says.

"My grandpa really likes you guys."

"We like him too," Damien says.

"It was nice to see him laughing with you, so thanks for being nice to him."

"You don't have to keep thanking us," Felix says.

"Oh, sorry."

"Don't apologize."

"Oh, sorry."

"What he means is, we're happy we can help."

"So I know you two must be busy. You don't have to stick around."

"We're not leaving you alone. Someone threatened you," Felix says.

"I'll be fine."

"I know you will. I'm going to make sure of it."

"I have a feeling there's no arguing with you, Felix."

"It would be pointless."

"Do you have jobs to get to?"

"I can take some time off," Felix says.

"And I can work from home."

"I can't ask you two to do that."

"It's already done."

"Guys, honestly, this is a little strange for me. I'm not sure why you're here."

"We're not leaving so stop trying to tiptoe around it. We're here. Deal with it."

My neck snaps back. "You don't have to talk to me like that."

"I think I do. Either you don't listen or you don't pay attention."

"I could say the same thing about you, Felix."

"Listen, I'm not going to abandon my mate in your time of need. If I had any idea anything like this was going to happen I would've had that ex of yours followed. I would've stopped this beforehand, but since I didn't, I'm going to see you through this. I'm trying to let the police handle this so I don't go to his house and kill him. I promised your grandfather that I'd look after you, and that's what I plan to do. Stop acting like you don't deserve our help and accept it. I'm done eating. I'm going to get back to work." He goes to the front of the salon and starts sweeping the glass from the broken windows. He's so sexy, but he's mean. I'm equally angry and aroused.

I wonder if Andre really did this. I wonder if it's a coincidence that he called me a whore and that's what's spray painted on my mirror. Whoever did this knows exactly which station is mine. Could it be a client? Is it possible that it's a coincidence?

"You'll have to excuse Felix. He's full of testosterone. He doesn't express himself very well. He fixes things for the people he cares about, and he really cares about you."

"How do I get him to leave?"

"He won't. He has to take action."

"You're so different. You're easy to talk to, and he's like a brick wall."

"We all complement one another. It makes us a good team."

"For the pack?"

"Yeah, and for you."

"Yeah, about that."

"I'm not going to pressure you, I promise, but I do need to tell you something."

"What?"

"We're going to take turns watching over you until this is resolved."

"No, you're not."

"Or you can stay with us. Whatever makes you more comfortable."

"I'd be comfortable alone."

"I'm sorry, luna. Your safety is more important than your feelings right now. We already cleared it with your grandfather."

"You what?"

"He said he'd feel better if you weren't alone."

"He can't make that decision."

"And we can't let anything happen to you. We'll stay out of your way. You have my word."

"No, you're crossing a line."

"I understand how you feel. Felix will keep watch first. I'll talk to him about his abrasiveness. I don't want to do anything against your will. Please let us help you. Darius will kill us if anything happens to you."

My heart skips a beat at the mention of his name. I'm sad because he's not here.

As if he's reading my mind, Damien grabs my hand. "He wants to be here, and it's killing him inside."

"He knows?"

"He does, and he's trusting us to guard his most precious treasure."

"If I'm so precious, why isn't he here?"

"I think you know the answer to that."

I've replayed our last conversation in my mind a million times. I know what Damien is talking about, but it's hard for me.

"Regardless of whether you choose to be with us or not, we're not going to let anyone harm you. Please let us do this. Think of us as bodyguards. Nothing romantic, we're just doing a job."

"Okay, but I can't be your mate. If you can understand that and accept it, you can help."

"You have a deal."

"As if I had a choice."

"You always have a choice."

Damien is still holding my hand, making my body warm and my skin tingle.

"Come on, let's get back to work."

"I need to call my assistant. Can you give me a minute?"

"Of course."

I call Tammy and let her know what's going on. The shop is closed on Sundays and Mondays, but the staff needs to be informed we'll be closed for a while. Tammy assures me that she'll handle that while I get things worked out. Damien and Felix are in the front of the shop so I stay in the back. With my AirPods in my ear, I grab a broom and turn on some music. I need an uptempo playlist. I bob my head to the beat as I sweep. I feel like I can relax now that I have some help and some protection.

Pretty soon the music begins to do its job. My mind is occupied with the beat and I feel the bass pulsing through my body. I dance with the broom handle when my favorite song comes on. Before I know it my eyes are closed as I hum along. I let loose and dance like no one is in the room. I think about Felix. He's so serious and so sexy. I imagine the broomstick is him. I would make it my mission to get him to loosen up. I grind my hips against the stick like I learned in a pole dancing class I took for fun. I laugh to myself as I imagine that hungry look in Felix's blue eyes, and him staring at me not knowing what to do with himself as I tempt him with my hips. He's so uptight. He wouldn't know how to function. I want him to touch me, to move to the music with me.

When the song is over, I open my eyes with the widest grin on my face which quickly fades when I see Felix staring at me. There's that hungry look I imagined. I've been caught. I stammer as Felix approaches me slowly with an animalistic gaze. My stomach tightens as lust surges through my body. I hear him growl as he stalks closer to me never breaking eye contact. He circles me like a predator. His desire is strong, and his scent wafts in my nose, fueling my fire. I might be a willing prey in this scenario. When he makes his way in front of me, I follow him with my body. What is he going to do next? He gently takes the broom from my hand.

"Let me handle the glass, sweetheart."

"Okay." I follow his gaze like a love sick puppy.

"Did you check to see if anything was missing?"

"Not yet."

"Why don't you do that?" He touches my arm.

"Okay." I let out the breath I was holding as he walks away.

I might be in over my head.

CHAPTER 14

Darius

I'm pissed that I'm not with my mate right now. She needs me, and I need her, but I have to trust Damien and Felix. I know they're capable, and they won't let anything happen to her. That doesn't stop me from wishing I was there giving her a shoulder to lean on. Unfortunately, I have to stick to the plan. It's the only chance we have at claiming our fated mate.

I'm still keeping tabs on the investigation and her safety. I don't want anything left to chance. The police questioned Andre, and he has an alibi. He was asleep, and his fiancé confirmed it. That doesn't mean he's not lying, but there's no proof at this point. They still regard him as a person of interest, but there's not much they can do. I'm having him watched now, and if he tries anything, I'll kill him with my bare hands.

He's a member of a small pack that no one knows much about. They could be responsible.

I take the threat on Audrey's salon mirror seriously, so until it's clear that this was some sort of hoax or some bored teenagers, I have people looking into the break-in.

I hope that Audrey comes around, but until then I have to take matters into my hands. I sit outside Alpha Donovan's house. As a sign of respect, I'm here to see him about his daughter, Nicole. She still lives with her father and is protected by his pack. She's groomed to be an alpha's mate, and her father treats her like a precious jewel. I'm not looking forward to this, but I have to do what I have to do.

I knock on the door to Donovan's spacious home. An omega maid answers the door. "Good afternoon. I'm Darius Huntington, here to see Alpha Donovan."

"I know who you are, alpha. Please come in." She

gives me a warm smile, and I scent her lust. As I walk past her, there's a glint in her eye. "Can I offer you something to drink, alpha?"

"No, thank you."

"If there's anything I can do for you, please don't hesitate to let me know. Alpha Donovan will be right with you. Follow me, please." She leads me to the drawing room and offers me a seat.

"Thank you," I say as I sit.

"If I may speak freely, you're kinder than I expected."

"What did you expect?"

"I'm not sure, an abrasive, no-nonsense disposition."

"I am all those things, but my father taught me to be a gentleman as well as an alpha."

"I'm grateful that he did."

"You may go now." Alpha Donovan dismisses the woman as he enters the room.

The maid bows and scurries away.

"Damn omegas. Can't keep their mouths or their legs closed. Am I right?" He laughs.

"I don't know about that. She was just being polite." I stand to greet Donovan, and I offer him a bottle of vintage wine.

"You let me know if she gets out of line."

I nod. "Alpha Donovan, thank you for seeing me. Please accept this gift."

"That's very nice, Alpha Darius. Take this to the cellar," he commands.

The maid appears in an instant to take the bottle. She bows as she enters and exits the room.

Alpha Donovan sits on the couch across from me. He's an older man with white hair and brown skin. I can tell he's the type of man who does what he wants when he wants. "To what do I owe the pleasure of your company?"

"The pleasure is all mine."

"Nonsense. No need to flatter me. Everyone knows about the legend of the white wolves. You're responsible for protecting our city from the tyranny of a rogue uprising. That's no small feat."

"I suppose it's not."

"What can I do for you?"

"I would like to meet with your daughter, Nicole."

He perks up. "Really?"

"For what purpose?"

"I won't beat around the bush. It's time that I found a mate for our triad, and I'd like to see if your daughter would be a match for us."

"I'm certain Nicole would be honored to hold such a prestigious position."

"Then I assume you'd have no objection to your daughter mating the three of us."

"None at all. Nicole would make a fine mate. I can't think of a better match. She's a special young woman. I've gone through great lengths to ensure that her virtue and her reputation remain untainted."

"I'm more interested in her ability to raise a family, unite a pack, and be an effective part of a quartet."

"Nicole would be perfect."

A younger man steps into the room with an entourage of three and sits next to Donovan. It's his son, Roman. He's no threat physically. He's average in height and thin. I did my research. Roman recently took over his father's pack. "Of course, if you want Nicole, there's business we'll need to discuss."

"Alpha Roman, how are you?" I have this smug bastard pegged the moment I see him. He's entitled and hungry for power, a bad combination.

"I was having a good day, Alpha Darius, until I realized you came to my father about pack business. I'm sure you're aware that I'm alpha now."

"I'm aware. I'm not here about pack business. I'm here about your sister. I wanted to speak with your father about meeting with her."

"I'm the one you should've come to. I don't appreciate you coming into my house without showing me the proper respect."

"I meant no disrespect. I only wanted to speak to Nicole."

"Nicole is my business, and any transaction involving her has to be approved by me."

"I'm not here about a transaction. With all due respect son, the adults are talking. Why don't you go play?"

Roman stares at me in stunned silence. I'm not moved, and I'm not the least bit apologetic. After some consideration, he laughs. On cue, his entourage laughs along with him. "You're funny," he says.

"Forgive my son," Donovan says.

"I can speak for myself, father. Won't you excuse us?"

Donovan rises. "It was nice to see you."

I shake my head. I'm surprised to see that Donovan is controlled by his younger idiot son. There's no way this boy is fit to lead, and if his son acts like this, I have a feeling the daughter won't be much of an option.

"As I was saying, my sister is pack business. If you want her, I have some conditions."

"You're in no position to make demands."

"Don't underestimate me."

I play along just for kicks. I want to know what this fool wants from me. "What are your conditions?"

"First and foremost, Nicole comes with a price tag. We'll call it a donation. Second, You must agree to a treaty between our packs. Your pack will respect me as a leader and you will agree to fight with us against any enemies."

"You must be kidding."

"I am not, Darius. I know Nicole's worth."

"You pathetic little pup. What makes you think my pack would ever follow your lead? You're not fit to wipe my pack's asses. I'm going to do you a favor and pretend you didn't just insult me with your insolence." I stand. "It's clear I've come to the wrong place. Consider my interest an error of judgment."

His entourage stands in front of me.

"Get the hell out of my way."

"I won't tolerate the disrespect," Roman says.

"Neither will I, and you have about five seconds before I really get angry. You don't want me to embarrass you in front of your little friends. You'd better tell them who the fuck I am."

"Let him go," Roman says after brief contemplation.

They step aside and allow me to pass.

I step to Roman and lightly slap his cheek twice. "Wise choice, alpha," I say with disgust. "Next time I'll make you bow like the little bitch you are."

That didn't go as planned. I open the door to my truck and step inside. This is going to be harder than I thought. I don't have time for this shit. I don't even want this shit. I want Audrey. I think about her the whole way home. When I pull into my driveway, I barely want to step out of the car. Fuck this. I want to lie in my bed, surrounded by the faint scent of her that lingers in my room, but there's another scent that's invading my nose right now. I step out of the truck and look in the truck bed. There's a woman lying face down.

"Nicole?"

She turns over and smiles like this isn't some weird shit. "I heard you wanted to talk to me."

"Wanted is right. My interests have changed."

She sits up. I can't remember the last time I saw her,

but she still looks and smells the same. She has long, black hair, gorgeous tawny skin, and the most beautiful amber eyes. "I'm here to ask you to reconsider." There's a pleading in her voice.

"I've had about enough of your family today. Just get your ass out of my truck and go home." I walk off and leave her sitting there.

She follows me to my front door. "Alpha Darius, please don't make me go back there."

"You people are mentally exhausting. What's wrong with you?"

"It was bad enough when my father was in charge. He was an ass, but my brother is an egotistical, heartless, ass, and he has no respect for me or anyone else."

"He seems reasonable. I'm sure you all can work it out."

"Please, you have to help me. He wants to auction me off to the highest bidder. All I am to him is property to be sold. I can't take it anymore."

"What do you expect me to do?"

"We can help one another. You need a mate, and I need an escape."

"Sorry, sweetheart. I can't be your hero right now. I have my own problems."

"You're telling me. Why is a man who's already mated looking for a mate?"

"That's a long story, and it's none of your business. Goodbye."

"Please, I'm begging."

"I can't mate you, and frankly after meeting you, I'm relieved it didn't work out."

She starts crying on my porch. I feel a little sympathy for her, but there's nothing I can do. "Cut the act," I say. "Fake crying is beneath you."

"I don't have anywhere to go."

"Have you thought about what your brother will do when he realizes you're missing?"

"I had to take a chance."

"How did you get away?"

"I jumped out the window. Can you protect me, Alpha Darius?"

"I can give you a moment to figure out your next move. That's all. There must be someone you can call. A friend?"

"I don't have anyone. They keep me isolated. With all the guards around, it became impossible to make real friends or have a life."

"Come inside."

"Thank you."

"Don't thank me. You have an hour to get your shit together."

"I'll take it."

Once we're inside, I fix her some tea.

"You got anything stronger?" she asks.

"No, you need to keep a clear head."

"Thank you."

"Your father and brother speak so highly of you. You should be making tea for me."

"Is that what you're looking for? An eager to please servant?"

"Not necessarily, but I need someone pliable. I don't want anything complicated."

"How romantic, Alpha Darius."

"I'm not looking for romance."

"Everyone wants romance."

"That's not realistic, Nicole. Sometimes we just have to do what we have to do."

"What kind of life is that?"

"It doesn't matter."

"It does matter. Don't you want passion and excitement? You need a woman who challenges you."

"She can challenge Felix and Damien. I've had enough excitement. I'm done."

"You're not dead."

"It feels like it. There's a phone. Call whoever you need to call. I want you gone by dusk or I'm driving you home."

I go for a run and stop at my greenhouse to water the plants. I need to clear my head. I miss my mate, and Nicole is going to be a thorn in my side. I'm aware that she isn't going to leave my home no matter how much I protest. Am I going to help her? I have no desire to get involved in her family drama. It's a disaster waiting to happen, but I can't ignore her pleas for help. Now I have to deal with this shit.

When I return home, the sun is setting. I find Nicole in my kitchen cooking.

"What are you doing in here?"

"I'm making you dinner, alpha."

"I don't want you making me dinner. Get out of my kitchen."

"She plates the food. I'm already done. You must be hungry."

"I'm not."

"Please eat. I wanted to say thank you, but I don't have anything to offer." She brings two plates to the table and two glasses of wine.

I sit after I get myself a glass of water. "Who did you call?"

"I couldn't think of anyone."

"You can't stay here."

"I can't go back there."

"What do you want to do with yourself, Nicole? You want to get away, but what are you reeling against?"

"I want to be in control of my life. I never got to go to college or work a job. I'd like to travel, pick my own mate, and I'd like to have sex."

I shake my head. "At this point, you might as well wait for someone special."

"I think you're special, Alpha Darius. You can teach me."

"It will come naturally when you're with someone you love."

"I could love someone like you."

"I love someone else."

"Where is she?"

"It's a long story, and it's complicated. I fucked up."

"What are you going to do about it?"

"I'm trying to fix it."

"By looking for another mate?"

"Contingency plan."

"I don't think that's what this woman would want."

"It's not what I want either, but sometimes we have to do what we have to do, don't we?"

"I guess."

"She would want you to fight for her, not replace her. I wish I had someone who'd fight for me, or right now I could really use some sex."

"What you want is someone who's consumed with you, and who will appreciate the precious gift you've been saving for him. As far as everything else, if you want control of your life, you have to take it."

"All I could think of was getting in your truck. I saw an opportunity and I took it."

"Now what will you do?"

"Ask you for help."

"Do you know what you're asking of me? Your brother is a loose cannon. The last thing I need right now is to make your problems mine."

"Please."

"I don't run, and I don't hide. You can stay here tonight, but we need to face this situation head on."

She smiles.

"Don't smile at me. I'm not sure how much trouble you've caused me yet."

CHAPTER 15

Audrey

Felix and Damien have worked tirelessly to help me with the shop. They managed to rally my stylists together and got members of their pack to help as well. They've handled damn near everything. They already have a construction crew working on the damage. I haven't had to worry about anything as they promised. The police haven't informed me of anything new at this point. I still don't know who did this. I haven't heard from Darius, and I'd really like to hear his voice, but it is what it is. He sent me a ton of plants and flowers for my Alaria line, and every day I get a huge bouquet of the most beautiful roses I've ever seen.

Felix has watched over me nonstop. For the past three nights, he's been camped out in my driveway in his car. He follows me to work, stays with me while I'm there, follows me anywhere I go. At first, it was awkward, but I've gotten used to him. He won't let me lift anything over five pounds, and as promised he doesn't get in my way. He's been a perfect gentleman. Every night he walks me to my door and tells me goodnight. I don't know if he takes breaks or not. I feel terrible that I haven't invited him inside.

I stare out the window at his car in my driveway. No one has ever done what he's done for me. I have a strong desire to reach out to him. I'm not sure if I say thank you enough or at all, but I appreciate his consistency. In the warmth of my home, I'm wearing shorts and a tank top, but it's cold outside, and Felix hasn't complained once. I contemplate putting on some clothes before I go outside, but I won't be out there for long. I grab a sweater that's hanging on a rack next to the front door and head toward his car.

When he sees me he quickly gets out of the car.

"Audrey, it's cold out here. What are you doing?" He reaches me before I get to his car, and instinctively wraps me in his arms.

His body heat is all the warmth I need. I close my eyes briefly lost in his scent and his embrace. I forgot why I came outside.

"Are you okay, Audrey?"

"I'm fine. I came to check on you."

"I'm fine. You should get inside. You're not wearing any shoes."

I look down at my feet. "I forgot."

He leads me back to the house. He makes sure I'm standing inside while he stands on the other side of the door. "Did you need something sweetheart?"

"No."

"Are you sure?"

"Yes."

"Okay. Go on back inside."

I hesitate for a moment.

"Audrey, what is it?"

"Do you want to come in?"

I see a light flicker in his eyes, but he doesn't say anything. My stomach flutters while the desire in his gaze burns a hole through me. He licks his lips, and I want to rip his clothes off with my teeth. I want to get my hands in his hair. I want to ride him like the stallion he is.

"No," he says.

I swear my heart drops into my stomach. I think I'm going to be sick. "Oh," is all I can say.

"Goodnight," he says.

"You too." I close the door and sit on the couch. What the fuck was that? I feel rejected. I feel stupid, but that's crazy. I shouldn't feel bad, I mean, I'm the one who said I didn't want to be with them. I was just trying to be nice to him. He's the one who wants me, or so he said. It's not like I was offering him my body. I just asked if he wanted to come in out of the cold. I was being nice to him and he turned me down, but why? What the hell? Who does he think he is? I pace across the living room floor. Maybe he lost interest. Does he think I'm mean? Whatever. Fuck Felix. He can take his ass home. I didn't even ask him to be here. That's what I get for trying to be nice. Before I know it I've marched outside again, headed for his car.

Once again he jumps out and meets me in the driveway. "What the hell are you doing?" he asks.

"What's your problem?" I ask.

"My problem is you're out here without any clothes on. Get your ass in the house before you get sick." He tries to move me, but I don't budge. "Audrey, get inside."

I don't move.

"Audrey, I'm not playing with you."

"I was trying to be nice to you, and you tell me no."

"Is that a word you're unfamiliar with?"

"Why are you so mean?"

"I didn't know I was."

"You are."

"Audrey, it's cold."

"I know it's cold. That's why I asked you to come inside, so you wouldn't have to sit in your car. I have three bedrooms. You don't have to stay outside in your car all night, but you'd rather sit in the cold than come into the house. What's wrong with you?"

"I was only trying to respect your wishes."

"I asked you to come in, didn't I?"

"You did, but we promised not to get in your way."

"You wouldn't be in the way, so you bring your ass in the house, Felix."

"Alright. Let me get my things."

I walk back inside and wait for him at the door. He

comes back carrying a backpack. "Can I take your jacket?" I ask.

"Sure." He takes off his jacket and hands it to me. He's wearing matching sweatpants and a white tank underneath. Good lord why? His muscles are solid and lick-able.

We stand in the entryway looking at one another. The heat in here isn't coming from my heater. "Come on in," I finally say.

He follows me into the living room and sits on the couch. I could sit on the opposite couch, but I choose to sit next to him.

"I was going to have a glass of wine. Would you like one?"

"Sure."

"Is red okay?"

"It's perfect."

"Are you hungry? I can fix you something to eat." I open a bottle and pour two glasses.

"I already ate."

I hand him a glass as I sit next to him. "Are you sure? It's the least I can do."

"I'm fine, sweetheart."

"You've been so amazing throughout all of this. I appreciate everything you've done for me. Why don't you let me cook for you tomorrow night? Before you tell me no, I have to warn you that's unacceptable."

The corner of his lip curls. He almost smiles. "If you insist."

"I do insist. I don't know what I would've done without you, and you've just been sitting outside watching over me. How can I repay you?"

"You don't have to."

"Sure I do."

"You don't owe me anything, but I appreciate you inviting me inside." He looks around my living room.

"You have a beautiful home."

"Thank you. I tried to decorate it myself. Sometimes I think it's lacking self expression."

"I like it. I think it reflects you perfectly."

"How so?"

"It's unique, a bit understated, but as you look around there are these things that catch your eye and draw you in, maybe even surprise you, like the bright pillows on that chair or that painting on the wall over there."

"I like the way the red umbrella is the only color in that black and white world."

"Me too."

"My mother says it's tacky."

"Your mother's wrong. I think you have excellent taste."

I smile. "Thank you. Would you like some more wine?" We're both near the bottom of our glasses.

"Yes."

I grab the bottle and pour us two more glasses.

We sit in awkward silence.

"Are you going to make me do all the work here?" I ask.

"What do you mean?"

"You have to talk to me."

"What do you want to talk about?"

"Something. Anything. What do you do for work?"

"I'm an appraiser."

"So you do what exactly?"

"I determine the value of expensive things."

"How?"

"I work for a lot of museums and auction houses."

"That sounds interesting."

"I'm glad someone thinks so."

"That's a powerful position to be in."

"What can I say? I like being in positions of power."

"How did you get into that?"

"I studied history, art, archeology, and I realized I had a knack for it, so I travel the world looking for beautiful things."

"What's the most special thing you found?" Our knees touch as he adjusts himself on the couch.

"You."

I blush. "You're just saying that. You don't even know me."

"I know value when I see it."

"And what value would you place on me?"

"Some things are priceless."

"And I'm one of those things?"

"Indeed you are."

"Why is that?"

"Because I said so, and I'm in the position of power. When I something is priceless, my word is final." His eyes flicker and passion flows through my body.

"Who am I to argue with the expert?"

"I wouldn't advise it."

"Is that what you do with women? You inspect them and appraise them."

"I suppose. It's efficient."

I laugh. "You're supposed to say no."

"Am I?"

"Yes, you are. That's not at all romantic."

"Romance is an illusion."

"How could you say that?"

"It doesn't matter. It's not real. Your body and your brain determine if you desire someone. The right person could buy you a box of chocolates and a dozen roses and it would be considered romantic. If the wrong person does the same thing, it would be considered an unwanted advance."

"So everything with you is technical as I suspected. Is there any passion behind the things you desire?"

"Desire is desire."

"What about love?"

"Love is an illusion."

"Felix, you're killing me."

"Why is that?"

"Don't you believe in love?"

"I believe that people believe that love is some magical force. It's not. Love doesn't change people's lives."

"It could."

"People use love as an excuse or a crutch."

"What do you believe in if not love?"

"Loyalty."

"Can I ask why did you want me?"

"You're my mate."

"And?"

"You were made for me."

"And you don't have any feelings for me? You just want me to have your children. You don't even like me. Everything you've done is because you're supposed to. Isn't it?"

"That's the purpose of mating."

"There has to be more to it."

"Why?"

"Don't you want to be with someone who wants to be with you? Haven't you ever been in love?"

"The past doesn't matter. I'm a single unmated man right now."

"And you're telling me you don't want to have romantic feelings for someone?"

"I don't know why you're getting all bent out of shape. You said you didn't want to be my mate, remember? And as far as I can tell, you're the one who doesn't like me."

"I wouldn't say I don't like you, I'm trying to understand you. I want to know that you feel something."

"I feel something, but that's not what's important to me."

"What's important to you?"

"Your safety and your happiness."

"That's kind of romantic. Darius said he was going to look for another mate for you guys."

"That makes you sad, doesn't it?"

"Why do you say that?"

"I can feel it."

"Three mates. is more than I signed up for. It's nothing personal."

"I don't take it personally."

"Good to know." I roll my eyes.

"What do you expect? You said you didn't want this."

"I expect that whoever I spend the rest of my life with wouldn't walk away from me so easily. I guess I expect someone who loves me enough not to give up."

"Isn't that what you've done?"

"No."

"We all want you. The only one who's given up is you."

"Yeah right. The minute I'm gone, you'll move on like I never existed and procreate with the next woman he brings around."

"I don't want to do that. I don't want to move on, neither does he. There's not another woman who will make me feel what I feel for you, but I can't force you to be with me."

I take a big sip. "You know what. This conversation took an unexpected turn. Let's change the subject. What do you like to do for fun?"

"Nothing."

"Do you have something against fun?"

"No, I just don't find many things to be fun. What

162

do you like to do?"

"I like to listen to live music."

"And dance," he says.

I blush. "I like to dance when no one's watching."

"I noticed."

"I'm not very good at it."

"I don't know about that. I liked what I saw."

I clear my throat. "I also like live entertainment like plays and performances, and I like to go to festivals and trade shows." I think about the hobby I discovered for picking plants, but I don't want to mention that right now. "I would also like to travel more. Maybe that'll be my New Year's resolution."

"Where would you like to go?"

"Paris, Greece, Spain, I don't know. Have you been to either of those?"

"Yes."

"Care to elaborate."

"They're beautiful cities filled with culture and history. Each has something unique to offer. I think you should visit all of them."

"Do you know them pretty well?"

"I could show you a thing or two."

"Oui oui."

"Quand tu dis oui, je veux t'emmener ici et maintenant, ma belle. Vous me torturez."

Shit. I think I just came. The passion in his eyes is enticing, and I can't turn away. My cheeks heat along with the rest of my body.

"Ne soyez pas timide." The words roll off his tongue.

"You speak French?" I ask.

"Oui."

"What did you say?"

"Something I shouldn't have."

"I'm intrigued. Teach me."

"You want me to teach you French?"

"Oui."

"If I do, you have to do exactly what I say. Can you follow directions?"

"Oui."

"Is that the only word you know?" he asks.

"Oui," I nod.

"Perfect. You should always say yes to me. I like a woman who knows her place."

"Felix." I slap his shoulder.

"Kidding." He takes our wine glasses and sits them on the coffee table. I turn my body to face his, and he turns to me. "Give me your hand."

I give him my hand.

"We can start with numbers." He holds one of my fingers. "Une."

"Une," I repeat.

He holds two of my fingers together. "Deux."

"Deux."

Three fingers. "Trois."

Each number sounds sexier than the last.

Repeat them back to me. He holds out his hand.

I touch his fingers like he touched mine. His large hands are well manicured. His fingers are long, and I remember what it was like to have those fingers inside me while he grunted and growled in my ear. "Une, deux, trois," I repeat.

"Very good."

I smile. "More," I whisper.

"Plus. More. Plus s'il vous plait. More please."

"Plus s'il vous plait," I repeat.

His dick jumps in his pants, but he keeps his eyes on me. He licks his lips. "Je veux te baiser pendant que tu mendie de plus en plus."

I don't know what he said, but I did pick up on more and more, and that's what I want from him. "Plus s'il vous plait."

He shuffles in his seat. "I think we should stop here. I can teach you more later."

"Plus s'il vous plait."

"What are you trying to do to me, Audrey?"

"I just want to learn."

"Is it French you want to learn, or something else?"

"What else can you teach me?" I look down at the bulge in his pants. His dick is sticking straight up. I desperately want to uncover it. I remove my hand from his and reach for it.

He grabs my wrist before I can reach his waistband. "It's getting late. You should go to bed. I need to get some work done."

"Are you serious?"

"Yes."

"I'm not tired, and you seem to be very awake."

"What is it that you want, Audrey?"

"I want to see."

He lifts the elastic on his pants and places it below his dick. It springs forward and stares at me. He's long, thick, and rock-hard. I'm intrigued by the two-toned color. The head and the top half are lighter. I want to put it in my mouth, but I suddenly feel shy.

"Now what?" he asks.

My tongue gets tangled.

"Get a good look," he says.

In my mind, I've grabbed and am stroking him. In reality, I'm frozen.

"I didn't come here for you to play games with me, Audrey."

"I'm not trying to play games."

"Aren't you? You want to tease me. Is that it? You want to see how much I want you. I want you this fucking much." He points at his dick. "Now what?"

"I, I was—"

165

"That's what I thought. I'm trying very hard to be respectful of your feelings and the position you've been put in. I want to fuck you right now. I want to take you against the wall or on this couch, or maybe on the kitchen island. We can do it all over this fucking room before I take you to your bed and we break that motherfucker, but I'm trying not to take advantage of your desire. I expect you to extend me the same courtesy. Don't try to play me. I'm not going to be used for your amusement."

"I wasn't trying to play you."

"Respect me enough to be real with me."

"I didn't mean—"

"It might be best if I go back to the car."

"You don't have to do that. I didn't mean to offend you."

"Don't worry about it. If you'd like I can have someone else come and watch you. Would you rather have Damien here?"

"Why would you ask me that?"

"I know you like him. You two get along well."

"I like you too."

"You don't have to say that."

"I do. You're strong, smart, protective, and you're really sweet in your own way. I'm just intimidated by you."

"You don't have to be."

"You have a strong personality."

"I'm sure you wish I were more sensitive."

"You are sensitive. You just hide it really, really well. You care deeply. It's okay though. I won't tell anyone."

"No one would believe you."

"But you do care, don't you?"

"I do. I care about you."

"It's nice to hear you say those words instead of

scolding me."

His demeanor softens. "Noted." He touches my cheek. "Of course, I care about you."

"I care about you too. I would never try to play you. Being here with you in this moment feels right. I don't know. I like being close to you."

"He veux être ici avec toi. I want to be here with you."

"Your dick is still out. If you don't want me to grab it, you'd better put it away."

"Shit," he says looking at my mouth.

I part my lips.

"Audrey, don't look at me like that."

I swear time stands still. I move my face closer to his. "You're going to have to be mad at me." I press my lips against his. Fire ignites in my body and electricity crackles through my skin.

He freezes for a moment before he pulls my body against his. "Embrasse-moi bébé," he whispers.

I rest my hands on his cheeks. Our kiss is slow and sensual. I close my eyes as his tongue explores mine. The kiss heats quickly. "Plus s'il vous plait." My mouth is hungry for his. "Plus," I demand.

We can't keep our lips off one another. His hands explore my body as he guides me onto his lap and squeezes my ass.

"Plus," I demand. One of my hands is tangled in his dreads and the other rubs his chest.

His dick is positioned between both of us. He slips his hand between our bodies. My shorts are loose fitting so it takes him no time to slip his hand beneath them. He rubs his fingers against the satin fabric of my panties. I moan. The protective layer of cotton is no match for the flood of moisture he caused. He kisses my neck and I grind against his hand. Before I know it, his finger has slipped past my panties and strokes between my labia. He slips and swirls his middle finger against me. My juices coat his hand as I grind against it.

"Plus," I demand. His finger immediately enters me and my head rolls back. He grabs my hair, exposing more of my neck to his mouth.

"Deux," I moan.

"Oh, shit," he growls in my ear. "You're a very good student." He inserts his index finger and plunges deeper inside me."

"Oui Felix," I moan.

"Oui," he says. He whispers in my ear in French. I imagine it's the dirtiest, filthiest thing he can think of, and I cum on his hand. My hips move to the rhythm of his fingers and I whimper and shout like a madwoman.

He kisses me intensely and keeps working my pussy. His thumb massages my clit and tension builds. I rest my head over his shoulder and rub his back.

"Trois," I moan.

He pulls his head back and looks me in the eyes.

"Trois," I say as I look into his eyes.

He slips another finger inside me and watches me as he strokes his dick with his free hand.

I don't break eye contact with him. I lift my shirt over my breasts and play with my nipples.

"Plus," he demands as he strokes furiously.

I squeeze and knead my breasts.

"Plus," he says again. His head pushes one of my hands away from my breast and his mouth demands it for himself. He clamps down and sucks my nipple sending a jolt through my body. He sucks and bites as I eagerly ride his hand and cry out his name.

This orgasm is more intense, and I bite down on his shoulder as I cum.

He growls in my ear and kisses me as I ride the wave. I rest my head for a moment. I steady myself as I lift my body high enough to linger over his dick. He holds my hips.

"Audrey," he pleads.

I hold my panties to the side. Before he can speak I've grabbed his shaft and slowly slid down his pole.

"Fuuuuck," he grunts. His fingers dig into my skin and his back snaps against the couch.

I moan as I sink to the base of his dick and lift myself.

His eyes are closed and he's biting down on his bottom lip. He whispers in French as I work my hips back and forth. He's defeated by the pussy. He's at my mercy. He reacts to every roll of my hips and every clutch of my pussy. Felix is mine. I press my chest against his and use my ass to work my hips as I kiss and suck his neck. Holding my ass cheeks he pulls me up and slams me down his dick. I cry out his name as I hold on to his hair.

"Plus," I scream.

His hips lift, plunging deeper into me from beneath.

"Oui," I moan. "Oui, Felix."

He slams his hips up and down with rapid thrusts taking my body on a ride of unlimited pleasure. With every thrust, I shout, pull, and grab to hold on to him. He doesn't stop. He only goes faster and harder, and I don't know how, but before I know it I'm flipped over on the floor. He's on top of me. My legs are in the air and he lifts my hips as he takes me to new heights. This time when I cum, it's strong. I scream like someone's killing me. He growls and lets my legs fall. He flips onto his back and lets me ride my high on his dick. My body bucks wildly against his and I lose control, jumping and shouting.

He lifts me off, and I sit next to him while he furiously strokes his dick. I quickly take him in my mouth. His shaft is warm like an oven, and I can taste myself on him. He growls, and I know it's coming. I stroke his dick with one hand and massage his balls with the other while he slams my head down and bucks his hips. He tenses and his warm liquid oozes into my mouth. He holds my hair lifts his hips as I swallow his seed. His body relaxes beneath me as he grunts and shivers at random.

I lie against his chest as he holds me with one arm. My head is cloudy from the multiple orgasms. There's no doubt we have a connection.

What the fuck did I just do? What does this say about me? I'm not this kind of girl.

Felix rubs my scalp. "I love your natural hair, my Nubian queen," he says.

"Thank you, but you have me beat. Your hair is gorgeous."

"I bought some of your shampoo so I could try it."

"I would've given you some."

"I wanted to support your business."

"Are you going to let me tighten your dreads when it's time?"

"I'll let you do it if you plan on sticking around. I can't lose a stylist."

"I would never neglect a client."

He interlocks his fingers with mine and kisses my hand. "How do you feel?"

"A little weird."

"Well, damn. Let me show myself out."

I laugh. "Don't you dare. I just mean I feel weird that I can feel the way I feel about him and feel the way I feel about you."

"How do you feel about me?" he asks.

"Smitten."

"How do you feel about me?"

"You had me the moment I saw you."

"I'd like to add that you're an excellent lover. Consider my mind blown. I'm not letting you out of my sight."

"You're not?"

"Nope. You're going to lie in bed with me, and spoon me, and cuddle with me."

"Normally I don't do that, but I'll make an exception for you."

"You're sweet."

"Are you too tired?" he asks.

"Too tired for what?"

"Plus." He flips me over and swiftly removes my clothes. He pins my arms and legs to the ground, and he takes me over and over again.

CHAPTER 16

Darius

As I walk through the Northern Forest, I'm impressed to see pairs of shifters sparring. I admire their discipline. Fog has settled amongst the trees, but I've already spotted a handful of traps meant to protect the pack. Nicole has been staying with me, and I've been teaching her to fight. Nothing too advanced, just some basic self defense techniques. She could learn a lot from the women here. The North Star Pack is known for its fierceness. Nicole needs some of what they've got if she's going to stand up to her brother.

I follow a trail that leads to a clearing and I see her in front of the horizon doing sun salutations.

"Alpha Darius, to what do I owe the pleasure?" she asks from a distance.

"Alpha Lauren, you're a hard woman to track down."

"Yet you found me."

"I was determined. I brought you a gift."

"I hope it's not flowers."

"Of course not."

She finally turns around and walks toward me. She's a beautiful woman with mocha skin. Her slicked back hair is short and wavy, and her physique is exquisite in a spandex sports bra and matching leggings. While her beauty is stunning, I'm more interested in her accomplishments. She leads a highly respected and revered pack of women. She's known for her prowess in battle, and a woman like Lauren will make a fine mate.

I present Lauren with a black box and lift the lid. Resting on black velvet lining is an ancient hunting dagger.

"Nice," she says. She lifts the dagger from the box

and studies it. My sources told me she has a collection. I hoped to make her smile, but no such luck.

"I'm glad you approve."

"You have my attention."

"My alpha triad is seeking a mate."

Her eyebrow lifts. "Do you want me to recommend someone?"

"I can't think of anyone more perfect than the great Alpha Lauren of the North Star Pack."

"I'm not looking to cater to the great white wolves, no matter how legendary you are."

"I wouldn't dream of asking someone of your stature to cater to anyone."

"Glad to hear it. Thanks for the gift."

"You won't consider being my mate."

"I don't have a reason to."

"Don't you want children to continue your legacy?"

"If I wanted to be someone's mother I would've made it happen. It seems like you're offering me the opportunity to take the next, what, five or six years to have your pups. After all I've accomplished, I'm only worthy if I'm a breeder. You disgust me."

"That's not what I'm saying."

"You should find someone else, someone who wants that life."

"I meant no offense. I thought that you and I could create something special."

She sniffs. "I smell human. Care to explain?"

"The situation is complex, to say the least."

"Please enlighten me."

"I'm mated to a human woman, but my triad is not."

"How did that happen? Did you trip and fall into her pussy?"

"I shouldn't get into it, but our bond may have to be severed, which is why I'm here."

"You're here to offer me the possibility of maybe

173

mating your triad if your current situation doesn't work out. Not only am I on standby, but I'm not even your first choice. Where do I sign up?"

"It's not as bad as it sounds."

"How dare you insult me with such a pathetic offer?"

"I do have a lot to offer."

"Please elaborate because the way I see it, your heart belongs to another."

"My triad and I will be loyal to our fourth. We would treat you with the utmost respect and honor, and you will have our allegiance."

"What will happen if your mate comes crawling back? Would you leave me and our children? Would you then be ready to break our bond? I don't want your scraps. I should kill you."

"I've always been a man of my word, Alpha Lauren. I wouldn't betray your trust, neither would Felix or Damien."

"They're great, but they're not you, Alpha Darius. Isn't the point to give you a child, the heir apparent?"

"We're equally important."

"What would happen to my pack?"

"What would you like to happen? Both our packs are powerful. We can rule together."

"And not me under you?"

"Unless that's what you want."

"I want to be alpha in charge."

"No."

"Is that any way to speak to your maybe, possible, backup plan, future mate?"

"I'm alpha in charge. That's not up for debate."

"I'll fight you for it."

"Does that mean you're interested?"

"I'm not sure, Alpha Darius. I don't think much about mating, but I imagined if I did I'd want a mate who wanted more than a business arrangement."

"I had no idea you were such a romantic."

"I'm not, but I'm a woman and I have the right to be complex."

"Any one of us can give you what you want, maybe even all three."

"I'm not so sure, Darius. I've had my eye on you for years. We could've had something, if only the most incredible sex of our lives, but you never looked twice at me, barely acknowledged me, and hardly spoke to me."

"I see where you're going with this. Let me lay my cards on the table. I was heartbroken for a long time, but I did notice you. I think you're beautiful, intelligent, and fierce. I always noticed you. That's why I'm here. The timing was never right. Things are different now. My eyes have been opened. My approach to this situation isn't romantic in the least. I have a list of women that I planned to visit. I visited Alpha Donovan about his daughter, not because I want her, but because she's a name on a list. That didn't go as planned and now I have a grown woman with the mentality of a teenager latching on to me. I want to call this off. I wish I didn't have to do this, but I fell in love with my mate, and I made a selfish choice. I fucked everything up. I hope she comes back to me, but if she doesn't choose the triad by New Year's, I have to do what's best for my pack and mankind."

"You're serious?"

"Very serious. I decided to say fuck the list and skip to the woman I wanted the most, the only name that truly matters, Lauren. I hope you can forgive my disrespect and look past the mess that I made. I need your help."

"I find your honesty refreshing."

"Will you consider?"

A figure in all black jumps from the trees. I grab the woman by the throat and slam her to the ground. She recovers and jumps to her feet. I swing and she ducks and blocks her face. Two more women emerge from the sides. One attacks Lauren and the other attacks me. I pull the one away from Lauren by the back of her neck and backhand the one in front of me. She stumbles into the third woman. I take the opportunity to trip the two women and knock them on their backs.

"What the hell is this?" I ask as I pin them all to the ground.

"Random surprise attack."

I let the women go. "That's an interesting method."

"If you stay ready, you never have to get ready."

I sniff the air. "I smell desire."

"You handle yourself very well. I like that."

I smile. "Enough to consider my offer?"

"Enough to consider a date. Pick me up tonight at eight. This time you may bring flowers."

"Let's go," she says to her pack as she walks away reprimanding them for their inability to sneak upon us effectively. I smile to myself. I knew there was a reason I liked her.

I like Lauren, but I love Audrey. I have to take Lauren on a date. I don't know how I expected to avoid these kinds of entanglements. If Lauren agrees to consider us under these conditions then one of my problems will be solved. I have no desire to keep looking for a replacement mate, especially since I only want the mate I have. I'm holding on to faith that after everything I've done she'll come back to me and be one with us. I want to be with her now, holding her, letting her know that everything will be okay, but I trust Felix and Damien. They deserve the time I stole from them, and I deserve to suffer.

Lauren deserves more than the scraps I've offered

her, and now I truly see the ramifications of my actions. What I've done affects more than me, more than my pack, more than my triad. There are women who have their hopes up, who think that there's a chance that I could give them all of me. I don't know if I can ever do that because right now all of me belongs to Audrey.

I'm in turmoil as I drive home. I don't want to hurt anyone else. As I approach my front door, I smell food. Nicole has cooked for me once again. I sigh as I open the door.

"How did it go?" she asks. Nicole stands in front of me naked.

"What are you doing?"

"I've decided that I want my first time to be with you."

"I've decided that's a horrible idea."

"Why is that? Don't you find me attractive?"

"You're very beautiful, Nicole."

"Thank you." She walks toward me and I back up.

"Stop, Nicole."

"You're not afraid, are you?"

"I'm not afraid. I'm also not interested."

"Is it something I said? Did I do something?"

"No, I'm in love with my mate."

"If you love your mate, why are you looking for another?"

"I have no choice, and as beautiful as I think you are, you're not the one for me."

"Why not? Don't you just need someone who says yes? You came looking for a mate. I'm saying yes."

"Put this on." I take off my button down shirt and hand it to Nicole. She throws it over her shoulders and leaves it open. "Sit down." I sit on the couch and she sits next to me.

"I can be whatever you need me to be, so stop looking and just go with me."

"Nicole, we could easily go with you, but doing so wouldn't be fair to you. You haven't experienced life. You have no idea what you want or who you are. Do you really want to be tied down to three mates who aren't fated to you?"

"Yes."

"You say that now, but what if you meet your fated mate tomorrow? Trust me, there's nothing like finding the one you were meant to be with. I don't want you to give that up."

"It's my choice to make."

"And this is my choice."

"I may not have life experience, but I know a good man when I meet one. There's no way my fated mate is better than the man standing in front of me. I'm willing to take that risk. I know how to cater to an alpha. I was made for this?"

"That's the lie your brother and father told you. It's okay for you to have things that you want to do. You're more than property to be passed around. It's time for you to live your own life."

"Are you thinking about mating this other woman?"

"Maybe, but I can't mate anyone while I'm still mated?"

"What does she have that I don't?"

"You aren't lacking. This is a woman who knows who she is and what she wants. I want that for you. I feel like I'd be wrong for taking away your identity when you haven't found yourself."

She stands. "You're right. I think I should find myself."

"I want to help you in any way I can."

"You have helped me. Although I wish you'd reconsider, I appreciate you not taking advantage."

"If it helps, I'm very tempted. So much that you should probably put some clothes on."

"If you'd like to give in, the offer stands."

"I'm going to work."

"Would you like some breakfast?"

"I'm not hungry."

I go to my greenhouse. I need to plant some more ora for Audrey. I'm trying to keep a healthy supply for her since she lost a lot of inventory after the break-in. I need to get Nicole out of my house. I don't know what to do with her. I think she should join Lauren's pack, but because of me, that's probably not possible.

I need to figure out what to do with Lauren. She asked for a date, and I'm sure she expects something special. She deserves something special, but I'm not in a position to give it to her. My wolf is silent most of the time these days. He wants Audrey, and so do I. I try to communicate that everything I'm doing is for her, but all he understands is she's not with us where she belongs. It's going to take all the energy I can muster to show her a good time. I haven't been on a date in a long time. I hope that Lauren and I can come to an understanding.

I spend the day outside and took a lot of time to work on my special breed of roses. When the sun sets I head back to my cabin to get ready to see Lauren.

Nicole looks surprised when I step out of my room wearing a black designer suit and no tie.

"Damn, you look good." Her mouth says one thing, but her face says another. She's not happy.

"I'll be out late."

"Where are you going?"

"Call me only if there's an emergency."

"Can I have a kiss goodbye?"

"I have to go."

She looks disappointed, but I can't think about that.

The drive to Lauren's home is short. I arrive with flowers in hand and ring the doorbell. She answers after making me wait for a few minutes.

"You look amazing." She's breathtaking in a tight black leather dress. Her hair is straightened, and she's wearing tasteful makeup and red lipstick.

She turns for me and smiles. "Thank you. You look handsome."

"These are for you." I hand her a bouquet of red roses.

"They're lovely," she says.

"I wouldn't dare bring you anything less."

"I'd kill you if you did."

"I'd expect nothing less. Are you ready to go?" I ask.

"Yes, let me grab my coat." She grabs a stylish leather trench coat and I help her put it on.

I open the door to my truck for her and help her climb in.

Once we drive off, she wastes no time. "Are you normally this attentive?" she asks.

"I don't know."

"I had no idea you were such a gentleman."

"I try."

"Where are we going?"

"I'm taking you to a nice restaurant, and I'm not telling you the name. You'll find out when we get there, and I won't tolerate any backtalk from you about it. I'm handling this date, Alpha Lauren. Do you have a problem with that?"

"Not at all."

I see her smile out of the corner of my eye. "How was your day?" I ask.

"Two of my pack members were sleeping with the same man. A fight broke out."

"How did you handle it?"

"I killed the man."

"Did you?"

"No, that's a joke. I let them fight. I told them to

handle it themselves. I don't have time for that nonsense. If we didn't need men for sex I swear I'd ban them."

"Ahhh."

"It was a good training exercise. Women don't fight over anything else quite like they fight over a man that doesn't belong to either of them."

"I like the way you see things," I say.

"How was your day?"

"I spent the day working."

"By working, do you mean planting flowers?"

"It's a little more complicated than that."

"Is it?"

"You really think I plant flowers all day? I'm a botanist, not a gardener."

"What does a botanist do?"

"I create."

"What do you create?"

"You liked the flowers I got you, didn't you?"

"Yes."

"I created those. I took the best parts of the best roses in the world and put them together to create something to complement your beauty." I look into her eyes. She has a big smile on her face. Damn, I didn't even know I still had it in me.

"Before I get swept away by your sexy swag, why don't you tell me about your situation. What happened with your mate and your triad. I need to know what I'm possibly getting into."

I pause. I owe it to Lauren to tell her the whole situation. If it had been anyone else I would've told them it was none of their business, but Lauren is different. Still, I can't decide if I should open up to her, or say forget the whole thing.

CHAPTER 17
Audrey

"Audrey, are you ready to go?"

"Almost. Do you like my dress?"

"It's fine."

"Maybe I should change."

"Why? You look beautiful."

"Do I look fine or beautiful?"

Felix gives me a blank stare. I should've known better than to ask for his opinion.

"Felix, how do I look?"

"I don't know what to say."

"Ugh. Give me a minute." I take off the blue dress I'm wearing and change into a long sleeved red knee length dress that hugs my curves. I pair it with black stilettos and look at myself in the mirror. Thanks to my Alaria conditioner my hair looks amazing.

I step into the living room.

He stands. "Are you ready?"

I roll my eyes.

"What's wrong?"

"How do I look?" I ask.

"You look fine."

"What's wrong with you?" I shout.

"I don't know what's happening right now."

I inhale and take a deep breath. "Felix, how would you appraise my look tonight?"

He looks me over. "Your hair is exquisite. Your curls look luscious. Your face is flawless. The color red looks perfect against your skin. This dress makes me want to fuck you right here and now, and don't even get me started on the shoes."

"You couldn't just say that?"

"Come here." He pulls me close. "I can show you better than I can tell you, but you might get mad if I rip your clothes off and mess up your makeup."

"I would take you up on that, but I'm starving."

"Me too."

"I wonder why."

His voice is husky. "Because I couldn't get out of bed for you."

"I didn't hear any complaints from you."

"And you never will."

I have a huge grin on my face and so does he. "What are you smiling at?" I ask him.

"I guess you have that effect on me."

I sneeze.

Felix places the back of his hand on my forehead. "I hope you're not getting sick."

"No, it was just a sneeze."

"Maybe we should order food."

"No, I'm already dressed. I'm ready to go."

"I don't want you going outside if you're under the weather, sweetheart."

"I'm fine. Stop worrying."

"Where's your coat?"

I point to the rack against the wall. Felix wraps me in my coat and ties it at the waist.

I pull him close and stare into his eyes while I button the second-to-top button of his shirt.

He grabs my hand. "What are you doing?"

"You forgot to button your shirt."

"No, I didn't."

"Yes, you did."

"I know how to dress myself."

"Baby, you look so good with it like this, and I don't want all the women in the restaurant looking at your sexy man chest."

"Do I tell you how to dress?"

"Did I tell you how turned on I am by a crisp buttoned shirt? A shirt like that makes me want to take my clothes off, except for my stilettos."

"I think I did forget to button it," he says.

He leads me to his car by my hand and opens the door for me. I thank him as I sit. He holds my hand as he drives.

"Where are we going?"

"McDonald's."

"Lies!" I shout.

"Oh yeah. I'm getting you a Big Mac so you can recharge, and we're getting right back to it."

"Don't play with me, Felix," I laugh.

When I look up, he's staring at me with a look I don't recognize.

"Why aren't you watching the road?"

"I don't want to take my eyes off of you."

I try not to smile too hard, but I can't help it. Felix is sweet when I least expect it. The two of us haven't been able to tear ourselves apart, but we're so wrapped up in one another that we forgot to eat. I offered to cook, but Felix insisted on going out.

As we walk through the restaurant, he keeps his arm around my waist, and I feel special when he holds me close. Once we're seated in a booth in the corner, I'm overcome with something. It's a feeling I can't put my finger on. I'm unsettled, and I'm anxious as I scan the room. This place is beautiful, spacious, and popular. The lighting is dim. Smooth piano music plays in the background.

"Are you okay?" Felix asks.

"Yeah, I think so." I sneeze.

"Bless you," he says.

I thank him as I look around. My mind is preoccupied with everything and nothing all at once. The waiter approaches to take our drink order.

"Would you like me to order a bottle of wine?" Felix asks.

"Huh?"

"Audrey, what's wrong?"

"Nothing's wrong. I didn't hear you."

"Wine?"

"Yes. Whatever you think is best. I'm sure you have impeccable taste."

"We'll take that one," he tells the waiter.

As the waiter walks away I see why I'm so anxious. Time stands still. My heart stops. I must've felt his presence. Darius is at a table across the room, eating, talking, and smiling with what may be the most beautiful woman I've ever seen. My stomach drops. I stand.

Felix reprimands me in a strong, stern voice. "Sit down," he says slowly and pronounced.

"Excuse me. I know you're not talking to me like that."

"You will not cause a scene."

"I'm not going to cause a scene. I'm just going to handle something."

"There's nothing to handle. You're better than that."

"What am I supposed to do? Sit here and watch? She stole my mate."

"She did not steal him."

"Of course she did. Look at her. Look at him."

"Look at you. He loves you. He's only doing what he told you he'd do."

"And I'm only going to say hi."

"You will not. Sit your ass down," he says.

I sit down. "Do you want her too? Maybe I should leave and you can all go on a group date."

"Listen to me," he says.

My foot bounces underneath the table. I can't concentrate. "I can't believe this." I try to hold it together, but tears fall from my eyes.

"Stop crying." Felix reprimands me.

185

"He's forgotten me."

"He hasn't forgotten you. Pull yourself together." Felix joins me on my side of the booth. He blocks my view of Darius with his body. I attempt to look past him, but it's no use. I can't see them. I need to see them. "Move," I command.

"No."

"What makes you think you can talk to me like that? Why are you so mean?"

"I'm not mean, sweetheart." He cups my cheek. "Concentrate on me for a minute. Close your eyes."

I close my eyes.

"Ma magnifique reine."

I open my eyes.

"Keep them closed," he whispers in a deep melodic tone.

"What does that mean?" I ask.

"My beautiful queen."

"I'm sorry. I'm sorry I ruined our evening. This place is so nice."

"You don't have to apologize for the way you feel. You never have to apologize to me for that. I understand what you're going through baby, but I need you to calm down. I don't want you to do something you'll regret. Okay."

"Okay."

"You're a strong woman, and everything will be alright, I promise, but first we need to leave."

"I'm not leaving."

"Yes, you are. Get your purse. Talk to me outside first, then you can do whatever you want."

"I need him."

"I know you do." He wraps me in his arms. "He needs you too. This is what happens when you mate. You become one, and your souls are bound together."

I open my eyes. "You know I —"

"Yes, I know."

"It's just that —"

"I know, sweetheart. You and I are okay," he assures me. "This doesn't change how I feel about you."

I hug him back and rest my head against his chest.

He kisses my forehead and I tilt my head to kiss him. His lips comfort me. He stands, pulling me up with him, and we walk outside the restaurant. He urges me to wait until the valet brings his car before we talk.

"If you still want to go inside, I'll bring you back," he says once we're seated in the car.

"Why are you acting so weird?" I ask.

"We couldn't talk in the restaurant because they might hear."

"He was sitting there with another woman like we never happened. He moved on. What am I supposed to do? He moved on."

"Our triad is connected. I know what Darius is feeling, just like I know what you're feeling. He's miserable, and if you pay attention, you'll feel that he's miserable too."

"He didn't look miserable."

"You don't know what's going on between them, and you can't jump to conclusions."

"Yeah right. If I were into women, I'd sleep with her."

He laughs. "He's not sleeping with her. He's doing what he told you he'd do. He's looking for a mate. If you choose not to be our mate, he has to pick another."

"Yes, someone who understands your ways. I remember very well."

"She is only one option, and she's a good one. Alpha Lauren is intelligent and formidable. You can't just go off and run upon her. She'll kill you."

"Alpha Lauren. You call her Alpha Lauren?"

"That is her title, one that is respected amongst our

kind. She is alpha of the North Star Pack, just like Darius is alpha of the Legacy Pack."

"Isn't that just great? I guess you're excited too. Who better to bear your alpha babies than Alpha Lauren?"

"I don't want her, and I'm sure I can speak for Darius when I say he sees her as a solution to a problem."

"Me. I'm the problem."

"You're the best solution we have. You're the one we want, the one we were meant to be with. She's many things, but no matter how strong and beautiful she is, she's not you. You are so much more to us, Audrey. There's no competition and nothing for you to worry about. Do you know how strong and beautiful you are?"

"Look man, I'm just trying to hold it together. I'm sure you think I'm beautiful, but I've been surrounded by beautiful people my whole life. My whole family looks like they stepped out of the pages of Essence magazine."

"So do you."

"No, not me. I'm not graceful or elegant or, you know what, it doesn't matter. I am who I am, and I'm okay with that."

"Who do you think you are?"

"I'm the average one. Everyone else is successful, beautiful, and married, and I'm the wayward thinker who doesn't want a corporate job. I'm the dreamer who can't find a husband and doesn't have a real career. They look at me like I'm something to be pitied, a cautionary tale. Kids, you don't want to end up like Aunt Audrey… alone. Make sure you straighten your hair and get a real job. I try to stay positive, but they make it hard."

"Maybe you should try not looking at yourself through their eyes. Why do you do what you do? You have hundreds of thousands of subscribers to your YouTube channel. What do you think they see when they look at you?"

"I don't know, another natural hair channel."

"People don't subscribe to just another channel. What sets you apart?"

"I don't know. I started it to document my natural hair journey."

"So it's real, raw, honest. It's something you care about."

"It is, but my family doesn't."

"What about the people that do? Audrey, not only are you stunningly beautiful, you're funny, you're passionate, and you have incredible hair. You're genuine, relatable, and sensitive. Those are the qualities that men like me appreciate, but we don't see them often. That's why Darius loves you."

"And you?"

"I'm yours." He kisses my hand.

I start singing. "And you, and you, and you. You're gonna love meeeeee."

We both double over laughing.

"Pull over here."

Felix pulls into a strip center. "Everything okay?"

"No it's not, but it will be."

He looks confused.

I continue. "I'm starving, and there's a spot right there with the best burgers you'll ever eat."

He and I eat, talk, and laugh. Felix surprises me every day. Despite my early impression of him, he's easy to talk to, and he managed to get me thinking about something other than Darius for a little while.

Once we're back at my house, I can barely get in the door before he removes my dress and rips off my bra and panties.

"I'm going to make you forget all about it," he

whispers in my ear.

My pussy drips with excitement.

He removes his clothes and carries me to the bedroom. He looks through my nightstand and finds a bottle of lube.

"What are you going to do with that?" I ask.

He's silent as he bends me over the foot of the bed and takes me from behind. I cry out with every thrust. This is just what I need. I lift my body while maintaining the arch in my back to grab the back of Felix's head. My hips grind against his, and we both moan in ecstasy. His dick slips out and I bend slightly, urging him to reenter me immediately. He holds his shaft and laps my pussy, pressing his head against me. My head rolls back as he pushes. Damn, he's at the wrong hole, but as he presses against me, I can't help but be curious. My body tingles with excitement, but I know he'll do what guys usually do, feel it out and go back to the pussy.

He pushes again. I don't object. I want to see where this goes. I wonder how much I can take. I wonder how painful it is. He stops and slides up and down again. Once again he comes back to ass and presses against my hole. I bend over the bed, and he grips my hips and pushes against me. I push my hips out and hold on to the covers. I can feel him sliding past my hole, teasing me. He suddenly pulls away and replaces his dick with his thumb. I wince as he slips it inside me and pushes in and out. This feels good. He removes his thumb and inserts his finger, then two fingers, thrusting in and out as I grip the sheets. He scissors his fingers while I moan his name.

Suddenly, he stops. He pulls away. I lift myself to see what's going on, but he commands me to put my head down and I obey. He gets on his knees and surprises me with a bite to my ass cheek. He holds me down when my body jerks. He spreads both cheeks with a possessive grip and licks my crack. His mouth circles the rim and he explores me with his tongue.

"That feels good," I moan as he teases me with tantalizing circles. I push my ass into his face. I want more. He growls and sucks my hole before he inserts his tongue and flicks. He slips his finger in my pussy and plays with both holes in tandem. I feel a wave of pleasure crash over me and I cry out as I bite down on the covers. He presses his finger against my clit in rapid pulses as I cum.

Once I catch my breath he stands and presses his rock hard dick against my ass. He pushes against me gently, breaching my back entrance. I moan. It's not as bad as I thought. He pulls out. This time when he pushes in, he slides a little easier with the help of the lube. I wince at the invasion of his huge dick, but I can handle it. I'm still as he moves his hips against me, and I moan my pleasure. He slides deeper. I hold my breath as he stretches me.

"You're going to take all this dick. Aren't you, mon chéri?"

"Oui."

"I'm almost halfway. Do you want more?"

"Plus s'il vous plait."

"Such a good student. I'm about to teach you how to take this dick."

"Oui," I groan.

He goes deeper.

"Oui," I moan. It hurts so good. I try to catch my breath and brace myself.

Deeper.

I cry out at the burst of pain.

"Take it all in," he says. "Tout prendre."

He slides out halfway and back in.

"Ummm," I moan at the merging of pain and

191

pleasure. "Plus," I demand.

He pulls all the way out and enters me slowly. "Are you okay?" he asks.

"Oui."

"If you want to stop, tell me now."

"No, don't stop."

He repeats the action of pulling out, taking his time, allowing me to get comfortable. He applies more lube and presses his body against mine. I feel his heartbeat, and his chest heave against my back. He smells divine, and he places his hand on top of mine and enters me with a rapid thrust as he bites my ear.

My body is stunned. My head feels light for a moment, and I cry out. He groans as his hips crash into my ass at a steady rhythm. Once I get used to it, I want more, and I tell him in French. He growls into my ear and I know he's about to unleash the beast. He lifts me onto the bed on all fours and climbs behind me. I arch my back and take all of him as he enters me. He's starved for me and his body lets me know how much he wants me, taking all of me, showing no mercy, slamming into me, forcing me to cry out his name into the night.

"Who do you belong to?"

"Felix," I shout over and over. "Felix," I scream his name as I cum. This feels different, amazing, maybe better, I'm still trying to decide.

He lowers me onto my stomach and drives into me. Our bodies are locked together as I meet his hips with mine. He holds me tight as he releases into me cursing the heavens as he cums. He keeps going until he's spent and we lie together face down.

"Would you do that again?" he asks.

"Hell yeah."

He carries me to the bathroom, and we shower together. Afterward, we fall asleep in my bed.

I hear my name over and over, waking me up suddenly. I look around the room to see what's going on. Felix is still asleep. Maybe I was dreaming.

Audrey. Audrey. Audrey.

It's Darius. I'm still a little foggy. Is he in the room? I look around.

Audrey. He's in my head, trying to get my attention.

What? What are you doing?

Come outside.

I look around. *What?*

I'm outside.

I panic. My stomach buzzes with anxiety. He's outside. I try not to jump so I don't wake Felix. I carefully move his arm and slide away from him. The light in the living room is on and my door is open so I can see a little bit. I put on my house slippers and tiptoe to my closet to grab a robe. Before I walk out the door I look back. Felix hasn't moved. I take a step out of the room.

"Tell Darius I said hi."

I jump before I realize it's Felix. I almost had a heart attack. This feels weird. What the hell am I doing? No time to think. I look out the window and Darius is standing in my driveway leaning against his truck. Damn, he's sexy. He's wearing a crisp white shirt and black slacks. My heart thumps. I can't believe he's here.

I open the door and run into his arms. He holds me tight and I bury my head in his chest. My voice is muffled as I tell him how much I missed him while tears stream down my face.

"Please don't cry, baby." His head is buried in my hair and he kisses my head.

I look up, and our lips crash. We kiss like we'd die if our lips didn't touch. After minutes, we pull away breathless. We stare at one another, and with all my might, I slap him across the face.

He growls at me. "Don't you ever do that again."

"You left me in the middle of the night. You lied to me."

"I know."

"How could you do that?"

"I had to. You know what's at stake."

"You didn't have to lie."

He hangs his head.

"I saw you tonight."

"I know."

"Who is she?"

"She's an associate."

"She's pretty. Do you like her?"

"Not in a romantic way."

"Do you want to replace me with her?"

"I don't want to. I want you, and I was very honest with her about my feelings for you. I thought it was important to be honest with her, too. I made it clear to her that I would honor and respect her if you decide not to be our mate, but my heart may always be yours."

"Do you mean that?"

"You know I do, Audrey."

"I don't know anything."

"I saw you too."

"You did?"

"You looked beautiful."

"Thank you."

"I was glad to see you smile. Do I have Felix to thank for that?"

I shrug.

"It's okay. You can tell me."

"He's been here for me ever since my shop got trashed."

"Looks like you two have gotten close."

I feel uneasy. I don't move, and I don't say anything.

"You two have been fucking."

I shuffle in his arms.

"You don't have to be coy. All that matters to me is that you're happy. Has he made you happy?"

"Yes, he has."

"Has he been good to you? I know Felix can be a prick."

"He's been good to me. He's been my rock, and he's really sweet."

Darius kisses my forehead. "That's all that matters."

"It doesn't bother you?" I ask.

"No, I meant what I said. You don't have to choose."

"What about you and Alpha Lauren? Did you sleep with her?"

"No, she's not my mate."

I breathe a sigh of relief. "Just so we're clear, I can't handle that."

"I know that baby. I know this situation is fucked up, but as long as we're mated, I wouldn't do that to you. Felix and Damien are as much yours as I am, and you can enjoy all of us whenever and however you want."

"I can't even fathom."

"But you can feel it, can't you? You've thought about it, dreamt about it. You're thinking about it now, and that's fine. Are you doing okay?"

"Yes, I am. Are you?"

"No. Staying away from you is killing me."

"You don't have to."

"I do, and I shouldn't have come tonight. Felix is going to flip out."

"He knows you're here. He told me to tell you hi."

"I see he's calmed down. He wanted to kill me. Must be this good pussy. I know it did a number on me."

I try not to smile. In my head, I'm doing a victory dance.

He whispers in my ear. "What's underneath this

robe?"

I whisper in his ear. "Felix's pussy."

"Nah, this my pussy. Isn't it?" He unties my belt.

I moan as he kisses my neck. "Here comes Felix with his hating ass," he says.

"I heard that." I hear Felix's voice behind me.

"What's up brother?" Darius asks.

"I think it's time for Audrey to come inside."

"We were just about to have some fun."

"Without me?" Felix asks.

"Audrey, do you want Felix?" Darius asks.

"Yes."

"Has he been fucking you right, baby?"

"Oui," I say.

"He got you speaking French and shit."

"Oui," I say as I turn around in Darius's arms. My robe spreads open, and I reach for Felix. He's wearing a pair of boxer briefs and nothing else.

He drags me to the front door. Darius follows. I wrap my arms around Felix's neck.

"Thank you for taking care of our mate. She speaks highly of you."

"I'm honored."

Damn, I'm horny. I should be depleted. I've never had so much sex in my life.

Felix reaches inside my robe and caresses my hips. He rubs my arms and slides the robe from my body. The chill of the crisp winter air is quickly masked by his heat as he presses his body against mine and kisses me. I'm lost in his lips when Darius presses his body against my back. I can feel the cold metal of his belt, and his dick pokes me. He gently pulls my face away from Felix and kisses me. His lips feel like the warmth of home. Felix kisses my neck and my body begs for more of their touches.

Felix whispers to me in French and Darius squeezes

my breasts and kisses my back. His hand moves up my body. He grabs my neck and squeezes lightly. I moan my delight.

"You like that?" Felix asks.

"Oui."

He speaks to Darius. "We discovered something else she likes tonight."

"What's that?" Darius asks.

"This dick in her ass."

"Is that right?" Darius asks in my ear.

My mind flashes to an image of Felix, Darius, and Damien all taking me at once. I'm overheated. "Yes," I whisper.

"She might be ready," Darius says.

"Close," Felix says.

"Ready for what?" I ask.

They're silent, but I feel like they're communicating without me.

"Mon chéri, kiss Darius goodnight. He has to go."

"No, don't go."

"I have to. I made a promise. I can't interfere."

"But I want you to stay. I want both of you."

"I want nothing more than to bury my dick inside you, but I have to go. Please don't be angry with me."

"But I just got you back."

"Felix is going to take good care of you baby. Kiss me."

I turn to him and hold him tight. He kisses me goodbye. "I love you mate," he whispers.

"I love you too."

I can't lose him. Would mating all three of them be the worst thing in the world? Maybe it's worth it if I get to keep that man. Am I actually thinking about doing this? Also, all of them are incredibly sexy and sweet. My thoughts are interrupted by Felix. He pulls me into the house, and as promised, he takes good care of me.

CHAPTER 18

Darius

I spent the night tossing and turning. When I got out of bed I was surprised that Nicole hasn't cooked. She usually wakes up before me and has breakfast waiting. I don't encourage this behavior, but I've come to expect it. The house was quiet and my gut told me to check on Nicole. The guest bedroom was empty.

There was a note on the bed with only one word. *Thanks.* I guess that's over. Good riddance. Why am I not relieved? I can't shake the feeling that something's not right. At this moment there's nothing I can do about it.

I told Lauren that I'd meet her in the forest for yoga this morning. I stand in front of the lake and take a deep breath. I'm excited about the possibilities that life has for me.

I scent Lauren as she approaches from behind. "Namaste," I say to her.

"Namaste, Darius."

She smiles at me when she sees me now, and she greets me with a hug and a kiss on the cheek. On our date, I opened up to Lauren and told her everything about Sarah and Audrey. I didn't realize she'd be so easy to talk to.

She guides me in meditation followed by sun salutations. "I didn't know you practiced." She seems impressed with my skill level.

"My father taught me from a young age. Now I dabble from time to time, but I've got nothing on you."

We finish our practice in silence, and when we both take a seat and look out over the water.

"I really enjoyed our date," Lauren says.

"I did as well. I'm glad I opened my eyes and took some time to get to know you."

"I'm glad that you didn't leave me high and dry when your mate showed up."

"You knew?"

"I did. You covered it up really well, but I knew something was up. You have a tell."

"I do? What is it?"

"I can't tell you. I have to keep you honest, but I appreciate you being a gentleman."

"I didn't want to disrespect you."

"She was there with Felix. She's pretty."

"She is, but she's so unaware of her beauty, it's ridiculous." I smile to myself. "She said you were pretty too."

"You couldn't stay away, could you? I knew it."

"I tried."

"You really do love her. It's all in your eyes."

"Yeah."

"I've seen her before on YouTube. She has one of those natural hair channels."

"She does, and there's something I want to talk to you about."

"You want to work it out with your mate."

"I hope I haven't offended you. I apologize."

"No need. I figured."

"I think she's coming around, and I don't want to go back and forth. That wouldn't be fair to you. It's so strange because I really like you."

"But only as a friend," she says.

"Are you okay with that?"

"I am. I got the vibe, but we can still fuck."

"Lauren, you know I can't do that."

"You're no fun."

"Neither are you."

"I'm happy for you." She reaches out for a hug.

"I appreciate that," I tell her as I return her hug.

"I'm going to get back, make sure my women are

training. I did want to ask you for a favor."

"Anything."

"Can you do some training with my fighters?"

"I can teach you a thing or two."

"That would be so amazing. When are you available?"

"How's Saturday morning at five?"

"If you want to sleep in. I guess we'll have to make do." She stands. "I'll see you then."

"Alright."

As Lauren walks away I can't stop thinking about Audrey. I know she loves Christmas, and she hasn't had a chance to celebrate with all she has going on. I think I should make sure Damien and Felix do something for her. Her tree still sits in my house, and regardless of what happens, she and I are going to spend Christmas together like we planned. We have a lot of time to make up for.

After I text Damien, I text Audrey to tell her I'm thinking about her. I have a smile on my face as I stand to head back to my cabin. Ever since I saw her I'm no longer concerned with cutting off all communication. Things are going well, so it should be okay.

I must admit my heart skips a beat when I see that she's typing a response to my text.

"Darius," my father shouts catching me off guard.

Somethings wrong. I look around and I see a group of men headed for me. I try to locate my father, but I don't see him. I feel a sharp pain in my neck. I touch the spot and find something sticking out. I pull it out and inspect it.

It's a tranquilizer dart.

Shit. I attempt to shift, but instead, I fall to the ground.

CHAPTER 19

Audrey

"Daddy's home." Damien stands in my doorway looking sexy as sin with a wicked smile on his face.

"Hi Damien," I give him a hug. I'm happy to see him.

"How's my luna?"

"I'm fine. I was under the weather, but I'm much better."

"Oh no, I wish I was here to take care of you."

"It's okay. I was in bed for two days, but Felix took excellent care of me every step of the way."

"Felix? Are we talking about the same Felix? Tall, dreads, uptight asshole?"

"Yes."

"He didn't run you off?"

"No, I was able to keep him in check."

"I'm sure you were."

"How are you, Damien?"

"I'm better now that I'm here with you, and I have good news for you."

"What's that?"

"Your shop will be finished tomorrow."

"Are you serious?" I jump up and down and hug him.

"I'm serious."

"Thank you so much."

I settle in his arms and squeeze him tight. He engulfs me in the comfort of his embrace. I'm overwhelmed with emotion. Tears stream from my eyes. The tighter he holds me, the closer I feel to him. The air between us is filled with calm intensity. He lifts my chin and the look in his grey eyes is endearing to me. I'm suddenly nervous as his head slowly moves toward mine. My lips meet his for a tender peck on the lips. I gently pull

201

his head closer and deepen the kiss. He eases me into the house and closes the door with his foot. He lifts me and I wrap my legs around his waist.

He carries me to the couch as his tongue tangles with mine until we pull away breathless.

"Why are you crying?"

"I'm so grateful. You and Felix have done so much for me. I don't deserve it."

"You do deserve it." He wipes my cheek. "Are you happy, luna?"

"Yes."

"That's all that matters. Now stop crying. You know tears confuse Felix."

I laugh. "They do, don't they?"

"Where is he?" Damien asks.

"He's on a work call."

"You look beautiful today."

I blush. "While Felix was working, I decided to do some work as well. I made a new video today."

"What kind?"

"I did flat twists using my new line. Do you like it?" I shake out my hair.

"I love it. I think you should take some photos like this for social media. Maybe over by the window, the light is perfect."

"Maybe you're right."

"I am. It'll be great for your website too. You look effortlessly beautiful."

"I guess I could take some selfies."

"Am I invisible? I can take them for you."

"You don't have to do that."

"Yes, I do. Let me take down the curtains." Once he takes down the curtains, he pulls out his cellphone. "Stand by the window for me."

I do as he says. I'm nervous being in front of him, but I try to act normal. I smile big with my hand on my hip. I hear the photo snap.

"That's good, but I need you to relax."

"Okay." I smile slightly less with my hand on my hip.

"Hands down," he commands.

"Laugh."

"No."

"Just do it."

"I can't."

"You've never laughed before?" he asks.

I laugh.

He snaps a photo.

"Wait." I hold my hand out. He snaps a couple of photos.

"Damien, stop."

He keeps snapping. "Turn your head to the left."

I follow his instructions.

"Good. Lift your chin slightly." He moves in closer. "Look straight ahead. Lips parted. Yes, just like that." He snaps photos as he circles me. "Okay, mouth closed." He reaches for me and grabs my hand. He positions my fingers against my chin. "Soft hands," he says. "Good. Turn your head toward me. Good." He kisses my lips and backs away. As I smile, he takes another photo. He sits his phone on the table and stands in front of me.

"Are we done?" I ask.

"Not yet. Do you trust me?" he asks sincerely.

"Yes."

"I'm going to take your shirt off."

I look down at my off the shoulder black top. I'm not wearing a bra. "Why?"

"Trust me."

He slowly removes my shirt and licks his lips as he stares at me. He takes my arms and positions them across my chest and picks up his phone. "Look at me.

203

Look into my eyes."

I obey, and he snaps three photos.

He walks up to me and fluffs my hair. Before he walks away he rubs his thumb down my lips. He snaps a photo. "Head back. Now, look at me. Pretend I'm touching you. My hand is pressed against your neck while I kiss your cheek. He snaps while he talks. I can't get enough of your sweet scent and I gently nibble your ear while I tell you all the nasty shit I want to do to you. My dick presses against your hip while my hands grope your breasts. Do you like it when I bite your nipple?"

I moan.

He snaps a photo. "Answer me, Audrey."

"Yes." I close my eyes. Electricity flows through my body.

He snaps a photo.

"What else?" I ask.

"I think I got it?"

"Got what?"

"Open your eyes, luna." He's standing over me with a sexy stare. He holds his phone out so I can see it.

"Wow," I start swiping through the photos. "I can't believe you did this with your cell phone. This is me?"

"That's you."

"I've never looked so good." There's a range of photos from girl next door to tastefully sexy vixen. "You should be a photographer."

"I do a little photography. Now I mostly do graphic design. If you want, I can help you with that tragedy you call a website."

"Hey buddy, don't talk about my website. I did that from scratch with no training."

"It looks good, and you should be proud, but I can make it better."

"You don't have to. The photos are phenomenal, and

204

you've already done so much."

"It's too late. I've been working on something for you, and with these photos, I can have it done tomorrow." He pulls up something on his phone and shows me a mockup website he created for me.

"I love this," I shout. I push the phone into his hands. "I can't. I can't accept anything else."

"What do you mean?"

"It's too much. You guys are great, and you've done so much for me, but this is not what I do. It's my responsibility to fix my website and get photos made, and take care of my shop, and hire security if I need to. I've already taken up your time and money. You have to stop."

"Why do we have to stop?" He sits on the couch.

"Because I could get used to this."

"And that would be a bad thing?"

I sit on the arm of the couch next to him. "I don't want to be spoiled. I've worked hard for everything I have."

"And you feel like if things are handed to you, they lose their value."

"No. Well yes. I guess. I don't need anything else. Thank you."

"Luna, I understand, but I need you to understand that I can't sit back and watch you work yourself to death when I know I can help. We all need help, and we all need kindness, but not everyone gets it. Instead of worrying about what you're losing, think about what you've gained."

"What have I gained?"

"New friends that care about you and want you to be happy. We only help because we can, and if you're looking for some kind of cosmic balance, you should help someone else that needs it."

"Are you a photographer or a philosopher?"

"Don't fight our kindness, pass it along."

"You do make a good point."

"Will you let me help you with this? It's what I do."

"I guess, but you get on my nerves."

"I know you don't mean that."

"Oh, yes I do." I stretch my neck and rub my shoulder.

"What's wrong with your neck?"

"Nothing."

"Come here." He slides over and pulls me next to him.

"Are you a masseuse as well?" I ask.

"I can do a little something, something. What's stressing you?" He rubs my shoulders.

"Everything is coming together perfectly, almost too perfectly thanks to you guys. The only other thing I'm worried about is who broke into my shop. Will they do it again? Are they after me?"

"That's why we're here. We won't let anything happen to you."

"It's been great, but you can't be with me every minute of every day. You have to get back to your lives."

"We're keeping an eye on things. We're not going to leave you hanging. I don't think there's anything for you to worry about. There haven't been any additional threats, and if it was your ex who did it, as I suspect, he knows you're off limits now."

"It's just like, I don't know. I've had trolls on my YouTube, but I can't imagine being hated this much. I've never done anything to anyone."

"That's why it hurts your feelings."

"Yeah."

"Unfortunately, we don't always find answers. Sometimes we have to learn to accept, process, and move on." He kneads between my collar bones.

"Letting go can be hard."

"But when you do, it's a relief." My neck rolls. His hands are magic. My body jerks when he hones in on a spot on my neck and rubs it out.

"Do you want the full body treatment?"

"I do, but—"

"I know. You don't want to accept anything else. Come with me." He takes my hand and leads me to my bedroom.

"Strip," he says. It won't be hard since I'm already topless.

"You have to strip too."

"Do I?"

"If I get one then you get one too, but mine first." I remove my pants and Damien removes his clothes.

He looks around my room and finds the all-natural body oil I made. "This smells good."

I don't care about the oil. My eyes are fixed on his ripped body.

"See something you like?" he asks.

"Nope."

"Damn," he says.

"You can still massage me though."

"I'm so lucky," he jokes. "Lie down on the bed."

I lie face down across the sides of the bed, and he straddles me. I know this is going to feel heavenly, and I can't wait. I hear him open the bottle of oil and rub his hands together. His palms rest on my back, and I moan as he spreads the oil over my skin. "That feels good," I whisper. His hands are strong and steady, and they grip my sides as they pass.

"Relax for me," he says.

I didn't know I was tense, but I feel how stiff I was when I try to loosen my body.

"Much better."

I rest my head in the covers and my arms at my

sides. He moves off the bed, and I wait. I don't know where he's gone, but I'm sure he'll be back. Music begins to play softly. Grown and sexy r&b takes my mind to another place. I sing along in my head as Damien rubs my body to the flow. I wonder if he knows how wet I am for him right now. I want to feel his dick pulsing inside my body instead of against my back.

"I can't leave you alone for a minute, can I?" That's Felix's voice. He must be done with work.

"Luna needed to relax."

"Why didn't you tell me? I could've helped with that."

"She didn't know."

"Well, I can take it from here," Felix says.

"Nah, I got her," Damien says.

I look up and Felix is naked in front of the bed. I'm in trouble. My body is on fire and it's both of them I want. I take deep breaths and return my face to the covers. *Just enjoy the massage, Audrey.* Felix stands in front of me. He spreads oil over my arms with his warm touch and massages my fingers. Damien slides back and massages my lower back.

I groan in pleasure. This isn't fair. Damien's hands move to my ass. He slaps his palms against my plump behind and kneads. He uses his elbows to work my lower back and comes back to my ass. Felix leans over me and strokes from my back to my neck. They work like a well oiled machine, moving their hands in tandem. I lose myself in the music and their touches. I can't stop my hips from moving when a sensual song starts. The room is quiet except for the music and the echoes of my moans.

Two hard dicks press against my skin. I open my eyes and look up. Felix's blue eyes sparkle. I look back. Damien's grey eyes flash.

Damien moves to my legs and Felix to my arms. I'm tempted to touch myself. Damien lifts my hips and his pelvis is pressed against mine. My ass is in the air and I arch my back. Damien works my back and Felix works underneath, rubbing my stomach, squeezing my breasts, driving me insane. Four hands touching me, caressing me, coating my body with oil, leaving nothing ignored, except for one major part of my anatomy. My body is overheated, and my desire is doubled.

Felix's dick stares at me, taunting me, begging to be sucked. I grab him with my palm and take him into my mouth. After he groans and the initial shock wears off, he grabs my hair with both hands. He pumps his hips, pushing his dick deeper into my mouth, and I'm eager to take it all in. I simultaneously suck and lick. The deeper he pushes, the tighter he grips my hair.

Damien's smoky voice melts into my ears. "Look at you taking that dick in your mouth. You're so fucking sexy, luna." He fingers me. "Fuck, your pussy is so wet, Luna. I think you want some more dick, don't you, luna." He scratches my back. "Don't you?"

I nod yes as I swirl my tongue around Felix's tip. "Please."

"You don't have to beg me, baby."

I feel the tip of his dick explore my pussy.

"I've been waiting for the privilege to fuck this pussy, but I don't know if you ready for this dick."

"I'm ready," I moan. I lift onto all fours.

Damien thrusts his dick inside my pussy and Felix thrusts his dick into my mouth. Oh shit, am I actually doing this? I try to create a rhythm. I suck Felix while Damien pounds me from behind. Damien grips my hips as he crashes into me. I hold my mouth open as I cry out in ecstasy. Felix strokes his dick as I attempt to catch it in my mouth.

"This pussy feels so good, luna. Shit, you feel good."

He leans over on top of my back and kisses my neck. I hear his grunts in my ear. He squeezes my breasts as he blesses me with long, agonizing strokes. He pulls me up and lays on his back. I ride him in reverse and rub my body while Felix watches.

Felix leans in and kisses me. I'm hungry for his kiss, for his touch. His lips travel my breasts and he circles my nipples with his tongue before he sucks like his life depends on it. I grab his hair and hold his head close to my chest as Damien drives into me from beneath.

"Cum on this dick, luna. I know you're close. Your pussy is gripping me so tight. Cum for daddy." He sinks his fingers into my waist as he moans.

Felix bites down on my nipple and I grind on his dick as I cum.

"Shit," Damien shouts. "Fuck," he groans as my hips drive into him and move in circles.

I squeeze my breasts as I cum hard. I bend over and take Felix into my mouth and moan on his dick as Damien circles his hips in rhythm with mine. I pull Felix into my throat as I grip his hips. Our collective moans and curses drown out the music playing. I lift myself off of Damien and turn to face him. "Move down." I direct him to slide down to the edge of the bed.

As I kiss his lips I climb on top of him and sink onto his dick. My ass is in the air as I ride him. I know exactly what I want, but does Felix. He smacks my ass and I turn my head.

"What are you waiting for?" I ask him. His look of surprise is quickly replaced with dark desire. Damien holds on to me as Felix spreads body oil over his dick. He takes his time and penetrates me slowly. Damien's dick pulses inside of me as Felix moves in. It's still a minor adjustment, but more pleasurable than painful. Every nerve in my body tingles as both men take their time, learning my body. With slow, sensual strokes they draw what their bodies need from mine, and I eagerly give and receive. I've never felt so much passion and power in my life. My pleasure spikes to new heights. I never knew I could feel so good.

Tension builds in Felix and he unleashes on me, pulling me against him as he crashes into me. Our bodies slap together. He spreads my cheeks and grips my ass, molding, and scratching while he growls and grunts. Once he's satisfied, he slows down and Damien thrusts into me from beneath, holding the back of my neck as he ravishes me.

"I'm going to cum," Damien announces.

I am too. He pulls me in and growls as he grips my body. His thrusts are hard, angry, forceful, and just what I need as I scream his name. Felix pounds me and my cries become desperate with both men depleting taking me savagely. I cum so hard water streams from the corner of my eyes. My legs shake and I can't move. Both of them pull out of me and stroke their dicks with fury while my body jerks on the bed. Damien's cum shoots out like a rocket as he strokes his dick. His head rolls back and it trickles down his hand. Felix cums in a steady stream, then drips down his dick as he squeezes. My body is showered with kisses before both men lie next to me.

I stare at the ceiling.

Damien speaks first. "How do you feel, Audrey?"

"Satisfied."

Both men howl, and I laugh. I almost forgot they were wolf shifters.

"What do you need?" Damien asks.

"What do you need?" I ask.

"I'm good," Damien says. "I asked about you."

"I need to know something."

"What's that?" Felix asks.

"Why hasn't anyone asked me?"

Felix sits up. "Asked you what?"

"I feel silly. Never mind. I don't need anything. I'm fine."

"Why hasn't anyone asked if you changed your mind?" Damien asks.

"How do you do that?" I ask him.

He only kisses me. I lose myself in his lips. He and I haven't had much time to spend together, and he excites me.

"Have you changed your mind?" Felix interrupts.

Damien and I slowly pull apart.

"Yes."

Felix jumps out of the bed. "No fucking way," he shouts.

I sit up with a smile on my face.

Damien sits up and kisses my cheek while he holds my waist. "We haven't asked you because we were waiting for you to tell us. The choice was always yours, luna. We didn't want to take that from you."

"What if I never told you?"

"Then we'd die," he jokes.

"Or you would've mated Alpha Lauren."

"Thankfully, we don't have to," Damien says with relief.

"Yeah, it would've been such a burden," I quip.

"The burden would've been losing you." Felix sits next to me.

"When did you get so sentimental?" Damien asks.

"I guess sometimes love has that effect on people," Felix replies.

Felix kisses me softly and rests his forehead against mine.

Damien speaks up. "You know you have me to thank for this."

"For what?" I ask.

"Damien insisted that I spend more time with you so that you could warm up to me, but I'm not that bad, am I?"

"Ummmm." I try to think of a good spin.

"You are," Damien says.

"Didn't you worry about the two of us?" I ask Damien.

"No, but we do have some lost time to make up for. When I have you to myself, I'm going to wear that ass out, respectfully."

"It's only fair," I say with a grin. I sigh.

"You miss Darius," Damien says.

"I do."

"The good news is you'll get to be with him as much as you want, and our pack has a luna."

"The pack? What about the pack?"

"Don't be nervous."

"I'll try not to be nervous around a pack of wolves."

"I have methods of calming you."

"I know you do, Damien."

He kisses my neck.

"I think I should give you two some alone time."

I blurt out. "We should tell Darius."

"He can wait a day or two. You two haven't had a chance to connect, and I think if it weren't for Damien, we would've lost you."

"You deserve a lot of the credit too," I assure Felix as he dresses.

"Come kiss me."

I wrap my arms around his neck and kiss him.

"I'll see you soon, mon chéri."

He walks out of the room and I turn to Damien. "What do you want to do?" I ask.

"You." He pulls me onto the bed and rolls on top of me.

"Audrey," Felix shouts.

"Yes."

"There's someone here to see you."

I push Damien off of me. "Just a minute," I shout. I scurry to put on some clothes. I dig through my drawers and pull out a pair of leggings and a t-shirt. "Who could that be?" I question out loud.

"Audrey!"

"Shit, it's my mom," I whisper to Damien as I pull up my pants. I smooth my clothes and throw my hair in a bun. I look around in a panic. My heart is pounding through my ears. "Shit." I stand in front of Damien. Stay in here and don't say anything. Where are your clothes?" I ask him.

"Over there," he says.

"Shhh," I urge. I don't know what I'm going to do. "Put them on and stay quiet."

He covers his mouth and laughs.

"Not funny," I whisper.

"Audrey!" My mother shouts.

I jump and run outside. "Yes, mom." I jump back when I see who she's standing with. "What is she doing here?"

"We'll get to that in a minute. Who is this man?"

"He was just leaving. Thank you," I say to Felix. I hold the door and usher him out. I hope I'm successful at hiding how jittery I am.

"Bye," Felix says.

I nod as he walks past me. As the door closes, I look at my cousin Michelle standing there with a smug face. "Why are you here?"

Ever poised, my mother stands in front of me in a trench coat and slacks with a suspicious face. "We haven't seen you in weeks."

"I wish you had called first."

"There's another car in your driveway. Whose is it?"

"What can I do for you two?"

214

"Is there some reason you haven't been around?"

"Mama, there's a lot going on. I have to get my business back up and running. I have a new product to launch and I've been dealing with my shop."

My mother looks around the room. "Are you going to invite us in, or do we have to stand in the doorway like common folk?"

I roll my eyes. I'm not in the mood. "That depends on why you're here."

"I know you're not talking to your mother like that, miss thing."

I squirm, but I resolve to stay strong. I stand tall with my feet firmly planted. My mother will not bring me down today. This is my house. "My apologies. I don't have time for visitors right now."

"That's too bad. Let's have a seat." My mother and Michelle walk past me to my couch, and I follow defeated.

"Please have a seat," I say sarcastically.

"You missed Sunday dinner. You missed my Christmas scavenger hunt. You usually help me get everything together. Mama just wants to know what happened."

"As I said, I've been busy."

Michelle looks like she's about to burst. "Aunt Maxine. I can't do this. I can't sit here and act like everything is okay."

"Lower your voice," I warn her.

She continues to yell. "You told the police that my fiancé vandalized your silly hair salon."

"What's your point?" I ask.

"I knew you were bitter and jealous, but I never thought you'd do something like that."

"I'm not jealous. I don't want Andre. The reason he's a person of interest is that he came here uninvited, he put his hands on me, and he called me a whore."

"He did what?" my mother asks.

"You're a liar. You can't stand to see us happy."

"I've never had anything to say about your relationship. I don't care what the two of you do. All I want is for both of you to stay away from me."

"Did he put his hands on you?" my mom asks.

"Yes," I shout.

"Of course not, Aunt Max, she's just an attention whore."

"What did you just say?" I ask.

"Michelle, that's enough. Audrey when did this happen?"

"A few days before the break-in."

"When did you see Andre?"

"He came here unannounced and refused to leave, and there was a witness. They got into a fight."

"Now my fiancé is fighting over you. You wish."

"Listen, ladies, you all are family, and you need to work this out. I won't tolerate this behavior."

"I'm sorry but I won't go anywhere if Andre is there."

"Honey, he's her fiancé. What do you expect her to do?"

"I don't expect anything from her, but mom you can't invite him to family functions. He's crazy."

Michelle stands. "You ruined his life. The police questioned him at work and he was suspended because of you. You're fucking with our lives."

"How? He's not your husband. He's suspended because of his actions."

"Fuck you. You fat, ugly, bitch."

I slap Michelle across her face.

She pushes my shoulder, gasps, and holds her cheek. "You are a whore. Who's the guy that just left here. He's not the same guy who I saw here that night, your so-called witness. It's not my fault you're being passed around like a cigarette."

My mother stands between us. "Audrey, what's gotten into you. We do not behave this way."

"We don't? How do we behave mother? Do we stand by one another no matter what? That's what family does, right? You're over here defending Michelle, but you couldn't be bothered to leave the house when my shop was trashed. You never even asked how I was doing. Now you're here for Michelle's sake. She hates me. She's always hated me. I'm your daughter and you always defend her. You two can have one another. Get the hell out of my house, both of you."

"You will not disrespect me. I'm the only mother you've got. My body was cut open to bring you into this world."

She starts crying, and I roll my eyes. This is what she does when she doesn't get her way. I will not be manipulated.

She continues. "All I ever did was try to give you a good life and try to teach you the best I could, and you want to put me out. I've never been so disrespected and ashamed. I don't know what's wrong with you, but I'm going to let you make it because you must be stressed. I will not let you tear this family apart. I'd better see you at Christmas, and you'd better fix your attitude."

She's unbelievable. Michelle comforts my mother as she guides her out of the room. They both agree that they don't know what's wrong with me while they exit. I lock the door behind them. Damien wraps his arms around me from behind.

"I'm so embarrassed."

He rocks me from side to side. "Don't be. Damn, you told me, but I had no idea how bad it really is. They should be ashamed of themselves. You can't keep subjecting yourself to that."

I turn around. "Why are you wearing clothes?"

"You told me to get dressed."

"Why did you listen to me?"

"You don't have to front for me, Audrey. I know you're hurting."

"I know you know, and you're going to make it all better, right?"

"That won't fix anything."

"But it'll be fun pretending it does. Now, please undress me."

We shed our clothes and he takes me against the door. When we're done, he takes me back to the bedroom and holds me until I fall asleep.

My mind keeps replaying my mother's visit. I sit up in the bed and gasp. "Damien," I shout.

"It was her."

"Who was what?"

"It was Michelle. She broke in and trashed my shop."

"How do you know that?"

"It's something she said, that Felix wasn't the guy that was here that night. How did she know that if Andre was never here like she claims?"

"You really think she did it?"

"I know she did."

"I'm going to call the detective."

"Don't. My mother was right. We're family, and we need to work this out. I wasn't going to go to Christmas, but now I think I will."

218

CHAPTER 20

Darius

As my eyes open, my head is pounding. I have no idea where I am, and I'm groggy. It's hard to keep my eyes open. I attempt to stand, but my body feels like it's being held underwater. It'll take me some time to focus and get my mind and my body to work together. I

Once I'm in a seated position, I look around. I'm in a cell in a dark room. You've got to be fucking kidding me. What kind of silly ass shit is this? I snicker as I shake my head. This is laughable. I can't take this seriously. I laugh uncontrollably. I'm pretty sure I know who did this. I knew Roman was an idiot the moment he opened his mouth.

"Darius," I hear a hoarse whisper.

"Dad."

He's on the ground. They must've tranquilized him too. He looks like I felt when I was trying to get my bearings moments ago. I reach out to help him stand.

"Where are we?" he asks.

"I'm not exactly sure."

"You should be. I taught you better than that."

"I just woke up one minute before you did."

"You should always be aware of your surroundings, Darius. You know that. You were distracted."

"I was. I was thinking about Audrey. I was texting her. Things are looking up."

"I'm happy for you son, but we can focus on that later." My father looks around, sniffs, and I join him.

I check my pockets to see if I have my phone, but of course, it's gone.

"We're not alone, and we're in the woods," I tell my father.

"Good. Which woods?"

"I don't know."

"Get it together boy."

"I'm sure we're in East Hollow territory. I'm pretty sure Alpha Roman is responsible. Are you familiar with him?"

"No."

"He's Alpha Donovan's son. He recently took over his father's pack."

"What beef do you have with him?"

"We had a few words but nothing that warrants all this. His sister snuck into my truck and she's been at my cabin, but there was nothing to that."

"Something must be up."

I rattle the bars on the cell and knock on the wall behind me. I put my face close to the bars and look down the room. There are more cells. "Who's there?" I shout.

"Hello." I hear a man's voice. "My name is Paul."

I hear another man's voice. "Hey, can anybody hear me? My name is Dominick."

"How long have you been here?"

Paul says, "I just woke up here. I don't know where I am."

"Same here. Who are you?"

"My name is Darius, and I'm here with my father. Who took you?"

Both men agree they don't know. "I was attacked by a group of men."

"Me too."

"Do either of you know Roman?"

"Roman," Dominick says.

"Yes," Paul says. "He and I went in on a business deal that went bad."

"Me too."

I knew this was Roman. "We need to find a way out of here," I say.

"We will," my father says.

"Nicole said something about her brother selling her to the highest bidder."

"What does that have to do with you?"

"I don't know. I told him I wasn't interested."

A door opens. I see sunlight, and I scent Nicole. She comes running to the cell I'm in. "Darius, he said you were here. I had to come see for myself."

"Who said?" I ask.

"Hello."

"Hello."

Nicole ignores the other two men and answers my question. "Roman, he said he captured you."

"Why?" I ask.

"I'm so sorry. This is all my fault."

"Can you get me out of here?"

"I can't. Roman is the only one with the key."

"Take it from him, Nicole."

"He'll kill me."

"Not if you're smart, and you're very smart, aren't you Nicole?"

"There's nothing I can do."

"Why does your brother have us here?" my father asks.

"I don't know why he has you, sir, but he said it was time for me to earn my keep."

"Meaning?" I ask.

"He wants money. He found out I was with you and he wants you to pay. He thinks you took me. He wouldn't listen to me. He's crazy."

"You need to get me out of here Nicole. I can take care of your brother. You know I can."

"I can't."

"Yes, you can."

"I can't. I'm sorry." She runs out of the door.

"Nicole, come back."

My words are in vain. She's gone.

My father looks at me. "She's lying."

"I know. I'm just trying to get her to let us out. It was worth a try."

"What do you think she wants?"

"Me."

"How do you know her?"

"I thought she was a potential mate for the triad before I met her brother and she snuck into my truck. She said she wanted to get away, that Roman was controlling and trying to sell her. I was clear that I wasn't interested, but I let her stay with me so she could figure things out, and then she left."

"Son, I really think that this bitch is crazy."

"I know that now."

The door opens, and Roman walks in. He wastes no time getting to the point.

"You're all here because you owe me money."

The other two men protest, but Roman tells them to be quiet. I choose not to react.

"What do you have to say, Alpha Darius?"

"Why is he here?" I point at my father.

"He got involved in something that wasn't his business. Be glad I didn't kill him. But I don't want to talk about him. I want to talk about you." Roman's eyes turn dark and angry. "You defiled my sister. You forced yourself on her."

I remain calm. "I never touched your sister. You know it, and she knows it."

"I know my sister came to me with tears in her eyes and torn clothes. She told me what you did to her. I don't know what you've gotten away with in the past, but you're going to pay for what you did."

"How much?"

"Excuse me."

"How much do you want?"

"Ten million."

"Fine. Let us out."

"In exchange for my sister. You will mate her."

"I'll give you fifteen million if you keep her."

"You took something that she can't get back. You will mate her."

"Am I supposed to be scared of you? I can't mate your sister. I'm already mated."

"There are ways around that."

"Sure, Roman whatever you say."

"And your pack will unite with mine."

I pause and grit my teeth. "That's not happening."

"Or," he pulls a gun out of his pocket and aims for my father's head. "I shoot your dear old dad in the head."

"Put the gun down, Roman. I'll do it."

"Son, you don't have to do what he says."

"I have n choice. It's fine." I look at Roman. "We have an agreement."

"Nicole," Roman shouts.

Moments later Nicole steps into the room with her head down.

"What's wrong, Nicole? Look at your future mate," I say to her.

Roman grabs her arm and yanks her forward. "You and Alpha Darius will be mates. Straighten up and greet him properly."

"But Roman," she objects.

"I said greet him properly. You're lucky he still wants you. He's paying a lot of money for you. Straighten up."

"Is this kid serious?" My father asks me.

I shrug and roll my eyes.

Roman raises his gun again. "Very serious, and I don't need you here."

"You do need him. If you hurt him, we have no deal, and you can find your sister another sponsor."

"Don't tempt me."

"Nicole, why won't you look at me? Is it because of what I did to you?"

She looks at the ground.

"I'm your mate. You will show me the proper respect. Look me in the eyes, woman."

She slowly lifts her head.

"What did I do to you?" I shout. My voice echoes through the room.

"I, I d—"

"Speak. Tell me what you told your brother."

"I told him what I needed to tell him." Nicole's demeanor changes and she smirks at me.

"What are you talking about?" Roman asks. His confusion is genuine.

"You're so stupid."

"What the fuck are you talking about?"

"I just want you to know that I hate you, and you were never qualified to be alpha." In the blink of an eye, she snatches Roman's gun and shoots him in the head.

Blood splatters across the room. Some lands on my face and my father's white shirt. The men in the other cells beg for their lives. Nicole kicks her brother's lifeless body. Hatred seeps from her pores.

I stand with my arms across my chest. "Let me out."

"I'm not as stupid as my little brother."

"What the fuck do you want from me?"

"I told you many times, but you kept ignoring me, and after all my father and brother put me through, I shouldn't have to beg any man to mate me. Obviously, they've got life fucked up. They surely got me fucked up."

"If you're going to kill me, then do it."

She laughs. "I don't want to kill you, Darius. I want to mate you."

224

"Whatever, let's do it then. Let's mate. Come on."

"I know how this works. You can't fully commit to me as long as your mate is still an issue."

"She's not."

"Isn't she." Nicole pulls my phone from her pocket. "I miss you, baby. I miss you too. Come talk to me. I neeeeed to see you." She's reading my text to Audrey. "It sounds like she's still a big issue." She kicks Roman's dead body again. "This is all his fault. If he hadn't interfered, you and I would've connected. He ruins everything." She flips his body and searches his pocket. His keys are in his shirt pocket. Nicole steps over his body and unlocks the two cells to my left.

Paul and Dominick step into focus. They bombard Nicole with their thanks.

"Get out of here, and don't tell anyone what happened here today. Do you understand?"

They assure her they won't tell anyone and they scurry past her. Before they can turn the door handle she shoots them in the back.

"It doesn't seem like you needed me to teach you anything."

"There's one thing you can still teach me, and you will, when we mate."

"Is that right? Well, let me out of here and we can talk."

"You men. You think you know everything. You think you're smarter than everybody. I can't let you out silly. I know you'll try to get away from me, and I can't have that."

"This bitch is crazy," my dad says.

She laughs like a maniac and she holds up my phone. "Baby, I'm on my way."

"Don't send that," I say.

"I'm in charge now, alpha. Actually, I'm the alpha too. So see, Darius, you were wrong about me. I know who I am and what I want. I even come with a pack. There's no reason you shouldn't want me."

"You're right, baby, but if you send that she'll know something's wrong. Felix and I agreed that I wouldn't see her until New Year's Eve. I promised him, and he knows I don't want to do anything to destroy my relationship with the triad. Felix won't let her out of his sight."

"Like I'm going to listen to you. I saw your little girlfriend. Damien sent you some lovely photos." She opens her photos and turns the phone to me. "Look at Audrey. Isn't she gorgeous?" She mocks me with kissing faces and noises.

"Don't hurt her, and I'll do whatever you want."

"I can't have her looming over our relationship. I can't have you sneaking out to meet her, so you're going to meet her one last time." She types on the phone then looks up at me. "Sent," she says.

I growl.

"I'm going to see Audrey. I'll be back dear."

"Nicole, don't touch my mate."

"That wolf of yours is so agitated. You'd better get him in line before New Years. You'll be locked in here until we mate. She opens the door.

Two guys are standing right outside and I scent more in the forest.

"Hey, idiots. This is no longer your alpha." She points to her brother, Roman, dead on the ground. "I am. Do you understand?"

They assure her they understand. "I have to go. Come with me. I have some fresh human meat for you. The alphas can't get enough of her and you two can have as much as you want in exchange for your loyalty." They all walk out.

I slam my fist into the cell door. "Nicole! Get back here." I rattle the bars and try to pull them off.

"Calm down son. You've been doing a good job at staying cool. Take a deep breath and look at this cell. We can get out of here."

I listen to my father. He's never steered me wrong. The wall behind us would take too long to break. The floor is not an option. The bars are pretty strong. The ceiling might be weak. As I take it all in, the easiest way out might be the door. I realize this cell is old as fuck, and that lock may as well be a toy. As strong as I am, I can get out of here in no time. Using some karate moves my father taught me as a child, I center myself, inhale, exhale, and let the energy flow through my foot. I aim for the lock and the metal cracks and the lock falls out the other side and crashes onto the floor. I repeat this action two more times and the door is loose. Two more times and the door slams on the ground.

I nod to my father. "That was good, but I could've done it in fewer kicks."

"I doubt it old man. Let's go."

We have to be careful and quiet. We open the front door slightly and peek outside. The wolves are out there. I can scent them. *Listen to me.* My dad speaks to my mind link. *If we get ambushed, I will fend them off and you go.*

No. Absolutely not. We go together.

I didn't ask you a question, son.

I won't leave you behind. It's not negotiable.

For the first time, I see tears in my father's eyes. *Son, don't be stupid.* His words are direct and clear. *Go get your mate.*

I cry as I hug my father. I know the pain he feels. I was a young boy when I lost my mother, and, he was never the same. Neither was I. I can't choose one over the other. I need my father, and I need my mate, but I understand why this is important to him. *Yes, sir.* Hopefully, it won't come to that.

Don't worry about me. I'm still the strongest motherfucker you know.

And you still have a lot of life to live dad. Take it from me. I have no doubt that there's a second chance out there for you. You hold on to that.

Are you ready?

I open the door and we shift into our wolves. His grey wolf nibbles on my white wolf's face before we enter the forest. I follow his lead because he spends more time in the woods in wolf form.

His wolf communicates with mine. We will not act like prey. We are the predators.

I know exactly what he means. Don't be hunted. We need to find them as we make our way out of the forest. We have to be stealth and quick. My father follows Nicole's scent and her tracks. I listen and scent the wolves and listen for their heartbeats and breathing while we run through the trees.

I signal my father. I scent three hiding behind bushes. We speed up and jump on top of them and wrestle them to the ground. My father taught me, when it's all on the line, don't fight, kill. I kick one off my back and sink my teeth into the other's neck. I turn and jump onto the other one. My father reaches him at the same time and rips his heart out.

He shifts. I'm confused, but I follow his lead quickly. We don't have time to second guess one another.

"Gun oil," he says.

I nod my agreement. We rush to the scent. These men left their guns and clothes behind trees. This is perfect. Thanks to my father's training, I'm an expert marksman, and with my enhanced sight and speed, we can get out of here quickly. We take guns, throw on some pants that are too tight, and some tennis shoes that almost fit, and I grab a cell phone and put it in the pocket. We take off, knocking off anything that approaches us. The pack catches on and we are under fire. It's a good thing they have no training. Their aim is horrible. We make it to the other side of the woods. There's a sports car with the door open. I hope there are keys inside, but I can hotwire it if I need to.

We get inside and the keys are in the ignition. The tires screech as I drive off. I call my warrior leader and inform him that I want to take down the East Hollow pack and I need some men to Audrey's address. I know he'll love this because he's wanted to increase our numbers for a while. Today is his lucky day. There's no more East Hollow pack and anyone who has a problem with it dies.

I call Felix as I hurry to Audrey.

"What's up?"

"Audrey's in danger."

I hear the alert in his voice. "What happened?"

"The East Hollow Pack is after her. I know there are three, but I don't know if they have reinforcements."

"Audrey's with Damien now. I'm on the way."

I call Damien. "Audrey's in danger. Don't let her out of your sight. The East Hollow pack is headed her way."

"I got her," Damien says.

"I'm driving as fast as I can. I'll be there soon."

CHAPTER 21

Audrey

"Audrey!" Damien shouts.

I jump. "Why are you shouting?"

"Come with me."

"I'm cooking."

"Turn the food off now." Damien rushes into the kitchen. I feel his urgency.

"I'm not done."

"Forget the food. You're in danger."

My heart jumps. "What do you mean? Are you joking?"

"No. We need to get away from the windows." He's forceful, not a hint of cheer in his voice. He's alpha.

I turn off the stove. I'm officially scared. "We have to get out of here. They may already be outside. We have reinforcements coming. Until then you hide in the bathroom tub. Don't come out for anyone or anything."

"What about you?"

"I'm going to make sure nothing happens to you."

"Damien, no."

"I need you to be brave, Audrey. You're the strongest woman I know. You're in charge of your own life, and you stood up to your mother. You can do this, and you don't have to be afraid. I got you."

"I don't want to hide."

"Now is not the time."

"We're in this together," I remind him.

He grabs my hand and leads me to his duffle bag. "Do you know how to use this?"

I turn off the safety of the handgun he places in my hand. I cock the gun and point it at his head.

He lowers the gun. "Not at me. Aim for the torso."

"You're assuming I'm not a good shot."

"Make sure that when you aim, you hit, smart-ass."

He grabs another gun and some knives. He also puts a pocketknife in my pocket. This is not the time to admit that I find him irresistible right now. I check him out as he checks out the doors and windows. He closes all the curtains and tells me to get down.

We wait. I'm crouched behind the couch. My heart was racing a mile a minute, but now I'm growing bored.

"Shouldn't they be here by now?"

"Are you in a hurry?"

"No, I just mean there's nothing going on. Is your information accurate?"

"All I know is what I was told. We have to remain vigilant until I find out more."

A ruckus outside causes me to jump to my feet.

"Darius, there's no one here."

Damien opens the front door and Darius charges in with a man I don't recognize. He's tall, muscular, and older. He's shirtless and he has sandy hair that's long and curly. Who the hell is this man? I can't help but stare at him. There's something familiar about him.

Felix walks in behind them. His voice is urgent. "What's going on?"

Darius rushes to me and inspects me. "Are you okay?"

"I'm fine. What happened to you?" I can sense his worry and that something is wrong.

Damien informs Darius, "There's been no activity. Are you sure you have the right information?"

"It's a long story, but they should've beaten us here."

"Who?" I ask.

I finally hear the other man's deep voice. "Some crazy bitch who threatened to kill you."

"Hello, I'm Audrey."

"Yes, I know. My son has been smitten with you for

quite some time. It's nice to finally put a face with a name." He walks over and hugs me. "My name is Jonas."

That's why Jonas looks familiar. Darius is his son.

"It's nice to meet you, Jonas. Who's after me this time?"

"Now, I'm not so sure. Nicole killed her brother Roman and claimed the title of Alpha of the East Hollow Pack."

"What does that have to do with me? Oh, wait. Is she one of your prospects?" I look at Darius.

"She was briefly considered and quickly ruled out."

"Unlike Alpha Lauren in all her fabulousness. You sure are in high demand, Alpha Darius."

"Call me that again."

"Maybe later. What is this girl's problem?" I ask.

"Lauren," Darius shouts.

"What?"

"You're not her only problem, Lauren is too. Dad, what do you think?"

"She's deceptive and crazy. She was likely trying to mislead you."

"I have to go," Darius says.

I grab his arm. "Go where?"

"Lauren's in danger."

"You can't go. Send someone else."

"She's my friend. I can't leave it up to someone else. I wouldn't be able to live with myself."

I hug him and squeeze tight. "Did they tell you yet?"

"I was ambushed and locked away. I haven't talked to anyone, and I don't have my phone."

"I changed my mind. I agreed to be your mate, all of yours."

"Baby, are you sure."

"I'm sure, so you have to come back to me. Go help your friend, and come back to me."

"I love you. I'm never leaving you again." I kiss her lips and spin her around. "Guys stay here with Audrey."

"I'm coming with you, son."

"Dad, I'll be alright. I have backup outside. You've helped me so much, not only today but everything you've taught me. I'm forever grateful. I've got this."

"I know you'll be okay, and I'm going to see this through with you. I'm proud of you son, and I'm happy for you Audrey."

As they rush out the door, I worry about my mate, but I have faith in him. I miss him already. Felix and Damien stand at my sides and wrap me in their arms, and I know I've made the right choice.

"Are you going to finish cooking?" Damien breaks the silence with the perfect dose of humor.

"Hell no."

"Come on. We'll do it together," Felix says.

"Felix, now is not the time," I joke.

"We can always make time," Felix says.

"Time to cook," I say.

I turn on some music and we dance and cook as I wait and try not to worry.

CHAPTER 22
Darius

"Careful, the forest is full of traps," I tell my father as he and I reach the North Star Territory.

I smell blood, my father says.

I hear fighting. The other cars pull up behind us. I let my pack know to protect Lauren's pack and to watch out for traps.

"Lauren," I shout as we run through the trees. Lauren's pack is doing a great job of defending their home, but with the power of Legacy Pack, we can get this done much quicker. My alphas show no mercy as they join forces to wipe out the threat.

"Lauren," I shout.

I run toward her scent with my dad on my heels.

"Darius," she shouts.

"Fuck you, Darius," Nicole shouts as I locate her.

"You wish," I say.

Lauren is being held down by the two men I saw earlier. She kicks her foot free from one of their grips and kicks him in the head. Nicole shifts and attacks Lauren.

Suddenly, my dad charges past me and shifts as he heads for them like a raging bull. It's a little excessive to me. His wolf is filled with rage. Lauren shifts and lunges for Nicole, but if she wants to kill Nicole, she'll have to beat my father to it. He jumps on Nicole from the side and pins her to the ground.

I stop in my tracks as he sinks his claws into her neck and her chest. In the blink of an eye, she's lifeless on the ground. Lauren shifts and snaps the neck of the man who had her held by the hands.

My father shifts and approaches Lauren.

"Who are you?" she asks.

"Jonas Huntington."

"What are you doing here?"

He pulls her close. "I came for you."

Before I can turn my head away, my father has his lips on Lauren's.

"Get the fuck out of here," I shout as I approach them.

They tear themselves apart breathing heavily as they stare into one another's eyes. I know that look all too well.

"Did you think I needed to be rescued, Alpha Darius?"

"I would never insult you in such a manner, Alpha Lauren. I just thought one friend could help another."

"Dad, are you ready to go?" I ask.

"I'm going to stick around here," my dad says. "Get back to Audrey. I can handle this."

"Are you sure?"

"I remember how to be in charge."

"I'm in charge around here," Lauren says.

"I have no problem with women in control," my father says.

"This is not weird at all. Congratulations, you two."

They're not paying me any attention as I walk away.

I give my pack instructions about East Hollow and inform them that we've found a luna. Their congratulations are loud and boisterous. We have a lot to celebrate. This is a big day for the Legacy Pack, and things will only get better from here.

I'd love to stick around and celebrate more, but I have to get back to Audrey.

When I reach her house, I find her, Damien, and Felix eating.

"Let me get your plate. I kept it warm for you." She pulls out a chair for me at the head of the table and hugs me from behind with a kiss on the cheek. "I'm glad you're okay."

I pull her onto my lap and squeeze her.

"What happened to you?" she asks.

I tell them about Nicole and Roman and everything that happened today while Audrey feeds me.

"You've had quite the adventure without us," Damien says.

Audrey hits my shoulder. "That's what you get for looking for another mate."

"You're absolutely right, but if none of this had happened, my father wouldn't have found his mate, and I wouldn't have gotten to keep mine."

"It's such a shame that Alpha Lauren will be off the market," Audrey says.

"My father has been alone for a long time. I'm happy for him."

"Me too. He seems like a nice guy."

Damien and Felix laugh.

"What's so funny?" Audrey asks.

Felix replies. "He was a pain in the ass when he found out we were a triad. He made us train day and night. He wanted to test out loyalty and ensure we would be able to have his son's back."

"Yeah, he's a good dad."

"And you're a good man."

"Fellas, I'd hate to do this to you, but—"

"You need your mate. We understand, don't we Felix?" Damien asks.

"I don't know. What does Audrey want?"

"I need some alone time with Darius."

"Then we will give it to you."

Felix and Damien clear the table and say their goodbyes.

Once the door closes I don't waste any time. I sit Audrey on top of the table and stand between her legs. I lean in for a kiss.

She pulls back. "You need a shower. I've been

suffering in silence this whole time."

I laugh as I put her over my shoulder and carry her to her bathroom. I've wanted to be close to my mate for so long. In between lathering my body and kissing me, she can't stop squeezing me in her arms, and it feels good to be wanted and loved by her.

"I can't believe you were going through all of that, and I had no idea."

"It was pretty crazy."

"Were you scared?"

"No, I knew I'd find my way back to you."

"I feel so guilty."

"Why?"

"I should've known, and I was over here having a good time."

"That's what you should've been doing."

"If something had happened to you, I don't know what I would've done."

"Same here."

"Let's get out of here."

Once we've dried off, I take Audrey to the bed. I kiss all over her body and take her slowly. The look of ecstasy is all over her face. We've needed one another so desperately.

"Tell me you love me."

"I love you, Darius."

"Tell me you need me."

"I need you. I need you so much." She wraps her legs around my waist and reaches for my hips with hers.

"You feel so good, baby. I hope you know you're not getting out of this bed tonight."

"Perfect."

"You are, love."

She sings my name as she cums all night. We've got a lot of time to make up for. When I've taken all I can get from her body, we hold one another and lie in bed.

"When will we mate?" she asks.

"New Year's Eve."

"That's soon."

"Are you okay with that?"

"I'm as ready as I'm going to be. I want this. I want to be with you all."

"I'm happy to hear you say that. I've kept things from you, and I know I shouldn't have done that. If you're ready to do this. There's one more thing you should know."

"Oh no. What is it?"

"You will transform when the mating ceremony is complete." Her body tenses.

"What do you mean, transform?"

"You will shift."

"Into a wolf."

"Yes. Are you okay with that?"

"Why? How?"

"Remember how powerful it was when we mated?"

"Yeah," she smiles."

"Imagine that times three. Plus, you will bear our children. Mine sooner rather than later and you will need the strength of a shifter."

"I hadn't thought about that."

"There's nothing to worry about. We have each other. That's what this is all about. We'll be there with you. We'll guide you and protect you. Do you trust us?"

"With my life."

"If you need to think about it some more, that's okay."

"I'm in."

"Are you sure, baby?"

"It's our destiny."

"That's right. We're lucky."

"I think so. I got some great mates and Felix."

I laugh.

"I'm just kidding. Felix has been great too."

"He's happier than I've ever seen him."

"You're welcome," she says.

"I've missed all this time with you. Tell me what's been going on while we were apart."

She fills me in on everything with her, Damien, and Felix. She tells me about her family and her mother and cousin. She thanks me for all the flowers, plants, and help we gave her.

We talk as we fall asleep clinging to one another. She is my mate, and I could've lost her. I'll never let that happen again. I will cherish her forever.

CHAPTER 23
Audrey

It's Christmas Eve and for the Stafford family, that means it's time for my mother's annual Christmas party. I haven't seen my mother or my cousin since I kicked them out of my house.

Darius touches me on my shoulder. "You ready?"

"Yes."

"You got this, mon chéri," Felix says as he squeezes my waist.

"I got this."

Damien smacks my ass. "Go get 'em, luna."

I hold my head high and square my shoulders. I open the door wide and step inside the foyer. I'm wearing a stylish black halter jumpsuit. My family is spread all over the house. I slide my coat off my shoulders and Darius grabs it and puts it on a coat rack.

Everyone stops and stares. Why wouldn't they? I look good, and I walked in here with three fine men. Darius stands by my side and Felix and Damien stand behind me. I walk around the room like everything is normal and hug my family members.

My sister comes running up to me. "Who are these men?"

"These are the men who stood by me, and tonight I have three dates, so I don't need to be set up."

"What's going on here though?"

"I said what I said, and anything else is none of your business. You look beautiful, sis." I kiss her cheek. "I'm going to make the rounds."

Her mouth hangs open as we walk by. Each of the men shake her hand and she doesn't know which one to stare at the most. I walk past the foyer greeting and hugging. I see my grandfather on the couch in the next room. I bypass everyone and walk over to him.

"Papa," I shout.

He stands and comes around the couch. "Hey, sweet pea. I was just wondering when you were going to show up."

I hug him tight. "Papa, this is Darius."

"It's an honor to meet you, sir. Audrey told me you're her favorite person."

"That's my sweet pea. I've heard a lot about you too, son."

Darius looks confused. "You have?"

"From these two."

"Have you all been in contact?" I ask Felix and Damien.

"Of course, we have," Damien says.

"He was adamant that we keep him abreast of everything concerning his sweet pea," Damien says.

"Papa, how much do you know?"

"Papa knows a lot. Now, I don't need to know all the details, but you deserve to be happy. That's what you deserve, and that's what I want for you. Long as you don't hurt nobody. These are fine young men. I still got to keep my eye on this one though." He points at Darius.

"Yes sir. I assure you that she's in good hands."

"Alright then."

Andre walks into the room with Michelle.

Darius growls.

"What is he doing here?" Andre asks.

"That's none of your business," I say.

My mother steps out of the kitchen and stands among us. I can tell she's salty with me. "Audrey, you made it."

"Hi, mom." I give her a hug and a kiss on the cheek.

"Who are these men in my house?"

"They're my guests. These men protected me when my shop was trashed. They watched over me, and they

241

made sure all the repairs got done. They helped me make products and promote. They were there for me when no one else was, and I'd like for them to be as welcome here as I am."

My mother rolls her eyes but forces a fake smile. "I suppose you all can stay for the party. Would you like some drinks?"

"Don't offer them drinks, Aunt Max. They need to leave. How do we know that it wasn't them who trashed the shop? It seems like an easy way to get into your pants. They've been taking care of you alright. What do they do, take turns?"

Gasps ring throughout the room.

"I know they didn't trash the shop, Michelle. Do you know how I know?"

"It wasn't my fiancé."

"No, it wasn't, but I had reason to believe it was when your fiancé, but you already know that, don't you?"

"What are you going on about now?"

I grab Michelle by the neck and push her head against the nearest wall.

"Let me go, you psycho."

The guys form a barrier between us and the rest of the guests.

"I know it wasn't Andre because it was you. Wasn't it?"

My dad comes into the room. "What the hell is going on here?"

"Michelle is about to admit what she did to me."

"Audrey, what's gotten into you," My mother shouts.

"These three," Michelle says.

I push her head into the wall. "Why did you do it?"

"I didn't do anything. Aunt Max, she's crazy."

"I've never seen you like this before, Audrey. Please

stop."

"I'll stop when she admits it. You always have something to say about me. If my life is so insignificant to you, why did you try to destroy it? My business is my life. I don't have anyone taking care of me."

"Get off of me." She tries to push me, but I have a firm grip on her.

"All your life you've tried to one up me, humiliate me, belittle me, and I've never done anything to you. Why would you do something like that to me?"

She rolls her eyes.

"Why? I never said anything when you got with my ex. I let you get your digs in and I've never done anything like this to you. Why do you hate me?"

"Because you have everything."

"What are you talking about?"

"You're so fucking basic and boring, but somehow you manage to have everything. Why does Audrey always get what she wants?"

"What the hell are you talking about? I worked for everything I have."

"Did you? Or do things just come easily for you. I thought once I took Andre, I'd finally best you, but nope. You still have him too. I saw the way he was looking at you, the way he always looks at you. He lingers. He has all this at home, but he still looks at you like you're the only woman in the world."

"He and I never even talked once you got together. What are you talking about?"

"I saw him at your house the night of the tree trimming party. You two were so into one another that you didn't know I was there. When he left here, he had that look in his eye, and I saw you two kissing. Tell me I'm lying."

Everyone gasps and whispers.

"I did not kiss him. He kissed me, and I stopped

him. I told him to leave. Did you see that part? I would never do that to you. We're family."

"I saw what I saw."

"That's why you trashed my shop."

"I trashed your shop because you're trash. He was acting funny and you know, women's tuition. I followed him. He thought I was asleep and there he was on your doorstep again. So wrapped up that he didn't notice I was across the street. There was my fiancé, fighting over his ex, begging at her doorstep. He got beat up by that thug." She points at Darius. "Over you."

"So you decided to take it all out on me. I have no control over what that man does. That's between you and Andre." I let her go.

She grabs her neck and rubs out the pain. "I hate you."

"I didn't tell the police about you, but I still can. Everyone in this room heard your confession. If you ever cross me again, they'll be hell to pay. You should thank these three for my generosity. Your ass should be in jail."

"You don't have to worry about me. I'm too fabulous to give you any more energy. Andre, let's get out of here."

"I'm leaving, but not with you. I want you out of my fucking house."

"Baby, I did this for us."

"You sat back and let me take the blame. That's fucked up. My life was almost ruined."

"Because of her."

He gets in Michelle's face and yells. "No, because of you."

He walks away and Michelle grabs his arm.

He jerks away. "Don't fucking touch me." He walks out of the house and slams the door.

Michelle looks at me. "Are you happy now?"

"Michelle, how could you?" My mother's disappointment is all over her face.

"Aunt Maxine, please don't be angry with me. You understand, right. It was her fault."

"No, no, no. My daughter does not deserve to be treated that way by you. I let you get away with so much because I loved my late sister, and I made a promise that I'd take care of you. What you've done to my child is unacceptable, and you need to get out of my house before I knock you into next week."

"Aunt Max, please don't."

My mother stands firm. "Please leave my home." She turns her back to Michelle. "Maybe these gentlemen can escort you out."

They face Michelle with their arms folded and their biceps protruding.

"Don't bother. I can show myself out. I don't need you. I don't need any of you."

She storms off.

"Michelle," I call after her. "We're your family, the only one you've got. You remember that. You know where to find us when you're ready to apologize."

"Hmph," she walks out.

I stand in the center of the room. Everyone's watching and whispering.

Darius stands at my side and puts his arm around my waist. I'm comforted by his warmth and his kiss to my cheek. I can hear people commenting about how cute we look together, and they want to know who he is.

"Miss Maxine," Damien approaches my mother.

"Yes, baby. What's your name?"

"My name is Damien. I'm a friend of Audrey's."

"It's nice to meet you, Damien."

"You have a beautiful home. I love this music. Will

you dance with me please?" He holds out his hand.

My mother blushes and giggles. "Boy, you'd better quit playing with me. My husband won't like that."

"Young man, take her off my hands," my father jokes.

Damien rocks from side to side and invites my mother to join him. My mom is shy at first, but she joins him, and she has a big grin on her face.

The tension in the room melts away. Darius holds my waist from behind and dances with me, and everyone starts to dance. Felix dances with one of my aunts and everyone just starts to have a good time like nothing happened. Damien has a gift.

When things settle down, my mother finds me standing alone, sipping on a glass of champagne.

"Don't worry, this is my first glass."

"Okay now," my mother says.

"This has been an interesting evening."

"It certainly has." My mother is more sincere than I've ever seen her. She runs her fingers through my curls and tears fall from her eyes. "My baby."

I can't stop myself from crying. Damn.

"Mama is so sorry."

"Why?"

"For not defending my child who I love more than myself, for making you feel like you were ever anything less than perfect because you are, even with all this hair. I never want you to think that I chose someone else over you or that you are not good enough. I'm sorry, and I've always been proud of you, baby."

My leg bounces up and down as the tears flow. My mother has never said these words to me, and I've always wanted her to. "Thank you."

"Please forgive me."

"I do. I love you. You're the only mama I have."

"And don't you ever forget it."

We hug one another tight.

"Mama loves you." She kisses my forehead. "I like that Darius. He's fine. You'd better hold on to that one, honey."

"Don't worry, I'm not letting him go anywhere."

"Didn't mama say you could do much better than Andre?"

"You did."

"See mama knows best."

I look at her affectionately and smooth her perfect hair. "I guess you do."

We hold hands and I lean against her shoulder as we watch the party.

CHAPTER 24

Darius

New Year's Eve, the time of year when people acknowledge the past and look forward to the future. There's no more perfect night for a full moon. The Legacy pack has gathered for a celebration of epic proportions.

Our triad will become a quad, and our pack will have a luna. Everyone's here, including my father and his mate, Lauren. Her pack came to celebrate with us.

The moon illuminates the forest like I've never seen before. Bonfires are set and lanterns are hung. Audrey looks radiant as she sits next to me and Felix with Damien next to Felix. I wear my alpha cloak proudly, and Audrey wears a matching cloak reserved and blessed for the luna along with a tiara. Felix and Damien also have ceremonial cloaks. We're served the finest foods and wines and honored with gifts and blessings.

We celebrate with the pack. We dance and drink. Everyone is excited to meet Audrey, and they love her. Why wouldn't they? She's everything we could've asked for and more. Time is winding down, and we must prepare for the ceremony.

Everyone gathers around the sacred pool. The healers bless the water, and we disrobe. I've already told Audrey about the process. We step into the brown water together. As we descend the stairs, the water turns clear. The pack howls. This means our union is blessed by the gods. We join hands in a circle and recite our sacred promise.

First, Felix, Damien, and I recite to Audrey. "I promise to honor, cherish, protect, and commit to you first above all others. My luna is my heart, and my heart will forever be bound to me."

Audrey recites to us. "I promise to honor, cherish, protect, and commit to my mates first above all others. You are my heart." She touches each of our hands. "My heart will forever be bound to you."

We ascend the other side of the pool and face the crowd on a stage. They bow to us and shower us with applause and congratulations. Behind the stage is a sacred tent, blessed by the elders and built like a palace. The four of us will be left alone to do what we've been dying to do, mate.

We go down the stairs first and hold our hands out to Audrey. The pheromones and the desire in the room are strong.

I take Audrey's hand and lead her to the mating bed decorated with luxury linens and pillows and any tools we may need. "You look more beautiful than I've ever seen you." I bow to her as she sits on the bed.

"Thank you, Alpha Darius. You may stay."

We laugh.

Felix approaches Audrey. "How may we serve you?"

Audrey sits back in the bed. "I want you to serve yourselves first." She spreads her legs. Damien climbs into the bed. He sucks her toes. Her eyes close and her head rolls back. He kisses up her leg, her thigh, and then her sweet pussy. I can imagine the taste and lick my lips as she moans and Damien slurps.

Felix steps into the bed. He kisses Audrey's neck and down to her breast. He takes her nipple into his mouth and sucks to her delight.

"Is my mate happy?" I ask.

"Very. Why don't you join?"

I climb onto the bed and tease her neck with my canines. She shivers beneath me when I toy with the spot where I bit her.

"Darius," she moans my name and rolls her neck.

Damien kisses his way up her stomach and takes her lips.

I lift her body. I stand in front of her. My dick stands at attention in front of her face. She pulls me to her and takes me in her mouth. She takes me all the way in as she moans. Felix moves his head underneath her body and tastes her ass and Damien moves back to her pussy.

Her body jerks and moves between them. I pinch her nipples as she sucks me. I'm ready for her. We all are.

"It's time," I inform her.

"Are you ready, luna?" Damien asks.

"I'm ready."

Felix holds her hand. "We will all take you at once. We will mark you and mate you, and you will be ours forever."

I hold her other hand. "Audrey, will you accept me as your mate?"

"I will."

Felix asks. "Audrey, will you accept me as your mate?"

"I will."

Damien asks. "Audrey, will you accept me as your mate?"

"I will."

"Alpha Darius, Felix, Damien, will you accept me as your mate?

"I will."

"I will."

"I will."

"Don't be nervous."

She nods.

Damien grabs lube from the table next to him.

I lie down on my back and position her on top of me. I run my fingers down her curves as my dick stretches her pussy. Her body is warm and wet, and she clenches me as she grinds my dick. I grab her breasts and squeeze.

Felix slips inside her from behind. Her body grips me, and I lift my hips off the bed. Her body moves back and forth between us while we caress her. She's tortured with ecstasy which only makes my dick harder. All of us want more of her. She cums on top of me. She cries out, and her juices pour onto my body. Damien enters her mouth. I guide her hips as she finds her rhythm between the three of us. She takes Damien all the way down her throat. I know this is a lot for her, but we appreciate the way she wants to please us all, and she pleases us all very well, and from her moans and wetness, she's pleased with us.

An alarm goes off, and she looks startled. It's time. One minute to midnight. I lift my head and tweak one of her nipples while I suck her breast. Her body bucks into a frenzy. I thrust deep into her pussy with vigor. Damien thrusts into her mouth and Felix thrust into her ass. Tension builds in my body, and I'm ready to explode. The countdown to the New Year rings through the tent from the crowd outside. When the clock strikes midnight, we each mark her back, sinking our claws into her skin, and our teeth into her neck. She's now mated and claimed by the three of us, and we all explode together. As she cries out and creams on my dick, my seed erupts inside her, then Felix, in her ass, and Damien in her mouth. She sinks her claws into my chest and scratches my skin. She marks me while she swallows Damien.

Her body convulses and we are swarmed with light and stars. Our souls become one with hers and we are bonded. Our minds are linked and we comfort her as her body relaxes. We assure her that she's alright and when she opens her eyes, she'll be like us. Using a basin by the bed we wipe her down and I carry her outside. The waiting members of the pack howl and cheer to celebrate our official mating to our luna.

They chant her name while she rests. I shift into my white wolf and so do Damien and Felix. We surround Audrey and sniff our scents on her body. We lick her to awaken her wolf, and we surround her. We lay next to her, Felix and Damien against her sides, and me at her feet. A blue light swirls around her and we rise together. Our triad is no longer three white wolves. Our quad is four white wolves.

The crowd gasps. I must admit I'm shocked as well. Alpha Audrey has emerged. The wolves of the Legacy Pack shift and howl to their luna. She howls back at her pack, and they are overjoyed, jumping and cheering for her. This is her home. She licks and nuzzles her mates and takes in our scents. My wolf is more in love than ever.

She holds her head and her tail high for the crowd as they adore her. Without warning, she jumps from the stage and runs. Myself, Felix, and Damien run after her, and she and I lead the pack in the midnight run through the forest. The excitement from the pack is contagious. Men, women, and children are all united and celebrate the future of the Legacy Pack.

I felt something when we mated, something that only I detected. I know it doesn't work like this, but she's pregnant. I feel it in my bones. She's pregnant with my first child.

EPILOGUE

Audrey

Five years and four children later, Darius and I live happily married in our much larger cabin. He and I had twins, and I have a child each for Felix and Damien. The kids are raised here with open access available to their fathers.

My relationships with my three mates are wonderful, and each is unique. My relationship with Darius is steady and constant. We manage to have love, family, and stability, and a spark that has never left. Our desire for one another has never faded and he will go to the ends of the earth to make me happy. Our twins, Jonah and Elijah were conceived pretty soon after the mating ceremony.

He steps into the house with a bouquet and hands them to me. He smells like the dirt from his greenhouse.

I smile. "What are these?"

"I've been working for years to capture you in a flower, and I finally got it. This soon to be award-winning, perfect rose is called Audrey."

"It's beautiful."

"Yes, you are?"

"Thank you, baby."

"Where are the kids?"

"The nannies took them out to play."

"That gives mommy and daddy time to play."

"Felix is on the way, remember. He just got back in town."

"Well, let's be quick."

He sits the flowers on the counter and begins removing my clothes. I could never resist him. I lift his dirt stained shirt from his chest and unbutton his jeans as he lowers me to the floor. We kiss passionately as he spreads my legs and works his magic tongue against me.

The door opens and Felix walks in. "You know I was coming to pick you up."

Darius lifts his head. "We got carried away."

I push his head back down.

"Viens ici mon amour," I tell Felix, come here my love, in French.

He replies, "mon plaisir." He removes his clothes and joins us.

Felix has maintained the life that he loves which works perfectly. He works and travels. Every once in a while I get to take a trip with him, but mostly we connect when he comes home. We did however take an amazingly romantic trip to Paris where he spoiled me with opulence and mind shattering orgasms. I'm sure our son, Bennet, was conceived in Paris.

"What the hell did I walk in on?" It's Damien. He removes his clothes as he witnesses the fire being produced on the floor and wastes no time joining in.

Damien and I have a son named Richard. Damien is always there when I need affection or adventure. He makes me feel alive. He takes me to exciting places and new heights.

It's nice that we can still have moments like this. I've come to rely on them. My life is hectic with work and kids. I have a thriving business, and four beautiful, rambunctious boys. Mama needs a release sometimes, and my mates know exactly how to please me.

The Legacy pack is thriving because they have an excellent leader. My family is my family. I will always love them. I'm no longer the single one anymore, but I made it clear that what goes on in my house is my business. They don't ask questions and I leave it at that.

I love my life the way it is, and just as promised, I don't have to choose.

Thank you for reading Claimed at the Stroke of Midnight. I hope you enjoyed this sizzling reverse harem and I truly appreciate your support. If you haven't already, check out these other Zoe Ray books.

Alpha Boss - Samantha Davis was on a mission to change her life, starting with a new career. She found herself in an elevator with a handsome jerk and she gives him a piece of her mind. Little did she know, she was yelling at the Boss. That kind of thing, Preston would never tolerate, but when it turns out the woman he offended is his fated mate, he's willing to do what it takes to claim her.

Mark of the Dragon (Discover the Dragon Book 1) - A sexy dragon shifter spin-off. Wade meets his fated mate, but he and is forced to choose between his one night rule and the woman he loves. Can Sam and Preston help this couple find their way?

Alliance- In the second Alpha Boss book Preston and Sam prepare for their wedding, but their lives and the lives of their friends begin to unravel. When Michael gets the opportunity of a lifetime his life-long friendship with Preston is questioned, and when he finds his mate his world falls apart. With forces of evil coming against them will Sam and Preston make it down the aisle, and will Michael find his happy ending?

Alpha Professor- Jeremiah Johnson is a proud alpha who doesn't want to accept his mate, Shante, but once Shante realizes Jeremiah is the man of her dreams, she'll stop at nothing to win his heart. With a little help from some new friends, Shante gets a crash course in dealing with her stubborn opponent.

Heart of the Dragon (Discover the Dragon Book 2) - Feeling pressure from those around him, Wade has to take a long, hard, look at himself which leads him on a journey he never imagined he'd take. With his life, relationship, and future, hanging in the balance, will Wade rise to the occasion or lose his spark?

STANDALONE

Stealing The Alpha's Mate - Desired, Betrayed, Mated & Captured. The passion can't be contained in this dark romance.

When notorious wolf shifter Red Paw meets Celeste, a human ballerina, he's overwhelmed with desire to claim his mate. Celeste wants nothing to do with the ruthless alpha — but can she deny their scorching chemistry?

ONE NIGHT STAND SERIES

Take Me: My Night With Preston

In this prequel to Alpha Boss by Zoe Ray, you find yourself alone when you're approached by a handsome stranger. Have you ever fantasized about what would happen if you met the man of your dreams from the pages of your favorite story? This is your opportunity to put yourself in the story and have an experience with your favorite leading man, Preston Jacobs.

Find out if Preston is everything you imagined he would be in this steamy story where you are the object of his desire, and the focus of his attention.

Teach Me: My Night with Wade

Can you handle a one night stand? Are you sure? One night with these alphas and you may not want to let them go. See more of Preston and Wade in my One Night Stand Series where the reader gets an experience their favorite characters for one night. What were Preston and Wade like before they met their mates?

Find out in these sensual novellas, but only if you can accept that it's for one night. (One of these ladies does show up in another book.)

Follow Zoe Ray on social media:

https://linktr.ee/zoeray

Website

http://www.sincerelyzoeray.com

BookBub

https://www.bookbub.com/profile/zoe-ray

Goodreads

https://www.goodreads.com/author/show/1477 3767.Zoe_Ray

Facebook

http://www.facebook.com/sincerelyzoeray

Instagram

http://www.instagram.com/sincerelyzoeray

Twitter

http://www.twitter.com/sincerelyzoeray

Amazon

https://www.amazon.com/author/zoeray